PRAISE FOR HANNAH GERSEN

"A talented and wise writer."
—Edan Lepucki, *New York Times* bestselling author of *Time's Mouth*

"Gersen's characters are so full, so gently flawed, and so deeply human that it's nearly impossible to resist falling into their world, with all its sorrow and all its subtle joy."
—*Kirkus Reviews*

"Gersen's writing walks a lyrical tightrope . . . [and] uncovers the unflinching truths in families that wound us and somehow, miraculously, save us."
—Robin Antalek, author of *The Grown Ups* and *The Summer We Fell Apart*

WE
WERE
PRETENDING

ALSO BY HANNAH GERSEN

Home Field

WE
WERE
PRETENDING

a novel

HANNAH GERSEN

Published by Little A, New York

www.apub.com

Amazon, the Amazon logo, and Little A are trademarks of Amazon.com, Inc., or its affiliates.

ISBN-13: 9781662515088 (hardcover)
ISBN-13: 9781662515101 (paperback)
ISBN-13: 9781662515095 (digital)

Cover design by Zoe Norvell
Cover images: © Linda Westin; © Alexander Andrews / Unsplash; © Arcady / Shutterstock

Printed in the United States of America

First edition

Spiritual readiness, by virtue of its transcendent nature, does not provide objective measures and metrics.
—10-29, *US Army Field Manual, Holistic Health and Fitness*

I never expected to see Jenny again. It had been years since she'd upended my life, and I'd come to think of her as a kind of mushroom: elusive, interesting, and potentially dangerous. My husband, Tim, disagrees. He thinks Jenny is just another out-of-work theater type. He doesn't trust actors; he says they lie for a living. Me, I've always had a high tolerance for pretension.

I suppose I could have walked away when I realized Jenny and I were together in the same crowded space. The cocktail reception was on a hotel rooftop in Brooklyn, and it would have been easy enough to avoid Jenny amid the partygoers sipping natural wine and surreptitiously glancing at name tags. It was the opening night of Tech in Healthcare, a conference that Tim and I were attending. We were slated to give a presentation about an AI-enabled fitness wearable we'd helped develop, but the real reason we were there was to report on the dozens of environmental protests that were occurring daily in New York City. The news media was ignoring them, but our boss at the Department of Defense wanted us to scout them for recruits to a top-secret initiative, Project Demeter.

The night of the reception, a small but scrappy protest was underway outside the hotel, with young people carrying handmade poster board signs that said things like CLEAN AIR IS HEALTHCARE and GREEN TECH IS A MYTH. They marched along walkways that had been installed alongside the Gowanus Canal—a toxic Superfund site whose murky waters were supposedly on the verge of supporting marine life. Above them, placards advertising a new luxury apartment complex optimistically depicted a future where residents might paddle kayaks along a crystal clear waterway. All the construction in the area—including the rooftop bar where I stood, drinking a glass of rosé—was billed as "sustainable," a word that had become as opaque as the canal's waters.

I was leaning against the railing at the edge of the balcony, looking down at the protesters, when I overheard a man grousing that "those kids" should be yelling outside an actual government building instead of hectoring entrepreneurs who couldn't write legislation. When a familiar voice agreed, I thought, *It can't be*, but I turned and there was Jenny. She looked different: older and more conventional, with tasteful clothing and a chin-length bob. Blonde highlights helped to blend the grays that had once corkscrewed from longer, messier hair. She wore a simple, sleeveless pantsuit and several gold bracelets. Around her neck was a pearl pendant as well as a lanyard with her name tag. I tried to read it even as I knew it was her. She must have felt my stare because she glanced over her shoulder.

"Leigh!" she exclaimed. "What are you doing here? You're looking well."

We embraced briefly. She felt thinner, but her woodsy perfume was familiar.

"You remember my husband, Emmett," she said, touching the elbow of the man who'd been complaining a moment before. I was thrown—I'd only heard her use his nickname, but I knew who he was. Years ago, I'd researched him, pulling up photos online. In real life, he was taller than I had expected, and his good features—clear skin, bright eyes, thick hair, straight teeth—were strangely inert, refusing to coalesce into handsomeness. He was the opposite of Jenny, whose bug eyes, flushed cheeks, and large mouth should not add up to beauty, but somehow always did.

"Good to meet you," he said, shaking my hand. "How do you two know each other?"

"Leigh and I went to high school together," Jenny quickly replied.

"You must have some stories to tell. Jennifer always makes it sound as though she grew up like the Beverly Hillbillies."

"Emmett, your references are dating you." Jenny gave him an indulgent, wifely smile. "Go get us another round, will you?"

Her face changed as soon as he was gone, some social veneer immediately dissolving. She spoke in a hurried rush. "I'm so sorry for the way we left off, for the way I left. I owe you an apology."

"It's okay," I said reflexively, wanting to reassure her—of what, I didn't know. We weren't friends, and perhaps we never had been, not in the way I had once believed.

"We reconnected at such a crazy time in my life," Jenny said, lowering her voice. "Emmett had given me that ultimatum, and I didn't know what to do."

I nodded sympathetically even though I wasn't sure what she was talking about. As always, I had the urge to agree with her.

"And then you came along, and I thought it was a sign. I used to be so prone to magical thinking. I'm a much more rational person now." She paused to adjust the clasp on her necklace. "Honestly, I feel like I've only just become an adult in my forties. It's like I'm finally settled. I think marriage can do that, really committing to one person. We're trying to have a baby, if it's not too late. You have a kid, right?"

"Yes, Rose," I said, looking in her eyes for a sign of recognition. How could she not remember my daughter? I was surprised—but I guess I shouldn't have been. "She just turned thirteen."

"Wow, a teenager. She's going to start hating you soon."

I heard this from other women more often than you'd think. Knowing Jenny's past, I assumed that she was probably just drawing from her own experience.

"So, what are you up to these days?" I asked her. "Are you still doing tree therapy?"

"God, no." She laughed. "I've put that behind me. I'm kind of embarrassed about it now. I feel like I was a psychic or a tarot card reader. No offense to either of those practices, I just didn't happen to know what I was doing."

"You helped a lot of people," I said, searching her face for signs of the Jenny I'd known years before—the sweet, enthusiastic woman who'd convinced me of so many things.

"If I did, it was purely by accident. Probably I just helped people get outside, soak up some vitamin D. Or maybe having someone pay attention to them made the difference."

"That's not nothing." I didn't like hearing her dismiss her talent. I still believed, despite everything, that she was a healer, capable of bringing people close to plants and trees and to the green, breathing pulse of the world. Nature, like Death, isn't picky. It will talk to anyone who listens.

"I mean, I still like plants," Jenny said wistfully. "But it's hard to keep them, you know? We travel so much. What about you? Still at the Pentagon?"

I nodded.

"Are you here to talk about giving psychedelic mushrooms to veterans? I read about funding going through for that."

"I'm not involved with that," I said. "I'm still working on AI applications for mental health care."

"Emmett's trying to pivot toward AI."

"What about me?" Emmett had returned with our drinks. I wasn't finished with my first and stood awkwardly holding my wine in one hand and a cocktail in the other while Jenny's husband explained how his pharmaceutical company was using AI to coordinate drone deliveries. The pandemic had accelerated everything. One day they hoped to deploy AI "prescribing agents." He spoke as if he were a guest on a podcast, invited to share his expertise. Jenny nodded and made affirmative noises. Her social manner had returned, a certain gloss and distance.

I was about to excuse myself when Tim approached, his bamboo plate laden with bread, hummus, and pickled vegetables. "Thought you might be hungry," he said, relieving me of my excess drink.

I made introductions. Eventually Emmett stopped talking, and Jenny mentioned a dinner reservation.

"Leigh, it was so good to run into you." Jenny touched my arm as she said goodbye, but there was no pretense of exchanging numbers and trying to stay in touch. I appreciated that, but I felt a little melancholy, too. I returned to my perch at the balcony railing, wondering if I'd catch a glimpse of her on the street. The protesters had dispersed, and the sidewalks were filling with commuters.

Tim followed me to the railing. "Was that who I think it was? The woman you almost threw your life away for?"

"She got me out of a rut, I'll give her that," I said, trying to joke. But it was still painful to remember the decisions I'd made during that time, the fantasies of escape I'd indulged.

Tim took my hand. "I'm ready to go if you are."

We headed outside into the warm spring evening. The trees were coming into leaf. I thought of the Larkin poem my mother had loved, and I thought of Walter, the little dogwood that had stood in the front yard of the condo I'd rented during some of the loneliest years of my life.

PART ONE

Jennifer Hex

1.

I had been researching Jennifer Hex for nearly an hour before I realized she was someone I used to know. Her Instagram feed sparked my memory, a photo of her dressed in green and relaxing in the shade of a sycamore tree. The dappled light made her appear slightly younger, reminding me of the teenager I'd known. *Jenny*, I realized. I was looking at Jenny Heck. This long-haired, casually glamorous guru had once been the tall new girl who'd slouched down the halls of Lost Falls Senior High. Now she was *Jennifer Hex: Tree Listener, Healer, Diviner of Green*. Her location, according to her profile, was "Los Angeles by way of Patience." Her website said she practiced something called "tree therapy." She had a yearlong waiting list. Probably a lot of unreported tax earnings, too, but that wasn't how she'd come to the government's attention.

I marveled at her transformation. In high school, she'd had a gap-toothed smile, round cheeks, and intense eyes that bugged out slightly. The effect had been almost comical. But in adulthood, her prominent cheekbones, straight teeth, and full eyebrows were striking. Her curly brown hair, which she had always worn in a messy nineties bob, was long, gently waved, and a lighter shade than I remembered. In every picture, she wore something green.

I lingered on a photo of her with her arms outstretched to reach the trailing branches of a weeping willow. She reminded me of her father, with his long silver braids and the heavy pink crystal he always wore around his neck. Everett Heck was regarded as a local crackpot who sold trinkets to gullible college girls in his New Age store, but I'd always believed he was sincere.

Like Jenny, he thought that connecting to nature could heal psychic pain. When my mother was dying, Everett was the one who'd told us about Hecate's Key, a rare mushroom that could take away the terror of terminal illness.

Maybe seeing Jenny reminded me of my mother, too. Maybe I'm always thinking about my mother, a little bit.

I knew I should ask for Jennifer Hex to be assigned to someone else on my team. We're not supposed to conduct interviews with people we know. At the bare minimum, we need to disclose prior relationships. But how well did I really know Jenny? She wasn't a close friend, or even a genuine confidante. She'd been two years ahead of me, and I'd looked up to her in the way that kids do in high school, when the divide between a senior and a sophomore is cavernous. We met doing theater together, and she had the kind of gawky, daring talent that's unforgettable. In my mind's eye, she was still the seventeen-year-old sauntering onstage in cutoff jeans and black tights. She was legendary for pretending to chew gum during her audition, a stunt that flummoxed the teachers, especially when she stuck the fake wad under her chair. (Later, she told me she'd gleaned this trick from a Barbra Streisand interview.) I believed with all my teenage heart that she would become a famous actor. She was dreamy—the type of person who could bring you into her dream.

Jenny was dropped into our little Maryland town for her senior year only. Apparently, her mother had dumped her with her estranged hippie father because she was such a troublemaker. But Jenny never struck me as rebellious. Just restless. When we drove home from rehearsals in her dad's bumper-stickered car with the windows down, blasting

"Gardening at Night," I sometimes worried—and perhaps secretly hoped—that she'd just keep on going north, right over the Mason-Dixon Line. We lost touch after she graduated. But she was one of those people who'd stayed in my mind since I'd left my hometown. I'd searched for her online a couple of times over the years, feeding her name to the internet, but nothing came up. It was uncanny to finally find her by accident through work.

I've been at the US Department of Defense for almost a decade now, but when I came across Jenny, the job still felt new. At that time, I was researching alternative therapies for inclusion in the military's *Field Manual for the Army*, incorporating holistic health into its fitness recommendations, with an emphasis on rest, recovery, and self-care. To the layperson, the updates are probably kind of obvious—soldiers are advised to try yoga, meditation, journaling, and napping—but it's a big step for the military to acknowledge that soldiers are human beings with emotions and moods.

In addition to the field manual, my department was conducting research for a wearable device—a complement to the manual. This has been an ongoing project, one that still hasn't been released to the public, but they're getting close. They're calling it an "Integrated Readiness Trainer for Holistic Health" (known in-house as IRTH2, pronounced like "earth two") and it will be akin to a fitness watch, with the ability to track and record diet and exercise goals. Unlike your typical wearable, IRTH2 will recommend individualized treatments for each soldier, whether they are deployed, on reserve, or retired. IRTH2 will also provide support for mental health and existential crises. It's the latter that has been hardest to incorporate. Treatment for spiritual malaise requires a level of discernment that is nearly impossible to program. It's just very difficult to know what will put someone on the path to transcendence.

I was working on the Spiritual Readiness problem when I found Jenny. I was supposed to be on the lookout for transcendent practices that exist outside the mainstream. My team leader, Marcos, has always been eager to include unconventional therapies, especially ones that involve the natural world. Marcos's theory is that, for many soldiers, communing with nature is the best and most accessible spiritual practice. The idea has real merit, and not only because many Americans have drifted away from organized religion. Humans have an innate connection to other living things; our nervous systems are soothed by time in nature. Even looking at a photo of a scenic vista can calm us. All this would seem to be common sense, and easy to fit into daily life, but people have become so disconnected from the natural world that they need a way back in. A frame. Jennifer Hex provided that. Her therapy consisted of speaking to trees out loud in a kind of open-air prayer. The idea was that the trees would hear you, and answer, but not in a way that you could consciously understand. It was hard for me to believe, even then, that her approach would be embraced by soldiers training for overseas deployment or recovering from a traumatic tour. But I was looking for an excuse to interview her. I told myself that if anyone could convince people to talk to trees, it would be Jenny.

I headed toward Marcos's office, down a fluorescent-lit hallway that revealed all the dinginess of government decor. He was on the phone and gestured for me to wait. Taking a seat on a vinyl-cushioned chair, I found myself eye to eye with his Sierra Club calendar, which hadn't yet been turned to March. I flipped it to reveal a classic portrait of California redwoods: camera pointed heavenward, light streaming down. Those trees had survived countless wildfires. They might even survive humanity. My mother had always wanted to see them in person, but she never had the chance—or maybe she felt there would be something hypocritical in burning jet fuel to make the pilgrimage. Mom knew the name of every tree species in our yard and was so committed to saving the old buckeye that she hired an arboreal surgeon to brace it with steel rods. When I was a kid, I would sit under it and husk horse chestnuts, peeling off rinds that, just like my mother, were spiky on the outside with a soft interior.

Marcos finished his call and turned to me. "What's up?"

"I think I know this woman," I said, holding up my phone. "We went to high school together."

"Really? That's wild—may I?" Marcos took my phone. "Oh, the tree therapist. I thought she might be interesting."

"I'd like to interview her in person, if that's okay."

"You looking to get away from this never-ending winter?" Marcos smiled as he handed back my phone. "Sure, go check her out."

"You don't think there's a conflict of interest?" I asked, feeling the need to double-check. I knew I wouldn't be asking for special permission to fly across the country if I didn't have such a personal connection to her. Maybe I also sensed it was a bad idea. At the same time, I think I wanted to believe there were subterranean forces at work, leading me back to Jenny.

"As long as she doesn't know you're with us, it's fine."

"Of course," I said. "I'll tell her I'm doing a piece for *Cerulean*."

"Perfect," Marcos said.

When I interview healers, I pretend I'm a journalist. Most alternative health practitioners are hostile to the military. For obvious reasons, they don't want their work being used to help soldiers kill other human beings, which is the Pentagon's number one fitness goal, at least as stated in the most recent draft of the field manual: *Holistic Health will help enhance Soldier lethality, prevent Soldier injury, and facilitate individualized treatment for Soldier readiness.*

"Any chance we'll see you at happy hour?" Marcos asked, when I stood up to leave. "We're going to that axe-throwing place."

"Not tonight, sorry. I need to pick Rose up from aftercare. I have her this weekend."

I spoke as if I were regretful, but I was glad to have an excuse. In the first couple of years after my divorce, I avoided socializing, ignoring those who said that I had to "get out there" to build confidence. I felt rejected, even though I was the one who'd blown up my marriage. Psychologically, I was totally lost. It was as if I had walked through the wrong door and into someone else's life.

"Leigh," Marcos said, "is this Jennifer Hex person literally talking to trees?"

"I'm not sure. I think she also listens."

"But it's not gardening therapy, right? We already have a lot of recommendations in that area."

"I think it's more like drama therapy," I said, waiting. I could see that Marcos was thinking something through, but I had no idea what it could be. I didn't know about Project Demeter then—and Marcos is always, as a rule, privy to lots of confidential projects. He's military brass, and I'm just a civilian contractor.

Marcos ran his hands through his graying curly hair. "When you apply for travel, say you're going to investigate mental as well as spiritual readiness. I'm thinking this might be one for CARP, too."

"I didn't know that was official." CARP stood for Climate Anxiety Readiness Pilot. There was a growing belief that IRTH2 should include treatments to address Climate Anxiety and depressive episodes related to Extinction Awareness. Soldiers were already reporting symptoms of burnout after being dispatched to help clean up after natural and unnatural disasters—like hurricanes and oil spills.

"I'm still trying to get funding," Marcos said. "We may have to wait until after the election, unfortunately. But we can bookmark things. When we get the okay, I want to be ready to roll."

"Consider Jennifer bookmarked," I said, even though I knew I wouldn't have any trouble remembering her. There are some people you never forget.

2.

The drive to Rose's school from Pentagon City usually took about a half hour. Traffic was light, and I pulled into Rose's elementary school parking lot a few minutes early. I walked toward the playground area, hoping the kids were outside, but a drizzle had defeated the teachers. It didn't take much. In Europe, there were forest schools where kindergarten classes spent the whole day in wooded parks, building stick forts and wading in streams and puddles. That was what I wanted for Rose, but after Carter and I split up, I learned it wasn't the kind of thing he was even willing to consider.

I headed to the entrance, where I arrived just in time to see Carter exiting, holding Rose's hand. Carter's newish girlfriend, Megan, followed behind, taking Rose's other hand as soon as they cleared the double doors.

For a few long seconds, I saw how they were a little family unto themselves when I wasn't around. Megan was tall, like Carter, with narrow hips, broad shoulders, and a head that I had decided was too small for her body. She was leaning toward Rose, and they were just about to swing her up in the air when Rose saw me.

"Mommy!" she yelled, dropping their hands and running toward me. "I knew you were coming!"

I knelt to hug her, and when I looked up, Megan and Carter were looming over me.

"What are you doing here?" Carter said. "Is something wrong?"

"I'm here to get Rose. It's my weekend."

Carter and Megan exchanged a quick, private glance. I felt like a child in my casual Friday outfit of "nice" jeans and a turtlenecked sweater. They were both dressed for their law firm jobs in dark, conservative suits. Megan's brown hair was in a low, neat ponytail that looked like it had just been brushed into place. If I'd known I was going to see her—and Carter—I would have put on some lipstick, making them wonder where I was coming from. Instead, I was showing up in a state of minor dishevelment, overly aware of the smell of my deodorant.

Rose swung my arm back and forth affectionately. "Are you coming with us to the Eastern Shore?"

"We're going to Chestertown to visit Megan's mother," Carter interjected. "It's her birthday."

"She's turning sixty-five," Megan added, a slight flush coming to her cheeks. It was only the second time we'd interacted with each other, after I'd insisted that Carter introduce her when she started spending time with Rose. I wanted to hate her, and in my lizard brain I did, but I couldn't deny that she seemed like a decent person. It helped, too, that she wasn't much younger than me—or any prettier. I might be uncombed, but I'm not above petty vanity.

"You can follow us in your car. We get to take the bridge tunnel!" Rose was grinning widely, and I realized that this was her fantasy: that we would all get along and go on trips together.

"I'm sorry, honey," I said. "But you're not going with them. Daddy made a mistake."

"I didn't make a mistake," Carter said, taking Rose's hand. "We've had this trip planned for a while."

"We switched weekends," I said. "Remember? Because of my flight being delayed?" Carter and I had worked out custody so that I got Rose on Wednesdays, Thursdays, Fridays, and alternate Saturdays. But between Carter's late nights at the office and my work trips, we made a lot of last-minute changes. I'd had to get Carter to cover for me the previous weekend when my flight home from a healing conference in

Buffalo got canceled due to an unusually powerful snowstorm—one of those once-in-fifty-years events that had started to come every other season.

"I remember that you *wanted* to switch weekends," Carter said, in a tone meant to communicate just how patient he was being. "I told you I'd have to check my calendar. I emailed you about this trip. You never replied."

"I never got an email. Did you send it to my work address? It probably got sent to spam."

Carter dismissed this. "Nobody's emails get sent to spam anymore."

"Mine do." I hated his condescending tone. "Our spam filter is very aggressive," I added, feeling ridiculous, even though it was true.

Megan smiled apologetically. "The good thing is you both remembered to pick her up. It could have been the other way around."

"No, it couldn't have." Carter and I spoke at the same time in the same sharp tone.

"Sorry, honey," Carter said to Megan, lightly touching her forearm. He turned to me. "You'll see Rose next weekend."

"Are you serious? This is my weekend." I couldn't believe he was going to steal Rose right out from under me, all because I didn't answer an email. He could have picked up the phone and called me; he could have just said yes in the first place.

"I'd rather we spoke privately about this," Carter said with a glance at Rose, who was standing very still, as though if she didn't move, we wouldn't fight.

"Fine, let's talk, just the two of us—if you don't mind, Megan?"

"Go ahead!" Megan said with a people pleaser's smile. Unlike Carter, she still cared about getting on my good side. "I'll wait with Rose."

"Thank you," I said, before Carter could disagree.

We went over to a scrubby row of laurel bushes that bordered the faded brick wall of Rose's school. Carter stopped walking and crossed his arms as soon as we were out of earshot.

"This isn't my fault," he said. "I'm well within my rights, according to our agreement."

"All I'm asking for is one extra day with Rose, which you got last week anyway, so it's not even extra. I don't understand why you're being such a stickler."

"I know I'm a boring rule follower," he said. "But some people actually like that about me."

He was baiting me, trying to turn this into an argument about the past, where we both knew I'd already lost the moral high ground. I felt like he was trying to distract me, that something else was at play.

"Why is it so important for Rose to go to Megan's mother's birthday?" I asked. "If it was your mother, I could understand."

"Oh, I'm sure you'd be thrilled if I said I was taking Rose to my mother's this weekend."

"I always liked your mother." This was true, even though I'd never had much in common with Mrs. Glenn. She was—and still is, as far as I know—a very traditional person, a homemaker who raised Carter and his siblings in a beautiful historic house in Savannah, Georgia, where she liked to host fundraisers for local, innocuous causes. When Carter and I first started dating, he was rebelling against his upbringing, attending antiwar marches with genuine fervor, whereas I was showing up out of a sense of obligation to my hippieish parents. Back then, I was drawn to his enthusiasm, his habit of looking for the best in everyone. But he stopped showing me that side of himself after we broke up.

"I'm sorry," Carter said in a case-closed voice, "but Megan and I had this planned."

"Is Megan's whole family going to be at this party?" I asked, pressing him. I had the sense I was onto something. "Because it's kind of a big step if you're going to be introducing Rose to all her relatives . . ." I stopped, realizing where I was headed, rhetorically. "Oh my god. Are you guys getting married?"

"No," Carter said quickly. "I mean, not right now." He glanced in Megan's direction, the light catching a hidden vein of silver in his sandy-blond hair. Now that I had the real context for the weekend, I understood the look they exchanged when they saw me coming their way. I felt even more left out.

"I can't believe you're thinking about getting married. It hasn't even been a year since we split up."

"It's been two years. More than that."

"I mean since it was official," I said, as if that were the point. I had always known Carter wanted to remarry, to replicate the stable life I'd upended, but that wasn't my plan, and I thought I would have more time to get used to being alone. I suppose my fantasy was that Carter would put off remarrying until I was totally secure as a human being and free of existential anxieties.

He looked at me with tired eyes. "I'm just trying to get on with my life."

"Are you doing this for your career?" I imagined him and Megan at some law firm function, Carter with his new ring, his golden-boy good looks.

"You're so cynical," he said, the contempt coming back into his voice. "I'm doing it because I like her—because I love her. And it will be good for Rose. Kids need stability."

"Okay, so I'm guessing you want to have another baby," I said flatly, in an assessing tone. "Maybe two—or three. And now you need to meet the mother this weekend to make sure you're not marrying into some crazy family. You don't want to make the same mistake twice."

"Are you really going to make this about you right now?" He was adopting the weary tone of a parent negotiating with a toddler.

"Fine," I said. "Take her." The futility of arguing with Carter was suddenly a crushing weight.

"I *am* sorry," Carter said. "If it weren't for Megan's mother's birthday—"

"Will you stop talking about her mother?" I snapped. Every time he mentioned Megan's mother, I thought of how much I missed my own.

"Leigh," Carter said gently, "don't take this the wrong way, but I think it could be good for you to get on with your life, too."

"I'm not sure how to take that in the right way."

"I just mean you seem a little down." He looked into my eyes, and for a second I remembered what it felt like to be close to him. Then he dropped his gaze. "What's done is done. You don't want to get stuck in the past."

"Thanks for your concern," I said dryly. He had no idea what was going on with me. I wasn't dwelling on the past; it was the future that obsessed me. I'd read the Pentagon's reports on the projected costs of global warming. They were planning for it even if the rest of the country wasn't.

"Never mind," Carter said. "I was trying to be nice, but forget it."

I watched him walk back to Rose and Megan. In the distance, the asphalt parking lot glittered in the spring sunlight. The whole world was getting steamrolled and smothered, it was a catastrophe. I hated my car, hated that I would be driving home alone in it. But I put those feelings away when I said goodbye to Rose. In those blissful thirty seconds, I savored her soft cheek, her sturdy legs wrapped around me after I lifted her into an embrace.

"My sweet wild Rose," I said. "Have fun at the party. Eat lots of cake."

3.

When I got home, my tidied apartment was a reminder of all I'd done to prepare for Rose's arrival. The refrigerator was stocked with the foods she liked best: orange juice, cottage cheese, tortellini, baby carrots, red peppers, spinach, strawberry jam, English muffins, raisin bread. None of it was anything I felt like eating. If I'd known Rose was going to be with her dad, I would have bought something nice to snack on, or else I would have stayed late at work and visited the fitness center, tried out one of the exercise and wellness classes in development for Physical Readiness. Maybe I would have even ventured to happy hour. I felt like I could use some axe throwing.

I texted my friend Tara to see if she was going. We work together, but not on the same project. She replied immediately: I skipped it to go on an app date which I may live to regret.

I sent a fingers-crossed emoji, then slumped onto my gray sectional to face the void of my evening. I didn't like being alone in my generic condo, one of a row of identical homes with small wooden decks and square crew-cut lawns. It wasn't any place I'd ever dreamed of living. With its vinyl siding and chemically doused landscaping, it was the opposite of the modest stone house that I'd grown up in, surrounded by swaying trees and an energetic jumble of flowers that changed with the seasons. Nothing was stopping me from planting such a garden in front of my townhome—except the feeling that my mother would never want me to be marooned in such a place.

Still clutching my phone, I did the one thing I shouldn't when I'm missing Rose: opened my photos. Scrolling, I traveled backward in time with terrifying speed, all the way to the videos from her babyhood. I watched one of her crawling, her little palms splayed like paws going *slap slap slap* on the floor. The pictures I liked best were the ones where she was just in her diaper, and I could see her smooth milk-fed skin. All that cushiony baby softness was gone now—she was a little girl with opinions and observations and memories folding behind her thoughts. In one video, I watched her climb onto our brown leather chair and rub the material with her hand, looking at me as if to say, "It's smooth, isn't it?" In the background, Carter called out, "Be careful on that chair, it's high up!"

Carter was the King of Careful, and I was the Queen of Reckless. That's what Carter would say, at least. I've always wondered what he told our friends about our breakup. Probably something boring, like I cheated on him, or we got married too fast. Anything but the weird truth, which was that, after he found out that I'd been selling "a Schedule I drug" on the side of my law-librarian job—he was through with me. "Drug" was his word, not mine. I never thought of myself as a drug dealer, which maybe makes me naive and overprivileged—even reckless. And maybe I was all those things. Maybe I put our life at risk for no good reason.

The truth is, I didn't expect Carter to understand. But I'd hoped he would forgive me—because it was me. Because it was us.

Our courtship started right after college, while we were both getting ready for law school. It was tentative but romantic. We went for long walks in DC—which is not a pedestrian's town. On rainy days, we treated the free museums like corridors, barely looking at the art and treasures, letting all the knowledge slide past us because the only history we cared about was each other's. We'd walk until the bottoms of our feet hurt, and then we'd get seven-and-sevens and baskets of salted peanuts in the shell at a nearby dive bar. At the end of the evening, we'd kiss like teenagers near the hedges outside my building, so often that, to this day, the spicy, herbal smell of boxwood shrubs brings back a feeling of erotic anticipation. Carter usually didn't stay the night but would call me when he got back to his apartment. We'd put our phones on speaker and watch Jon Stewart together while I sipped chamomile tea and he had a nightcap. Maybe I was happiest then, I don't know. All I remember is that during that time, I stopped caring about law school. Carter was feeling the same way, though he ended up attending Georgetown that fall. His parents were paying but only if he started that year.

I married Carter because I'd wanted a baby more than anything in the world, but on the eve of our wedding, I stayed up late reading about projected temperatures in 2050, when I would be in my seventies and my hypothetical child would be entering middle age. I wanted grandchildren, too. A stable future seemed untenable then, and it's only become more so in the intervening years, with coral reefs dying, algae choking Lake Erie, fires tearing through the West, and, somehow, even *more* fossil fuels being burned, more methane leaking into the atmosphere. Carter had no patience for my despair. He never really understood where it was coming from.

My thumb swiped up, taking me further into the past. I was getting into the danger zone, the photos of my mother in the months leading up to her death.

I decided to call my dad. I guess my logic was: I'm already feeling agitated, so why not go whole hog?

Dad's phone rang endlessly. He's never had an answering machine; his method of screening is to see who will endure. Finally: "This is Steve Bowers."

"Dad."

"Leigh! Are you calling from a landline?"

"I'm on my cell."

"You know how I feel about that. Call me back when you're home."

"I am home. I don't have a landline."

"How can you not have a landline?"

"It's new construction, we've been over this. I'm not going to get cancer from one cell phone call."

"It's *cumulative*," he said.

I ignored this. "Do you remember Jenny Heck?" I asked. "I came across her online."

"Of course I remember Jenny. I just saw Everett a couple of weeks ago. I got a dog from him, some kind of Airedale mix. I named him Harold."

"I didn't know you wanted a dog," I said, though I wasn't surprised he'd gotten a pet from Everett. Jenny's dad was known for collecting stray animals. The Heck house was in an isolated section of woods where people often abandoned their pets. Everett would find them when he was out hiking and bring them home with him. Jenny used to complain about it, but in an admiring way.

"I ran into Everett in Lambert when he was out walking him, and he said, 'You like him? You can have him!' Somebody had just dumped him, and Everett already has his hands full. So I took him. It's been good. He takes me out for walks every day. Maude's not too thrilled about it, but she'll get used to it."

Maude was our ancient housecat, who had never been known to thrill at anything.

"You should see all the animals Everett has," my dad went on. "He's still living out there in the woods, doing his neo-hippie thing, sporting those Willie Nelson pigtails."

"That's his style," I said vaguely. I couldn't decide if it was meaningful that Everett Heck had shown up in my dad's life around the same time that Jenny had shown up in mine. He and Everett worked within a few blocks of each other, yet neither of them had much reason to venture into each other's worlds. Dad spent most of his time on campus, while Everett stayed behind the counter at Phases of the Moon, recommending crystals to Dad's students.

"So what is Jenny up to these days? The last I heard, she was trying to be an actor in New York."

"She's still doing that," I lied, to avoid bringing up my work. Like almost everyone in my life, my dad was under the impression that I worked for the Pentagon Library. I hadn't worked up the nerve to tell him that I was helping to develop new technologies for the military. He wouldn't approve.

"Dad," I began, as casually as I could, "did you ever tell Everett that we got Hecate's Key for Mom?"

"I thought we decided not to mention it to anyone."

"I know, but it's been a while. Don't you think he'd like to know that we were able to track it down?"

"I don't want it getting out that your mother used a mushroom. You know how people are around here. She has a good reputation—it doesn't need to be tarnished by small-minded gossip."

I felt deflated by his paranoia.

"When are you and Rose going to come up for a visit?" he asked. "Don't you have Easter break soon?"

"I can't come then, I have to split that week with Carter," I said. But truthfully, I just wasn't in the mood to go back to my parents' house. It was harder in the years after my marriage ended; it was as if my grief over Mom had resurfaced in the aftermath.

"We'll come this summer," I promised. "The last week of August."

"We should get off the phone. I don't want to keep you on your cell. I hope you've been using a headset, at least."

"I always do," I said. I never do. "Bye, Dad."

"Bye, sweetheart."

I hung up and sank into what Rose called "the cozy corner" of the sectional. But it didn't feel cozy by myself. I missed having a partner in life. My mother wrote to my father in her last Valentine's Day card, in 2009, "You're always just about to go off the deep end, but so am I. I picture us standing there at the edge, holding hands, and looking down at the troubled waters. Sometimes, though, the water is calm and smooth as glass, and I see your reflection smiling at mine, as if you know this life is an illusion."

4.

Alone for the night, I started working on my travel form so that I could visit Jenny. To support travel for an in-person interview, I needed to show that Jenny's therapies were best understood face-to-face and related to at least one of the domains of health readiness: Physical, Mental, Spiritual, or Sleep. Our team focuses on spiritual treatments, but Jenny's therapy was, as Marcos suggested, probably effective for mental readiness as well.

As I browsed online looking for a good argument to justify a plane ride, I wondered how I could have missed her all these years. "Jennifer Hex" had been featured in alternative-health publications that I regularly read, as well as lifestyle magazines and blogs I monitor for work. She'd even been mentioned on a podcast I regularly listen to, in which the hosts try out a self-help routine for two weeks and then dissect it.

Looking at Jenny's timeline, I started to think the real reason I hadn't noticed her star rising had to do with my divorce, which had been finalized in late 2014. Jenny's popularity had peaked around the same time. While Jenny had been enjoying her press honeymoon, I was dealing with months of lawyers, motels, and finding a new place to live. I landed in my blanched condo in January 2015. It was the beginning of an empty season in my life, a time when I longed for winter storms because I wanted the quiet tenderness of snow.

Jennifer Hex's most accessible therapy was called "Say Hi to the Locals." For a small fee or an item of barter, Jennifer would FaceTime with you while you took her on a tour of your yard, block, or nearby park. Then she would advise you to form a relationship with a certain tree, one that would help you "get on the path to healing." How the relationship would evolve was hard to say, but Jennifer Hex had a lot of positive testimonials on her website. "Say Hi to the Locals" was evidently very good at helping people deal with anxiety and low-grade depression. Another of her treatments, "Ancestral Forest Walking"— which, as best as I could tell, was hiking barefoot—was recommended for severe afflictions brought on by PTSD and TBIs. There was also a category of tree therapies devoted to fertility issues. But Jennifer Hex wouldn't guarantee outcomes or make any promises about her methods. They were just something to guide you onto a *path*—an important word to Jennifer Hex. In an interview with *Seeker Magazine*, Jennifer Hex said, "I choose the word 'path' over 'journey' because *path* doesn't suggest a destination, as *journey* inevitably does."

Many things Jennifer Hex said about her methodology sounded absurd out of context, which made her perfect for the internet—or terrible, depending on your point of view. When she was profiled by *Crystals and Croissants*, a wellness blog targeted at foodies, she was quoted as saying, "Americans are obsessed with their digestive systems, with chewing and shitting. Trees don't eat, they synthesize. We could learn a lot from them."

As a result of that interview, Jennifer Hex was accused of promoting disordered eating, and her name was dragged through numerous tweetstorms. I spent a good half hour digging up old tweets and getting angry on Jenny's behalf, as commenters railing against a misogynist culture with impossible beauty standards assumed she was a dumb, vain woman. No one even bothered to look at the original interview. Their careless assumptions were a different kind of misogyny altogether.

Jennifer Hex didn't respond to her critics until she did a Q&A with *Moon Child*, a beloved/reviled email newsletter run by a famous actress. It was Jenny's most recent interview, as far as I could find online:

Moon Child: You've said you don't like the idea of "gut instincts"—can you talk more about that?

Jennifer Hex: By the time you feel something in your gut, that's an alarm system going off. It would be like making all your life decisions by calling 911. Your gut has no subtlety. You think with your immune system, and with your skin.

MC: What do you mean by that?

JH: Your skin is where your body meets the world. It's porous, and it gives you so much information. It practically breathes. There are theories that there is an organ beneath your skin, which I believe connects to your third eye. I might even go so far as to say that this organ is related to your consciousness.

MC: Does your therapy work by tapping into this consciousness?

JH: I couldn't really tell you how any of my treatments work. I'm just talking about the way consciousness functions. Consciousness is the story of a particular living thing. It's a kind of reading. We as a species have lost our ability to speak the language of plants and animals. When I say I teach people to communicate with trees, I just mean that I teach people to break down that superficial border between themselves and the world. People need to let the world in.

MC: Why focus on trees instead of, say, the animals and insects in a particular area, or the grasses?

JH: I grew up with trees, so I know how to listen to them. If I'd grown up on the prairie, maybe I'd be really into dirt or clouds or birds. I like trees because they're old, and they've weathered a lot of storms. The ones that survive, especially the ones in cities, they've seen some shit, you know? Where are you based?

MC: Today? Brooklyn.

JH: A tree that grows in Brooklyn—really any tree that grows in New York City—is a very smart tree, a tree worth listening to. It's very difficult to be a street tree. There's pollution and cars and dogs peeing on you. I lived in New York for a while, when I was trying to be an actor, and there was this one sidewalk plot on my block where the trees just wouldn't grow. They must have planted six seedlings, and they would always die. I was like, what happened in that spot? Because I felt there was a spiritual reason.

MC: Or it could have been that there was some kind of deep chemical or industrial pollution.

JH: To me that's a spiritual reason. Whenever I visit New York I'm so haunted by its past, by the forest that was there—and freshwater springs, the ponds, the swamps, the wildlife. It was probably one of the most beautiful islands on earth, but now it's transmogrified. I think it's haunted by its own beauty, and I think everyone who lives there is haunted by it.

MC: What about LA? Isn't it haunted?

JH: Yes, of course, but it's a desert, so the energy is much different.

MC: I was going to ask about that. How does a tree therapist end up in a desert?

JH: The acting thing again. It took me a while to shake that. When I was young, it was like I couldn't be myself until I was walking in the woods or on a stage. The stage gave me permission to be in the world as fully as I wanted to be, to let down those borders that I was talking about. To play. I think I was actually a pretty good actor. The problem was that I was never what casting agents were looking for. I'm too tall and broad, and my face isn't pretty in a marketable way.

MC: But you're so beautiful!

JH: See, you're still stuck in the Hollywood mind-set, you feel a need to say that. Who cares if I am or not? All those years of rejection in New York and LA forced me to find a way to be myself in the world without being onstage. And then I could see there were all these other rejected actors who had the same problem. I started doing group therapies with actors and other artists, trying to help them reconnect to the green divine. And that's how it all got started.

MC: Everything happens for a reason.

JH: Oh no, I would never say that. Everything happens. Leave it at that.

I reread the last part of her interview about quitting acting. It was the part of her biography I was most curious about. When I'd known her, she'd been dead set on pursuing a career in the theater. She'd been crushed when she wasn't chosen for a lead role in our school production of *A Midsummer Night's Dream*—that was how we'd become friends. When I congratulated her for being cast as Titania, the Queen of the Fairies, she said, "I tried out for Hermia. I didn't get it because I'm taller than Paul and he's Lysander. It's fascist patriarchal bullshit."

I'd wanted to agree but hadn't been totally sure of the definition of "fascist." Or "patriarchal." I shyly told her I was Cobweb, one of the fairies, and was thrilled when she seemed genuinely pleased. She was so magnetic, even back then.

"I was worried I'd be stuck with a bunch of freshman girls I don't know," she said, slinging her dark-green JanSport over one shoulder. "I gotta go outside and wait for my dad. You need a ride?"

I shook my head. "I go home with my mom."

I followed her to the cement benches outside the auditorium. "Do you want one?" She offered me a slender brown cigarette, a kind I had never seen before. "They're cloves."

I shook my head, flattered that she would think I might.

"My mom smokes, but she won't let me. She's such a hypocrite." Jenny exhaled fumes that smelled like Christmas. "I can't figure what there is to do around here for fun."

I shrugged. "Go to the movies?"

"You need a car for that," she said. "You need a car for everything around here. I miss the Metro."

Her father arrived in his beat-up Honda Accord, covered in bumper stickers that said things like KILL YOUR TV and LIVE SIMPLY SO THAT OTHERS MAY SIMPLY LIVE. They were the kind of slogans my mother might have brandished if she weren't a teacher. Her Volvo was a sitting duck in the high school parking lot. I realized then that Jenny and I were from the same kind of family, the children of parents who prowled health food stores and dreamed of utopia. The children of parents who didn't fit in.

Jenny had surprised me that day with a hug goodbye. "I'll see you tomorrow for the read-through."

I treasured our weeks of rehearsal. Jenny could make people laugh with just a facial expression or an offhand gesture. She stole every scene she was in, and no one minded. She seemed to do it without trying.

Jenny's parents attended different performances. Her father came on the first night with her younger brother, who was visiting for the weekend. The two of them looked like they were dressed for Freaky Friday, with Everett Heck in stone-washed jeans and a wildlife-themed T-shirt, and Jenny's brother wearing a collared shirt tucked into belted khakis.

Jenny's mother, Suzanne, showed up alone on Saturday night. She came backstage after the curtain call and gave Jenny a mixed bouquet, saying, "Your father left this in the car overnight, that's why the flowers are wilted." Then she told Jenny to hurry up and meet her in the parking lot because she wanted to drive back to Bethesda that night. Jenny was upset that she couldn't go straight to the cast party, that she had to go home and say goodbye to her brother when he hadn't even bothered to come that night.

"Jenny, no one wants to see Shakespeare two nights in a row," Suzanne said sharply. "Just wash your face, okay?"

I followed Jenny to the bathroom, where a bunch of girls were standing at the sinks.

"She wants me to meet her at the car so she can smoke while she waits," Jenny said, rubbing Noxzema on her cheeks and forehead. "She couldn't even bring herself to say that I was good. I *was* good, wasn't I?"

"Jenny, you were so, so good. Everyone thought so."

She nodded, her eyes welling up. "I'm going to be so much better than her, and she knows it. I'm going to be free and not stuck in some dumb government job filing papers for the FEMA people. I'm going to travel all over the world. I'm going to meet famous people and see famous places. I'm not letting her say who I am or what I can be."

Jenny's tears mingled with cold cream, and her face was a red mess.

"I can't go out to her like this," she said. "Will you go talk to her? Tell her I can't go now because I promised I'd take you to the party."

"Of course," I said, my heart flying.

I found Jenny's mom in the parking lot, leaning against her car, smoking, her handbag balanced on the hood.

"Mrs. Heck? Jenny wanted me to tell you that she's going to take me home."

"Why didn't she come out here herself?"

I shrugged, pulling tight the sides of my cardigan. It was a cool evening in late spring, with insect sounds that I took for granted.

"Never mind, she doesn't want to talk to me, I get it. I don't know why she has to drag you into it." Mrs. Heck exhaled, moving her head so the smoke wafted away from me. "Don't ever start smoking. It's addictive."

"I know."

She laughed. "I guess that's beyond obvious. I've tried to quit, I even went into therapy for it. You know what the therapist told me?" Suzanne paused for dramatic effect—and to exhale. "She said I was trying to control my own death. *A slow suicide,* she called it. And the crazy thing is, that didn't stop me. It just made me understand myself better. Which wasn't what I wanted. I don't think anyone does. What good does that do?"

I struggled to answer her question.

"Maybe it helps when you die," I said. "Maybe if you know yourself, it's a little easier to let go."

"Well, that's morbid." Suzanne dropped her spent cigarette. "Tell Jenny that I'll see her next weekend. And tell her she was really good."

Jenny wasn't in the bathroom when I returned, but she found me there a few minutes later, and she was as happy as she'd been sad, fifteen minutes before. Our director had said she should be an actor, move to New York.

She grasped my forearms. "Are you ready to celebrate?"

We hurried out to Jenny's dad's car with all the bumper stickers on it. People called across the parking lot about the party, and we waved back like *Yeah, we'll be there.* As we got in the car, Jenny lit one of her cloves, rolling down the window to ash it. Then she handed it to me so she could get the car started.

"Go ahead," she said. "One puff won't kill you."

I took a drag. It was sweet. "You didn't tell me these were dessert cigarettes."

"Keep it for yourself!"

I ashed out the window, like she did. The cool night air whipped through the car. We listened to a mixtape, turning it up loud as we coasted the empty, rolling country roads. Above us the sky was marvelously dark, every star pinpricked into place. The gibbous moon looked like something you could grab hold of.

"I don't want to go to the party," Jenny said suddenly. "It's just going to be beers in someone's basement. I want to do something different, something special. This is the night my life really begins."

I nodded, even though I still had two years of high school left to go. But I could see something was changing for her.

We drove to Lost Falls, our town's namesake. It was near Jenny's house, and she knew the hike to the falls well. The trail was flat and easy, about a mile through a pine and deciduous forest. When we pulled into the parking lot, there was no one else there. A sign warned us that the park was closed after sunset and that camping was prohibited. "It doesn't say anything about night-swimming!" Jenny said.

The path to the falls was well trodden, and we were so thrilled by our own daring that we pretty much ran there. Jenny kept the flashlight she'd found in the trunk fixed on the ground, and we jumped over protruding roots and knobby rocks. The trees seemed to flow past us as we ran, propelling us. After a few minutes, we could hear the falls.

It was called "Lost" Falls because it was slightly hidden by a turn in the creek and a limestone boulder that jutted into the water. The water tumbled from a height of about fifteen feet, a curtain that spilled into a rocky pool. In the summer, you could usually find people wading in the pool. It was very much a local's spot, though. Like our town, it was not dramatic or unique enough to make it onto tourist maps.

In the daylight, the falls caught the sunlight, and you could see rainbows in the spray. The surrounding rocks were covered in a deep-green moss. But at night, the mosses were bluish in the dim light, and the falls had a silver cast. The sound of the rushing water seemed to be magnified by the darkness and the smell of the woods. Most magical of all was the little pool, which held a reflection of the moon, a white orb floating delicately, like a flower petal.

"It's even more beautiful than I thought it would be," Jenny said. She turned off the flashlight and started to take off her clothes. "Are you going in?"

"I don't know," I admitted. "I'm a little cold."

"Leigh! Are you joking?" She had already stripped down to her underwear and a tank top. "You have to go in. You'll regret it for the rest of your life if you don't!"

"I know . . . I've just never gone skinny-dipping before."

"Me neither!" Jenny laughed, then did a little dance after she took off her tank top to make her small breasts shake.

"Bring the blankets over at least!" she called back to me, and I grabbed the fringed yoga blankets that had been on the back seat. She wobbled as she stepped from stone to stone, making her way toward the water.

I took off my clothes, wrapping one of the blankets around me and draping one over my arm as I shivered in the dark. Ahead of me, Jenny was stepping into the pool, up to her ankles. She yelped as she got to waist height, and then she surprised me by suddenly going up to her neck and then going under. She surfaced after a few seconds, her hair slicked back. "It's deeper than I thought!"

I forced myself to run in. The water was so cold that it stung. But then it was like something under my skin warmed up and a mellow calm took over. Jenny and I swam to the bubbly, churned-up area in the wake of the falls. I tipped my head back to look up at the fine mist of the Milky Way, the falls so close that the sound of the water was almost like a physical wall that surrounded us.

Jenny dunked her head again, pushing her hair out of her face as she surfaced. "This is so much better than getting drunk at a cast party."

I just nodded, because I'd never been drunk or even been invited to a party where consuming alcohol was a possibility. I was a nobody sophomore, best known as "the science teacher's daughter."

"I wish we could do the play another night," Jenny said. "I wish we could do it every weekend until school is out. Athletes get to play every week, why shouldn't we?"

"Because this is America. Sports are wholesome. Theater is weird."

"Theater goes back to the freaking Stone Age," Jenny said. "People around here are so puritanical."

"Not everyone," I said, feeling the need to defend Lost Falls, my home. "Your dad isn't."

"Honestly, I don't get why he stays here."

"My mom says she likes being near the woods, near nature."

"If I had to choose between nature and being around people who like theater and art and all different kinds of music and religion and poetry, I'm going to choose that, you know?"

"Yeah, I know," I said, even though I hadn't known, not until that moment, that I would probably never come back to Lost Falls after graduation.

"I think if I stayed here, I would just die of loneliness," Jenny said, her voice high and sincere. "I mean, the woods don't talk."

We hurried to the yoga blankets, drying ourselves quickly and then using them as shawls once we were dressed. The temperature had dropped, and we were still cold from the water.

We stopped at a Denny's on the way home and ate eggs and bacon and buttered toast. The waitress kept giving us coffee refills, and we kept talking about the future. When I finally got home, five hours late for my curfew, my mother was angrier than I'd ever seen her, and barely able to speak through sobs of relief.

"I thought you were dead!" she said. "I thought you were in a car crash. I thought the police were coming to my door."

"I'm not dead," I said, unable to stifle my smile. I was the polar opposite; I was wildly alive.

"Get that smirk off your face! Where were you? Why is your hair wet?"

Everyone rebels from their parents at some point, and that night was the beginning of my era of mild defiance. I stopped trying to live up to my parents' environmental ideals, embracing the consumerism that my peers enjoyed, buying new clothes and makeup, glossy magazines, and CDs in plastic jewel cases that my mother despised. I insisted on driving lessons, and began to save for my first car. I yearned to drive nowhere in particular, for no good reason.

Jenny left early that summer, and I got a postcard from her months later, a photo of the diner from *Seinfeld*. On the back of the card, Jenny wrote, "I live right near here—come visit! Love, Jenny." That was it. No phone number. No address. I decided she was careless, because it hurt too much to know that she didn't really want me to find her.

She left in an age when it was still possible for people to disappear.

But here she was, gazing at me from my computer screen. As I stared at her photo, wondering how she'd ended up in California, my phone buzzed to alert me to a new message from Tara: HELP. I need to be done with this date.

I wrote back: Tell him the babysitter texted to come back.

I don't have kids

But does he know that??

Ha idk. Stay up okay? I'll be over soon

5.

Tara was wearing her standard first-date outfit: a black-and-white patterned blouse, silver jewelry, black jeans, and heeled boots that she took off as soon as she was inside. Her socks were striped wool.

She sank onto my sectional as if she'd just gotten back from a tough session at the gym. I offered her wine or tea.

"Wine, please. Give me a Tami Taylor pour." She checked the dark-green band on her wrist. Tara is one of a small group of army reservists testing a version of IRTH2 that is limited to fitness and nutrition coaching.

"Do you ever just not tell it what you ate?" I brought a can of salted cashews over with the wine.

"I did it all the time at first, but it's smart. It knows something's off. Or worse, it doesn't realize, and then it starts adjusting your calorie budget based on fudged numbers." Tara examined her wineglass. "What do you think this is, six ounces?"

It looked like a drag to keep track of every morsel, but Tara claimed to like it, especially the newest feature that paired her wearable with a "smart" fridge and pantry that recommended healthy meals based on what Tara had in stock. It could also generate grocery lists and online orders.

After Tara typed in the wine, a warm baritone voice emanated from her wearable, reminding her that she might not be fit to drive.

"Is that . . . George Clooney?" I asked.

"Yes! Isn't that hilarious? If I log a second glass, he's going to ask me if I really want another drink." Tara held up her glass. "I do, George!"

We toasted each other and then exchanged our stories of minor humiliation: I told her about discovering Carter's proto-engagement plans, and she described her boring date. She'd met the guy online and screened him in advance with her usual method—limiting text messages and insisting on a phone conversation ASAP. Also, Tara calls her dates during her morning commute, so if the guy isn't up by seven thirty, no dice—no matter how good-looking. If he can hold a fifteen-minute conversation on the phone, and if she laughs, she'll ask for a date. Her first encounter is always a drink or a coffee at a place in her neighborhood, and then, if she likes him, dinner.

This guy had made it through the gauntlet all the way to a cute little farm-to-table restaurant in the city. *Then* he started talking about the upcoming election. It wasn't that Tara disagreed with his politics; it was just that he was so overheated, and it was only March. He was reading polls, listening to podcasts, following so-and-so on Twitter. And he wasn't even a journalist or a staffer. He was an IT person at a consulting firm. He was clearly disappointed that Tara wasn't more "politically engaged." He thought she would care more, considering that she was in the military.

"I told him I have to accept whoever gets elected, so why get emotionally involved when that person is going to be my boss? He didn't get that. I was like, a little distance is for my own mental health. He didn't get that, either." Tara poured out another dose of wine. "You want some?"

"No, thanks." I was still nursing my first glass. Some nights you just know alcohol is going to take you straight to the valley of sad-ass songs. Or to a website that maps dead zones in the ocean. I needed sleep.

"When you go on dates," Tara said, "what do you tell people about your job?"

"I don't tell anyone anything," I said, "because I don't date."

"Okay," Tara said, "but on that beautiful day when you finally let me make your dating profile, what are you going to say?"

"Librarian?" I shrugged. That was what I'd told Carter. Like my father, he thought I worked at the Pentagon Library. It was easier than explaining what I really did, and Marcos had advised me to be vague, in general.

"That's good. Guys like that. Smart, but behind the scenes. I don't know what to say. The stuff I'm doing is so cool, but I basically have to say that I'm training dogs. And people don't respect that."

"Can you tell them about the PTSD therapy?"

Tara worked with the IRTH2 programmers to teach therapy dogs to incorporate feedback from the wearable device. As far as I knew, that part of her job was not classified.

"I do, but they see it as, I don't know, soft. Like I'm teaching people to pet dogs or something. Or they go off on a tangent about other people's emotional support animals on planes. Which is a real red flag, honestly. Whenever someone gets upset about emotional support animals, I'm like, this person has emotional needs that aren't being addressed."

She seemed more down after this dud date than usual.

"Sometimes I think all the good guys got married. I'm stuck with the damaged divorcés."

"Thanks a lot," I said lightly. I knew she wasn't talking about me, but I worried about how I would be perceived if and when I ever started dating again.

"When I meet a woman who's divorced, I always assume she had a good reason," Tara insisted. "Or there was something wrong with the guy who left her."

"You wouldn't say that about Carter if you met him." I could just picture him on a date, wearing his suit and shimmering with the confidence of fatherhood and career success—and the knowledge that he'd been the one wronged in our marriage.

"Oh, forget about him," Tara said, taking a handful of cashews. "He's just another pompous lawyer guy. Trust me, I've gone out with his type."

"He's actually kind of a good person."

"He left you!"

"Yeah, I guess so," I said evasively. She didn't know the whole story of why Carter had left, or how I'd come to work for the DOD. No one really did.

Tara had a tentative look on her face. "I've been thinking about freezing my eggs," she said. "The army will pay for it."

"You should," I said, sensing that she wanted approval—or at least the feeling that she had options. "That's great that it's covered."

"They're trying to be more female friendly. They have a postpartum option in here for workouts," Tara said, tapping her wearable. "But no period tracker . . ."

"Did you tell them to add one?"

"I told them it should be an option. I'm pretty sure it's an easy thing to program. There's already a ton out there. But they said it's a privacy issue for women. I think they just don't want to know about any lady's cycle."

"Don't ask, don't tell," I said, trying to keep things light. But I felt heavy. "Do you ever think we're just total hypocrites?"

Tara laughed at my non sequitur. "What do you mean?"

"Like, we're trying to come up with these technologies to deal with the climate crisis, but the military is like, the worst offender in terms of emissions."

"They're trying to be greener," Tara said. "But there's not a lot of options for fueling an F-16."

"They could stop building so many."

"Yeah, sure. Tell that to Lockheed Martin."

"Sometimes," I said, "I just wonder what I'm doing with my life."

"I've been there." Tara picked up the remote. "You want to watch a movie?"

"*Top Gun*?" I joked.

We flipped around until we found *Mermaids*, that movie from the nineties with Winona Ryder and Cher.

Tara stayed over, sleeping in Rose's room. I was tired, too, but I couldn't fall asleep, despite sticking to that one glass of wine. The movie had stirred something up. I remembered being so bowled over by the glamour of Cher—the idea of *Cher* as a mother—when I saw it as a kid. She was the opposite of my science-teacher mother, whose bywords were "sensible" and "practical." Other mothers took their daughters school shopping or installed aboveground pools so they could tan and have friends over; my mother took me to demonstrations for the preservation of an old-growth forest in the Allegheny Mountains. No one wanted to eat dinner at our house because we were such strict vegetarians. We ate so much soup, so much salad with sunflower seeds sprinkled on top, and so many types of beans. Black beans. Kidney beans. Lima beans. Red beans. Lentils—obviously, lentils. I had to carry a canvas lunch bag—anything disposable was contemptible—and eat mushy-looking concoctions like brown rice mixed with yogurt and ground flax seed or chickpea-and-tomato salads. None of it was packed in Tupperware; my mother insisted on miniature mason jars. I always felt like such a weirdo, unscrewing my glass jars and taking out my metal spoon. On top of that, we had an outdoor composting toilet, and my parents mixed our waste with peat moss for the flower garden. When people expressed incredulity or even disgust at the way we lived, my mother would shrug and say, "You're the one who is completely reliant on public utilities."

It's hard for me to gauge now how extreme my mother was in her thinking. She spent her entire adult life taking heed of ecologists' observations about the delicate balance of nature upended, but I don't remember her having the apocalyptic mindset of today's preppers, who think that society is on the verge of collapse. The only time I remember her expressing thoughts about national politics was when Gore lost. "He was the only one who seemed to have any sense of urgency," my mother said. "They've known for almost twenty years now, and they've done nothing. Now they never will."

"Maybe there could be some kind of legal action," I said. "Some kind of litigation against the oil companies."

"You really think lawyers are going to save us? They're the ones who defended DuPont and Exxon Mobil."

At the time, I felt personally implicated by her pessimism. I knew the planet was being destroyed, but I didn't want to be an activist or a scientist, I wanted to go to law school, I wanted to move to a city and rent an apartment on a high floor. I had a hunger for the luxuries I saw in magazines: suede boots, restaurant meals, manicures, cashmere, airplane travel—all the things my parents disdained.

I gave up on sleep and went outside into the chilly night, walking around to the front of the condo, where a lone sapling stood. It was a dogwood. There was exactly one flowering dogwood planted in the front yard of every condo, and in pretty much the same spot, as if the developers had put an "X" on their blueprint and written "decorative tree." I examined the twiggy end of a branch, looking for where the leaves had grown the previous year. From Jenny's website, I had learned that trees produce special cells to snip the leaves free. After they fall, another kind of cell repairs the tiny cut, protecting the exposed area from winter's harsh weather. A textbook example of self-healing, if trees have selves.

"Hey," I whispered to the tree. "What's your name?"

Hey yourself, I imagined him replying. *I go by Walter, Walt to my friends.*

"Walt," I whispered. "Am I getting depressed?"

No, he said. *It's just March.*

I wished Walter really could speak. Maybe he *was* talking to me, and I just couldn't hear him. I'd read somewhere that mice and bats can hear the noises that plants and flowers make. Apparently, they speak at a volume similar to the human voice, but the frequency is out of our range of hearing.

There were buds at the tips of Walter's twigs. He would blossom soon, emitting a melody I wouldn't be able to hear.

It hit me then that my mother had died in the spring, though I hadn't exactly forgotten. Every year the anniversary seemed to sneak up on me.

The next morning, I made breakfast for Tara. The sun was streaming into the dining area, and for once I appreciated where I lived. Someone had put thought into the placement of the window.

Tara stirred her oatmeal without eating it. Her face was a little puffy, and in the bright morning light, her unlined eyes seemed vulnerable and young.

"What's the matter?" I asked. "Do you want some milk? Some raisins? I think I have some cinnamon sugar somewhere."

"No, it's fine, stop fussing over me. Just sit down, drink your coffee. I need to tell you something."

It was strange to have an adult across from me first thing in the morning. I was used to being alone, or with Rose, who could barely sit still long enough to eat her meals.

"I'm leaving town for a while," she said. "They're sending me back to Camp David. I go on Tuesday. They want me to stay through the summer."

"All summer? Why?"

"They have a new iteration of CATI. It's the real deal this time. They think they finally have it working."

CATI stood for Canine Assisted Therapeutic Intelligence, pronounced like the woman's name. And that was pretty much the extent of my knowledge of it, at that time—another classified project, above my pay grade.

"Well, that's good, right?" I said, trying to sound upbeat even though I was disappointed. My one good friend was leaving town. There were other people I could call, but no one else who would drop by spontaneously, no one else who would tell me that my ex was a jerk and I needed to get out more.

"I'm going to put in a request for you to visit," Tara said. "The dogs need to interact with other people besides just me. And *I* do, too."

"I doubt I have a high enough security clearance to go."

"Maybe they can make an exception. Otherwise, I'm hardly going to see you for months. I mean, I'll still come back on days off, but—"

"It won't be the same," I finished. We were old enough to know that adult friendships could die on less.

"I'm sorry," she said. "I just found out yesterday."

"Did you tell your date?"

"I would have if I'd liked him. In a way I was glad I didn't." She stood up. "Hang on, I have something in the car for you—for Rose, for her birthday."

She hurried outside and came back with a Lego set called "Lava Island: Velociraptor Family." The box pictured a winged dinosaur perched at the edge of a nest that held three large white eggs. In the background was an ingeniously designed volcano modeled from dozens of red, brown, orange, and black Lego pieces—a scene of extinction made from a substance that was a contributing factor to our own accelerated demise. I tried not to dwell on the irony and instead told Tara that Rose would love it, which was true. And it wasn't as if I didn't buy her plastic toys or purchase clothing woven with polyester fibers. Unlike my mother, I had forfeited the fight against synthetic materials.

After Tara left, I attempted to give myself some tree therapy by standing beneath Walter's brittle-looking branches. I could not bring myself to talk to him in the daylight, but I tried to get to know him, to intuit his story. I wondered if he was happy to be planted there, or if he was confused. He'd probably had a pleasant saplinghood in a nursery, surrounded by other trees, watered daily, properly fertilized, pruned, and pollinated. Then one day he was uprooted, literally, and loaded into the back of a truck with a burlap sack around his nether regions. That had to be a shock.

I wondered if I was just projecting all my issues onto poor little Walter, who, for all I knew, had been glad to leave the nursery. Maybe being planted in a pot had been boring. Maybe he was excited to be in the ground, finally able to stretch out his roots. Maybe we could both learn to be happy on this arbitrary plot of land.

I was pretty sure I was doing tree therapy all wrong.

I went inside and checked Jenny's social media feeds. There was a new post on Instagram, a selfie of Jenny lying on a bed of dark-green moss. Large ferns drooped at the edges of the frame. Her long hair was down, and she wore a black fleece jacket that wasn't particularly stylish. She was smiling in a genuine way. It wasn't your typical wellness vanity shot, and even as I knew I was being taken in by a curated authenticity, I wanted to be where she was, walking beneath old trees, breathing in cool air, feeling moss beneath my fingertips. Whatever she was selling was working on me.

Maybe it was all nostalgia. I didn't care. I missed Rose, I missed my mother, and I couldn't figure out how to be happy in this dying world. But maybe Jenny knew.

6.

Usually I enjoy flying, the blank timelessness of being in the air, but on my flight to Los Angeles I couldn't relax. I was too worried about my interview with "Jennifer Hex." I'd arranged our meeting over email, telling her that I was writing an article about nature-based wellness trends. For this fictional piece of beauty journalism, I would be speaking to her as well as other Los Angeles healers "in the wellness space." I didn't want Jenny to think I'd flown out only to see her. Jenny had been warm over email, sincere. She'd even mentioned my mother, saying that she remembered her class fondly. When I read that, I was tempted to pick up the phone and call Jenny, to tell her the truth of why I was visiting. But I didn't know how I would even begin. She would know right away how odd it was that I was working for the Pentagon. She would want an explanation.

I leaned my head against the rounded window to look down at cloud cover so thick that you couldn't see the land below. We could be anywhere; we could be in heaven. My mother used to say it made more sense for hell to be up in the lonely sky and for paradise to be underground, mixed into the soil's rich stew.

I felt like everything always came back to Mom. I had tried so hard to take a different path from her, to be practical in all the ways she wasn't. In college, I majored in psychology, which I thought would be a useful degree for a lawyer. After graduation, I took a job as a paralegal in a DC firm. My plan was to work for two years, save money, and take the LSAT. Then I would go to law school and graduate at twenty-seven. I would find someone to marry in graduate school, and we would have two children in our thirties. I genuinely thought life could be planned in that way.

I wanted comfort and I got it. I will never again be as mindlessly happy as I was during my first summer out of college. Everything was easy: my paralegal tasks were simpler than my undergraduate assignments, and I got paid to do them. I made new friends, bought nice clothes, and rented a studio apartment in a new building with a gym and a sauna. For the first time in my life, I had cable TV. I ordered takeout in plastic and Styrofoam containers and watched *The West Wing* and *Six Feet Under* and *Sex and the City*. I painted my nails, went to a salon for highlights, and learned to order Prosecco when I went out with my work friends. My life was ordinary, but I felt glamorous.

Then 9/11 happened, and my contentment seemed frivolous. People forget that DC was a target. While military police in flak jackets armed with automatic weapons patrolled the city, I dabbled in activism, chanting "No blood for oil!" at antiwar marches. That's where I met Carter. Actually, I met him at a bar after a march. A mutual friend introduced us on the pretense that we were both waiting to hear back from law schools, though I later found out Carter had asked around until he found someone at the bar who knew me. Which I liked. It would be glib to say I was drawn to Carter because he was the kind of guy you wanted to grab a drink with, but he was the first person I dated who was extroverted and eager to strike up a conversation with strangers. Before him, I'd dated boys who were moody, shy, holier-than-thou. Carter was so agreeable, so easy to be around.

Instead of going to law school, I decided to give myself another year to figure out what I really wanted to do. I switched to a large corporate firm where I could earn a bigger salary. I didn't mind the work, though I hated the atmosphere—a cubicle warren in the basement, as if the paralegals were the firm's dirty secret. Maybe we were. As far as I could tell, we were drafting most of the documents, even the big-ticket merger agreements. One night a partner came down to our under-world to goad us into working faster, angry that we had taken time off for dinner instead of scarfing sandwiches at our keyboards. *Don't you understand that this is the single biggest merger in the history of the United States?* She was the only female partner, and whatever insults she had to swallow to ascend to that position had caused her to run through the patience allotted to mortals at birth. I was terrified of her, but the other paralegals just laughed. Apparently, "single biggest merger" was a record broken every six months, along with "biggest real estate deal." Eventually the Pacific would merge with the Atlantic, and we'd be the ones to put the terms down on paper.

One day, looking for an excuse to leave my basement cubicle, I took the elevator up to the thirty-second floor to pick up a book from the library. When I got there, I was struck by how serene it was compared to the rest of the firm. It was an early winter day, with a soft, clear blue sky that enhanced the quiet atmosphere. The mahogany bookshelves were tall, well dusted, and lined with leather-bound volumes. I felt like I had climbed to the top of a tree, where the branches thin out and you can feel the breeze.

That night, I downloaded applications to library school and completed them over the weekend. Carter was supportive. I think he was secretly relieved that he was going to be the one with the high-powered career. We had a City Hall marriage shortly after I started my graduate program. We'd been dating for a little over a year, and it was impulsive. We were usually so cautious that getting married made us feel like the most exciting versions of ourselves.

Two years later I was hired as a librarian at a corporate law firm. Carter was an associate at a different big firm. He'd decided that he was only going to stay there for a few years and wouldn't try to kill himself trying to make partner. Sometimes, though, if you refuse to compete, you become accidentally powerful, and that's what happened to him. Soon he was in high demand, and definitely on the Partner Track, but in his mind, he was just working a lot. I didn't see him much during those years. Still, we were saving to buy a house for all the kids we were going to have. Carter came from a big family that he wanted to replicate, while I wanted a household where the optimism of youth could keep the pessimism of the parents in check.

When Carter and I were both verging on thirty and starting to think about getting pregnant—"the next step," as we obnoxiously called it—I got the news that my mother had been diagnosed with stage IV ovarian cancer. Among the first things I thought when my mother told me how far her disease had progressed was: *If I get pregnant now, it would probably still be too late.*

I couldn't believe how quickly my mother's surgery and chemotherapy started after diagnosis. One day I was going through my kitchen cabinets, looking to see if we had any baking soda, the next minute my cell phone was buzzing—*Mom* illuminated on the screen—and then suddenly I was standing outside the OR, waving to my mother, who was as high as cirrus clouds on whatever they give people before surgery. "I love you so much, my little Leigh, I adore you!" When she emerged, hours later, she was groggy, sad, irritable, and terribly diminished in her whisper-thin hospital gown. It didn't make sense that the next step was to pump her body full of toxic chemicals, but that was the plan.

All summer long in 2008, she went to Johns Hopkins for treatments. Sometimes she and my father would stay overnight, and Carter and I would meet them for dinner, bringing news of the outside world. The financial markets were collapsing, not that my parents cared. Their detachment was in eerie contrast to the attorneys in my office, whose BlackBerrys wouldn't stop beeping, buzzing, and vibrating as they slunk down the beige hallways of our office, looking like spooked dogs. One of the normally garrulous older partners started coming to the library on his lunch break to sit in the silence. You weren't supposed to eat in the stacks, but I didn't say anything. I started calling him Peanut Chews, because that was his favorite candy bar. It came in six pieces, and he always ate two, gave me two, and saved two pieces for later. He confided to me that the world economy was in danger of collapsing.

He worried about the times in the past when he hadn't understood the financial products that his clients were selling. "They had computer models that were supposed to do the math. Now it's all hanging by the thread of a thread."

"It will be okay," I promised. His plain terror reminded me of my father, who sat by my mother's bedside working on a hooked rug, pushing each strip of felt into place. Dad always had craft projects going, usually related to the classes he taught. The rug he made now rests in his kitchen, but it will always remind me of the hospital.

In October, the doctors announced that the chemo had slowed the cancer's growth but hadn't stopped it. My mother declined experimental treatments after reading about the side effects. She was already suffering from joint pain in the wake of the chemo, was balding, and had lost weight, strength, and even a certain resonant timbre in her voice. Then there were the headaches that shattered her ability to concentrate. "If I only have a few months left in this world, I'd like to be able to listen to music," she said. "And hold conversations with your father."

The day she made the decision to forgo further treatment, we were all weirdly jubilant. It felt dignified, a refusal to buy into an American culture that wouldn't acknowledge death and decay. But it didn't take long for the fear to creep in. As the physical side effects of the chemo began to lessen, my mother had room for contemplation, and soon ice-cold existential questions began to twist their way around her thoughts.

"I'm not ready to go," she would moan during the day. "Why can't I stay?" At night she just sobbed. Her crying reminded me of the heavy rains that came at the end of the days in the hottest part of July: Maryland summers, saturated with cicada song; Maryland summers, where the heat is something you have to reside in to survive. Maybe death was like summer; you had to relax into it.

A hospice nurse was assigned to my mother. I imagined some kindly, borderline elderly woman with a Mrs. Claus physique and twinkle.

Instead, we got a woman in her midthirties, Teresa. She had a tattoo of a medical cross on the inside of her right arm, and on the left was the inscription *primum non nocere*. She looked like a bit of a gym rat, but as I got to know her, I found out she did something called Log Fit, where you lift logs instead of weights and run trails through the woods. She made her own granola and yogurt and believed coconut oil could heal pretty much anything. I liked her, and my father liked her, too. But it didn't matter. My mother was still in agony every night.

"It's normal to cry a lot," Teresa said. "Especially when the patient is relatively young, like your mom. It would be good if she could come to some kind of acceptance, but a lot of times people don't get there. You have to be like, a Buddhist monk with years of meditation under your belt."

"I just want her to have some kind of peace."

"Some people have their faith," Teresa said. "And that helps. But your mother tells me she's not religious."

I shook my head. I remembered asking her about the possibility of God when I was a kid. Her answer: *I believe in plants and animals, not God.*

"Try to focus on the positive moments of your visits," Teresa said. "That's all you can really do."

Like all good advice, it was trite, banal, and difficult to follow. Still, I tried. Every weekend I drove up from DC to visit her, sometimes with Carter but usually without. Those lonely drives will never leave my memory. The gray highway, the radio always tuned to talk of the upcoming election, and outside the leaves going through their vibrant dying as they let the green go, leaving behind vermillion, scarlet, fuchsia, maroon, red, and gold. It seemed as if my mother's death would be the same, as her milder emotions fell away and left a rage that no painkillers could touch.

My mother had stopped teaching, but she kept improving her ongoing lesson plan about the climate crisis. She downloaded and printed computer-modeled images of what our state might look like after sea levels rose, poring over strange maps that showed a Maryland without an Eastern Shore or a Chesapeake Bay. A Maryland that might not be able to sustain a population of blue crabs—its culinary mascot—because if the water continued to warm at current rates, the eelgrass would die, and the crabs would have no place to hide from their enemies. I don't know who she thought would use these lesson plans; even then, she was one of the only teachers who talked about global warming. Maybe it was a way for her to think about the future without contemplating her own death.

Once, when Carter visited, he overheard one of her nighttime crying jags. On the drive home, he told me that I should talk to Teresa about putting my mother on antianxiety medication.

"I already did. She said it doesn't help existential grief." But I asked again. Teresa said she would do what she could do to ease the physical symptoms and help her to get a good night's sleep. Then, when she was finishing up her shift, she slipped me a phone number. "You didn't hear it from me, but you can try marijuana. If it were legal, I would prescribe it."

I gave the number to my father the next morning.

"We tried weed," he said. "It just made her giggly. As always."

"Oh. Well, laughing is good, right?"

"In the moment, sure. But she needs something that's going to change her heart."

"I don't know how we can do that."

"I actually have an idea." My father looked nervously around the room, as if he suspected bugging. "Let's go for a walk, okay?"

We went out to the backyard, with dry, unraked leaves underfoot, leaves that my father would in a normal year use to bed down the garden. I was a little bit chilly, and the air smelled of cold and smoke, and I remember thinking that my father's paranoid tendencies were taking a turn toward, well, actual paranoia. Then he told me about Hecate's Key.

My dad had dropped by Phases of the Moon one evening after work, looking for something for my mother. Everett was working there that day, and my father asked him if there were any crystals that helped people face anxiety about death. Everett pointed him toward lepidolite, and then, when he was ringing up my father's Hail Mary purchase, he mentioned Hecate's Key, an underground treatment he'd heard about at the VA, of all places. Apparently, when ingested, it took away the fear of death. Permanently.

My dad didn't take Everett's suggestion very seriously in the moment. But when he got home and typed "Hecate's Key" into the abyss of the internet, he found out that what Everett said was true. In the Netherlands, where it was legal, it was occasionally prescribed to terminally ill patients. Those who took it reported feeling deep gratitude in their final months, a sense that there was meaning, after all. My mother wanted to try it. The problem was that they didn't know how to find it. They wondered if I knew anyone.

With that one question, my life took a hairpin turn.

7.

The GPS in my rideshare showed that we were approaching Jennifer Hex's house. I didn't feel glam enough to be convincing as a beauty reporter. Despite a nap and shower at my hotel, my hair was limp and my skin dull. My clothes, high-waisted skinny jeans and a striped sweater, were too heavy for the heat.

Fuchsia bougainvillea climbed the walls and tumbled over the garden gates of the houses we passed. My driver had gotten off the freeway and was driving through a suburban neighborhood of well-kept single-family homes painted in a blushing palette of peach, pink, and terra-cotta. Palm trees swayed, reaching toward a cloudless, still sky. There was a sense of spaciousness that I never felt on the East Coast.

"This is it," the driver said, pulling over rather suddenly in front of a house surrounded by a tall white wall. Cacti peeped over the top, hinting at a garden. "Nice place."

With that, he drove off, leaving me in front of Jennifer Hex's wrought iron gate. I peered through the bars to admire a crowded garden of flowering succulents. When I rang the electronic bell, the gate opened immediately, retracting into a cavity in the wall. A stone path led to her front door, and as I stepped onto it, I felt queasy with stage fright, knowing I had to pretend to be someone I wasn't.

"Leigh!" Jenny opened the door and smiled widely, arms outstretched. "You look just the same!"

I knew this could not be true. When she'd last seen me, I was a skinny adolescent, flat-chested with overplucked eyebrows. I'd hoped to stand in front of her as the best version of my adult self, but instead I felt wilted, defeated by air travel and budget hotels and divorce.

Jenny was even more glamourous in person. She was LA-pretty, with white teeth and long wavy hair, but also Jenny-pretty, with freckles on her cheeks and coarse strands of gray hair that curled away from her head. Her feet were bare and tanned, and she wore a loose-fitting pale-green jumpsuit that looked to be made from silk. A delicate gold necklace rested on her clavicle.

I realized then that she had money. The unfussy luxury of her gardens should have been a tip-off, but it wasn't until I saw her standing on her doorstep, aglow with understated beauty, that I felt the undertow of wealth. It threw me off. There was no way tree therapy was lucrative. I knew there was no familial trust fund. Someone had to be bankrolling her. I wondered who.

Jenny led me inside, down a long hallway awash in sunlight from enormous skylights. Her perfume, a blend of pine and bergamot, filled the space as we walked toward a square courtyard that was open to the sky. There, another meticulously planned succulent garden incorporated several abstract sculptures mounted on slabs of granite. A patio was also nestled among the cacti and yucca, with wicker chairs and a wooden table set for tea. Everything was carefully arranged, as if for a photo shoot. In addition to the tea tray, there were several small ceramic bowls filled with snacks: raw almonds, roasted pumpkin seeds, and squares of dark chocolate studded with sea salt.

"Would you like some tea?" Jenny began pouring me a cup before I could answer. "It's very nourishing after travel—and there's no caffeine, don't worry."

"Thank you, this is so nice." I was genuinely flattered by the effort she had made, even as I was still trying to make sense of the casual opulence that surrounded us. Something about it felt off. "This is such a beautiful space," I ventured. "It's like a museum garden."

"It kind of is. I mean, this isn't my stuff." Jenny gestured to a somber block of polished metal behind her. "I rent it, sort of. It's good for meeting with clients."

"Well, it's a great find." I hated how bland I sounded. I hadn't flown all the way to LA to have a conversation about real estate.

"Do you like the tea?" Jenny asked. "It's chaga, a mushroom that grows on birch trees. I think it's better than coffee."

"I thought I recognized it." It had an earthy flavor that was slightly bitter. "I did a story on mushroom powders."

"For *Cerulean*?" Jenny asked, with an amused expression.

I nodded. *Cerulean* was my go-to fake byline. It was just the right amount of obscure and expensive. "I mostly write for them."

"It's funny, I wouldn't have guessed you'd end up writing about beauty products. I mean, knowing you, knowing your mom. What does *she* think?"

Jenny's expression was genuinely curious, and it took me a minute to realize that she didn't know my mother had passed away. She really *had* left Lost Falls behind.

"What is it?" Jenny said. "Did something happen to your mom?"

When I told her, she looked stricken.

"I wish I'd known," she said softly. "My dad never mentioned it. Not that he would know. He's in his own world with all his rescues. It's not just dogs anymore. Somebody let loose a bunch of parakeets . . ." Jenny paused. "I can't even believe about your mom. She was such a good teacher. She knew so much, you could ask her anything. Everything I know about trees, about plant biology, it started with her."

I just nodded, my eyes welling up. It had been such a long time since I'd talked with anyone who knew my mother.

"How did she die, if you don't mind my asking?"

A familiar numbness took over, my coping mechanism. I'd never told anyone the whole story, but I gave Jenny more details than I would have with most healers: ovarian cancer, which hadn't been caught until late, so she'd had limited options. Ultimately, she had opted to stop treatment early so she could die in the comfort of her home.

"I respect that," Jenny said. "Most people can't think rationally when faced with death, but I'm not surprised your mom could."

"It was still hard for her," I said, thinking how she couldn't have done it without Hecate's Key. Part of me wanted to tell Jenny all about it—after all, it had been her father who had recommended it. I felt like she would understand better than other people. Because she knew my mother, and because she knew me when I was young—before I'd become such a compromised version of myself.

"Do you ever see people who are terminally ill?" I asked, trying to get a sense of her comfort level.

"Not really," Jenny said. "Sometimes people with cancer will come to me for stress relief, but they're not expecting a cure. I guess you could say I do palliative care. Any contact with nature is therapeutic."

"What does your treatment consist of, usually?"

"It depends on the person." Jenny looked at me. "Are we doing the interview now? For your article?"

"Yes, let me just get my notebook." I made a show of taking things from my bag. "Is it okay to record on my phone?"

"I'd rather not."

"Okay, I'll take notes and we can fact-check later." I was certain I'd never in my life been less convincing as a journalist. "So, um, how did you learn so much about plants and trees? Did you take a class on herbal medicine?"

"I've only ever taken acting classes," Jenny said. "I started doing this therapy with actors, trying to give them a different perspective on their lives. With them, I could say things like 'talk to trees' and 'listen to flowers,' and it wasn't that bizarre of an exercise."

"Do you frame it that way when you're working with non-actors? Do you tell people it's a role-playing exercise?"

"No, I tell them it's real. Because it is."

I couldn't tell if Jenny was being deliberately obtuse or merely inarticulate. I wanted to tell her that it was fine with me if her therapy was completely made up, as long as it got soldiers to go outside and take a walk in the woods. Instead, I pressed on, asking her about her typical client.

"I get all kinds," Jenny said. "People struggling with anxiety, with depression. I get people with autoimmune issues, people with chronic illnesses. I get people who are just trying to manage their stress. Trauma is another big one."

"If I came to you, how would you start my treatment?"

"First, we'd just talk. I'd try to find out what's bothering you. With you being recently divorced, I'd probably start there."

"My divorce?" I felt like I'd been called on unexpectedly in a meeting. "How do you know about that?"

"It's on your intake form," Jenny said.

"Oh, right." I had forgotten that I'd filled out her patient questionnaire before my interview. I had planned for her to do her therapy with me; that was how I usually approached interview subjects. But I hadn't anticipated how personal it would feel with Jenny.

"I guessed it had to be recent, from the way you wrote about it," Jenny said. "And from Rose's age. I love her name, by the way. So old-fashioned. Do you have any pictures?"

I was relieved to have a moment to gather my wits as I pulled up a photo of Rose on my phone. I found one of her standing in front of a bed of daffodils, dimples fully activated. Jenny looked closely at the picture, declaring that Rose looked a bit like my mother.

"Yeah, I guess she does." I glanced at her one more time before putting my phone away. I'd always thought she looked more like Carter's side of the family, with her golden hair and fair, freckled skin.

"Is she with her dad right now?" Jenny asked.

"Yeah, we have joint custody." I felt disconcerted by Jenny's sudden, intense focus on me. "I'm still not used to that, to her not always being in my house. I feel like it's finally sinking in. At first, I was distracted by all the logistics. We had to figure out a schedule, and I had to move out—"

"*You* had to move out? It's usually the father, isn't it?"

"Yeah, it got ugly . . ." I looked down at my tea. Once again, I was wrestling with the urge to tell her everything. "It was kind of my fault that we broke up."

"What happened? Did you fall in love with someone else?"

"No, nothing like that. I still love him, in a way. Which is completely stupid. He's moved on. He's dating someone else now. They're talking about getting married." I was getting teary again. It was as if my teenage self had been summoned to the surface. "I think I'm still kind of hung up on him."

"Why wouldn't you be? He's the father of your child." Jenny handed me a cloth napkin to dry my eyes. "And you don't have your mom. You need your mom in a time of transition. This is something I've learned from trees. Not from my own life—god knows my mother was never there for me. But yours would have been. She was very rooted. The way trees are. They're not solitary, stoic creatures."

I wiped my eyes, feeling ridiculous. But what she was saying was so true. I'd never longed for my mother's presence as much as I had after my divorce—not even in childbirth, or the first weeks of motherhood. It was in my stupid beige condo that I wished for her most. It was when I looked out the window at puny little Walter—a tree I'd *named*, that's how lonely I was. "I'm sorry," I said, blowing my nose. "I'm ruining your napkin."

"Don't be sorry! Your mom was amazing. Honestly, Leigh, I think of her a lot now, with climate stuff finally in the news. She was the first person I knew who talked about global warming. I have these Silicon Valley guys who come to me for treatments, and they think they're on the cutting edge of this stuff, but I'm like, you're twenty years behind." Jenny leaned forward and lowered her voice. "Every single one of them is buying land in Canada. They're all making their escape plans."

"Do you get a lot of Silicon Valley clients?" I asked, trying to steer the conversation back to intellectual territory.

"They bring me up for corporate retreats. They're really into nature, as like, a concept. I just got asked to consult on a virtual forest project. I was like, what's wrong with the real ones?"

"So you don't like working with them?"

"I want to help anyone who's interested. I just don't want to become a luxury service. That's why I'm wary of being featured in magazines." She looked at me, and then down at my notebook, where I'd only written a few lines. "You're not really from *Cerulean*, are you?"

"What do you mean?"

"Leigh," she said, "I'm not going to sit here and keep pretending."

"Pretend what?"

"That you're a reporter."

"But I am," I said, trying to stay calm. Inside, I was panicking.

"I looked you up after you called," Jenny said. "I thought, Whatever happened to Leigh Bowers? When I googled, I found your wedding announcement. It said you were a librarian—not a journalist."

"I used to be a librarian." I reached for an almond as I spoke, trying to come off as casual. "But I got bored, so I started freelancing and ended up writing about beauty."

"The thing is, I couldn't find any articles by you."

"I use a pen name." I felt like Jenny was looking directly at the acne scar on my right cheek, from when my face broke out after Carter left, after I got caught selling Hecate's Key.

"Even if that's true," Jenny said, "and even if you're going to give me some name that checks out, I just don't believe *you* care about beauty treatments. Or *wellness*. It just doesn't make sense."

I held her gaze. "There are things about you that don't make sense, either."

"Like what?" She seemed taken aback.

"Like, how do you afford this place?"

"I told you, I'm renting it, I know the owner. It's almost like a barter situation."

We both knew there was no amount of tree therapy that was equivalent to a house whose pristine upkeep suggested at least a part-time gardener and housekeeper. I looked at Jenny, uncertain of where to take our conversation. I wasn't trying to accuse her of anything nefarious. I just figured there was more to the story; there always is.

"You're not wrong to be skeptical," Jenny said, breaking the silence. "But I don't think I am, either."

"Okay," I admitted. "I don't write for *Cerulean*." I hoped there was a needle I could thread; maybe I could tell her enough that she would feel validated, but not so much that I would get myself into trouble. "I'm not actually a journalist. I just say that because it's easier. I'm doing research into nature-based wellness treatments. The people I work for, they want to bring tech into health care, sort of."

"And who are the people you work for?" Jenny asked. "Is it a pharmaceutical?"

"No, nothing like that."

"One of the big health insurance companies? Facebook?"

I shook my head, afraid that if I spoke, I would give myself away. I didn't like being vague, I felt like I was cutting myself off from a conversation I needed to have. But from a work standpoint, there was no good reason to tell her the truth. Yes, she would likely reveal more about herself, but I doubted there was anything earth-shaking beneath her apparent wealth. Probably she was funded by some VC with money to burn. Maybe he had a crush on her.

"Come on," Jenny said. "It's me. Who am I going to tell?" She smiled at me as if we were in on the same joke, and I felt fifteen again. Her connection to my past was like a contact high. I wondered if I should just get up and leave as an act of self-preservation.

Jenny must have sensed my exit strategy, because she suddenly stood up. "I have an idea," she said. "Are you free tonight? I have a house up the coast. It's not mine, really, but I'm allowed to borrow it. We could go up there and talk—for real."

"*Another* house?" I'd never met anyone with so many empty residences at their disposal.

Jenny ignored my teasing. "You have to see it, it's gorgeous—and there's a whirlpool right near a grove of cedar trees. You can sit out there, under the stars. There's nothing more relaxing."

"I can't. I have a flight first thing in the morning."

"I'll get you back in time, I promise." She looked at me with her wide-set brown eyes. I was wavering and she could tell.

"I *have* to catch that flight. It's Rose's spring break."

"I promise, you won't miss it," Jenny said.

I knew if I went with her, I would, without a doubt, step over the line of professional behavior. It was bad enough that I had finagled a trip to see an old friend. Then again, I had flown all the way to California. It didn't make sense to turn back right when things were getting interesting. And it was okay to slack off every now and again. In the right light, if you squinted, maybe it was even subversive.

"Okay," I said. "Let's go."

8.

My rolling suitcase was still packed, open on my bed, the clothing nestled inside. All I had to do was zip it up. I felt giddy as I walked past the front desk. It felt so good to escape my hotel, to leave the coffee pods untouched, the plastic cups wrapped in plastic. It was like I was saying goodbye to a certain sanitized version of my life.

Jenny was waiting outside in her dark-green Volkswagen Beetle convertible, one of the newer models.

"I always wanted one of these in high school," I said, admiring the clean, polished interior. It seemed almost new.

"Oh my god, me too," Jenny said. "Remember my dad's car?"

"The one held together by bumper stickers?"

"And it was a clutch," Jenny said. "It took me forever to learn to drive, I don't know if you remember. Living in New York City didn't help."

"What was it like when you moved there? I mean, you were like eighteen, right?" I was still impressed that she'd moved there at such a young age, without knowing anyone.

"I had no idea what I was doing," Jenny said. "Probably that was a good thing. If I had known what I was up against, I never would have tried."

Jenny smiled fondly, recalling her ignorance, and as we drove out of Los Angeles, heading north on roads that quickly became dark and narrow, she told me the parts of her story that had been left out of profiles.

When Jenny landed in New York in the midnineties, you could still find cheap rent, and there were plenty of temp jobs. She got by on a few days of work per week, and the rest of her time went to her acting career. She did all the things a young actor is supposed to do: classes, headshots, open auditions, improv comedy—and this was back when improv was still misfit territory, before marketing and sales types started doing it to self-actualize. She met all the comedic stars before *SNL* snapped them up. Her own career was going nowhere, despite her best efforts.

In 2000, after nearly four years in New York, Jenny went to LA to pursue film and TV roles. She tried to be savvier about her look, auditioning for the "Weird Girl" parts. But that only brought her into rooms of people who looked just like her.

"It was disturbing to my ego," she said. "I didn't realize how much I had always clung to the idea that I was special, and that all I needed was for someone to recognize it and lift it up."

"Doesn't everyone feel that way?" I asked.

"I thought it was just an actor thing." Jenny looked over at me from the driver's seat. "Do *you* feel that way?"

I had to think about it. No, I realized, I didn't. I felt special enough. It was a gift from my mother—and maybe from Rose, too. When she was born, I went around telling people she was heaven on earth, because everything about her was soft, tender, subtle, mysterious, and vaguely but thrillingly terrifying, like the velveted paw of a lion. I felt like I was the most astonishing woman in Washington, DC, to have birthed such a perfect creature.

"I think I need to feel like I'm doing the right thing," I said. "Like I'm on the right path. It's hard to know, sometimes. Especially when you get older. Things aren't as simple as they seemed."

Of course, I was thinking of my job. I tried not to dwell on the cognitive dissonance of researching spiritual practices to *enhance soldier lethality*. Some researchers think that self-delusion is the secret sauce to positive mental health outcomes. *Useful delusion*, they call it. I felt like mine had outgrown its usefulness.

"Everyone has regrets," Jenny said. "You have to lean into your mistakes and imperfections, all the stuff that makes you different. That's what I was doing wrong when I was younger. I was trying to fit the mold."

After months of rejections in LA, Jenny started volunteering in a nursing home. It was something she'd done in high school, with her father. He would bring his crystals and do numerology readings, pet therapy; he even organized a solstice ceremony in the winter. As a volunteer, Jenny brought meals to people, did puzzles, played cards, knitted, and chatted. Her life felt knotted beyond repair, but visiting the nursing home was calming. It gave her perspective. She was twenty-five.

One of the women in the old folks' home, Dorothy, lived in a suite full of plants that the other residents referred to as "the green cave." Every flat surface and piece of shelving was crowded with plants. Dorothy would play Barbra Streisand, Maria Callas, and Johnny Hartman records for the plants, claiming that it helped them to grow. The room had a funky but not unpleasant smell.

One day Dorothy asked Jenny to bring her a cutting of one of her houseplants. When Jenny admitted she didn't have any, Dorothy insisted that she purchase one. Dorothy was very old, the nurses said. Older than she seemed. Jenny guessed late seventies. The nurses said she was in her late nineties.

Jenny went to a nursery to find a plant for Dorothy, and after much consideration—she wanted to impress the old woman—she selected a succulent with long, curling purplish leaves. She brought the whole plant in because she didn't know how to take a cutting.

Dorothy said her choice was auspicious, and when she broke off one of the smaller stems, dark violet liquid dripped from it, just a few drops, which Dorothy rubbed on her lips, tinting them dark pink. The plant, she said, was known as Dark Heart Sunday. It was very hard to find. She offered Jenny a cutting, which Jenny dutifully accepted, carrying her specimen home in a waxed paper cup. But it shriveled up and died, even though she'd followed Dorothy's instructions to a T.

Over the next few months, Dorothy taught Jenny the names of all the plants in her room while sharing episodes from her life. Dorothy had once been indispensable, a makeup artist to the stars. She became interested in plants when she started to mix face masks to deal with her clients' skin problems. Just about everyone's face was ravaged from years of heavy cosmetics, not to mention the stress of being a performer. Sometimes Dorothy did masks just to give her clients a chance to sit still and close their eyes.

After people left Dorothy's house, they felt calmer. They didn't know why—they just did. Dorothy gave them simple, commonsense advice, like *Eat more vegetables* and *Take walks outdoors*. She told them to grow plants in their home and to observe their way of living, both underground and aboveground. Meanwhile, Dorothy began to expand her own collection of greenery. She coddled her plants, playing music to them, telling them jokes, and chatting with them about her day. She began to feel as if she were learning from them.

Styles changed, and Dorothy's contacts in the business got old, retired, and died. Still, people kept coming to her to sit in her verdant bungalow to drink tea and talk. They told Dorothy their dreams and obsessions, their worries and their vanities. Dorothy listened and didn't say much. The plants listened and said nothing most humans can hear. It didn't matter. People felt better when they left. Much better. They paid her in meals, movie tickets, clothing, artwork, jewelry, books, and plants—lots and lots of plants.

Jenny brought plant specimens every time she came to see Dorothy, foraged from other people's yards and gardens, or gathered from hikes. There was never a plant that Dorothy couldn't identify or didn't know a little something about. Jenny took notes and practiced recipes at home. Soon Jenny was brewing herself cups of argyte tea for menstrual pain, using linnera paste for her torn cuticles, and taking rubrarium baths to ease sore muscles. On days when she was anxious, Jenny undertook elaborate gardening chores. The smell of soil soothed her nerves, or maybe it was talking to Dorothy, or the plant vibrations, or the color green, or all of it together. The years of rejections slid off her like a skin of tired, old rumors. Jenny felt she was part of a bigger story. She got her confidence back.

A year passed with Jenny learning from Dorothy and surviving on wages from a part-time job at a New Age boutique very much like her father's. She wasn't as interested in acting anymore, but she landed a recurring commercial gig for a brand of high-protein energy bars. It was a big enough paycheck that she could take a break from retail. She told Dorothy she was thinking of doing some traveling to visit wild areas in the Pacific Northwest. That's when Dorothy told her that she was feeling ill and thought that her time to die was drawing near. When Jenny asked how she knew, Dorothy claimed it was because Jenny brought her Dark Heart Sunday.

Dorothy explained that the plant was a death omen. If someone gave it to you, then death was coming, and that person was someone who could make use of your life's wisdom. Dark Heart Sunday was rare, a plant that grew exclusively in the decomposing matter of a fallen tree—usually a very old tree.

Dorothy had never seen one before Jenny came. She told Jenny that healing was drama, and Jenny had the drama. That people would listen to her.

Jenny was doubtful. She'd never had that sense of herself. She felt like she was an unwelcome person—hadn't she been kicked out of her own house? Her own mother had hidden her away in the woods.

To her embarrassment, Jenny started to sob, right there in Dorothy's room.

"Oh, honey," Dorothy said. "I'm not leaving you. I'm just dying."

Jenny didn't realize that when Dorothy said that death was drawing near, she meant that night. When she came to visit Dorothy a few days later, the old woman was gone, and a cleaning woman was vacuuming her empty room. The nurses had already thrown out Dorothy's plants, and Jenny ran to the dumpster to rescue them. She wanted to be sure to save the Dark Heart Sunday, but it was gone.

Jenny went back to the nursery where she had bought the plant, but the shop assistant said she'd never heard of Dark Heart Sunday.

She spent hours searching for it on the internet. Nothing matched. Word and image searches drew a blank. She called other nurseries. Nothing. People seemed to hold her questions at arm's length, like she'd lost touch with reality. Maybe she had.

Dark Heart Sunday, Jenny decided, was an angel of death. She shouldn't want to get it back. But getting over Dorothy was a different story.

Jenny was grieving, for the first time in her life. Not only for Dorothy, but for her parents' marriage, for her childhood, for her mother's unhappiness, and for the distance between her and her brother. It was agonizing, but it also felt like a rebirth. Like she was getting in touch with the truth of who she really was.

During this time, Jenny started making Dorothy's teas and elixirs to share with other people. Then she decided to host a class based on Dorothy's teachings. She also mixed in some ideas from her father, who had taught her simple things like how to walk very quietly through the forest, how to read the clouds, and, more generally, how to be open-minded. The class would heal her and maybe help others. She knew a lot of actors and artists who were downhearted after years of failure.

This, of course, was the beginning of Jenny's public biography—her early work with actors and artists, during which she developed her green therapy. She spent three years honing her treatments, which she designed so that anyone could do them, anywhere. A lot of her clients traveled frequently, and she taught them to find stability in the trees and plants that they met along the way. She gave people houseplants to care for, and explained how the plants would care for them, expelling oxygen. She poured cup after cup of tea. Like Dorothy, she barely made any money, surviving instead on donations and bartered arrangements with friends. She was happy.

Jenny did not advertise until late 2010, when one of her clients offered to create a website for her as a barter payment. Another client helped with her branding strategy and suggested that she call herself Jennifer Hex. But it wasn't until Devony Patterson, one of the actresses Jenny first worked with, mentioned Jenny in an interview in *Moon Child* that Jenny's therapies reached an audience beyond Los Angeles. Suddenly Jenny was in the culture, if not quite the mainstream. Her website crashed with sign-ups. The press requests came next, which Jenny was quite happy to accommodate. But soon she was in over her head. She couldn't handle the notoriety—not logistically and definitely not existentially.

"Everyone assumed I was trying to expand my business, and I started thinking that was what I was supposed to do, even though I didn't actually want to *be* a business," Jenny said. "Then I started getting this whole new caliber of customer. People would fly me to their properties, and I'd help them pick out plants and trees for inside their houses. At first, I just went with it, because it was fun and . . . I don't know, I didn't think I could say no. But after a while, I felt like I was becoming a glorified decorator.

"After, I don't know, two years of this, I was totally burned out. Also, I was in debt. I'd rented this bigger space that I couldn't afford, and I was buying all this new stuff—new clothes, new makeup, new jewelry—I felt like I had to be beautiful and stylish and successful-looking. I just totally lost track of myself. I was telling my clients to get outside and be present in nature, and meanwhile I was spending all my time inside, shopping online and answering emails. You can't have your inner and outer worlds so misaligned. You feel worse than just hypocritical, you feel like you're not real. I was like, I need a *break*. I want to be anonymous again."

We'd been off the highway for some time and were driving up a winding two-lane road with few houses. The landscape was bare and sparsely vegetated with a few trees here and there, clumped together in shadowy groups.

"So, where you live now, is that where you moved when you started to get big?" I was trying to get a sense of where in her trajectory I'd met her.

"No, I was in a different location," Jenny said. "I've moved a lot in the past few years—too much. Hang on, this is our turn coming up."

Jenny slowed down, turning right onto a single-lane gravel road marked "Private Drive." The road became even narrower as the elevation climbed. As we crested the hill, Jenny took a remote from the visor above her and clicked a button. All at once, I could see the lights of a low-lying but expansive building. It was eerie, beautiful, and modern—all at once. Jenny parked in the gravel drive, and we stepped out into the chilly night air that smelled of eucalyptus, sage, and a hint of smoke. Above—an ocean of stars. I was suddenly aware that I was out, alone, in the middle of the night in a location I couldn't find on a map. I had the giddy, childish feeling of staying up too late. I wasn't afraid, exactly. It was more like I'd slipped out of time.

We followed a curving path to the front door, which opened to a foyer where gray felt slippers were neatly lined up against the wall. After trading our shoes, we walked down a short flight of stairs into a large, open room with vaulted ceilings. Golden beams of wood spanned the ceiling, echoing the wood floors. The far wall held large windows that faced west, toward the Pacific, whose distant and mysterious expanse I could sense if not see. Jenny went around the room, turning on lights. She opened the sliding glass door. "Do you want to check out the gardens?"

"Sure, why not?" I said with a self-conscious laugh. Even though I'd been expecting something luxurious, I was bowled over by how refined everything was. I didn't know anyone who lived this way.

We stepped out onto a small stone patio. The house had been constructed on a steep hill with landscaping that spilled down to a formal lawn; below, there was a trellis and chairs for lounging.

"There were plans to build a pool down there, but it never happened," Jenny said. "Kip put in the hot tub as a compromise." She pointed to a small, enclosed area to the right, just beyond the garden. "We can go in later."

"Who's Kip?" The way she said it, he sounded like a boyfriend.

"He's the guy who owns this place."

"Are you sure it's okay to be here?" I asked, still overwhelmed by the surroundings.

"Don't worry, it's fine. He likes it when I visit. He needs someone to keep an eye on it."

I followed her back inside to a large built-in hallway closet, where a dozen bathrobes were hanging, all of them the same dove gray. Fluffy towels in muted shades of ochre and indigo were stacked neatly on the upper shelves.

Jenny handed me a robe. "You can wear this over your swimsuit—and there should be some here . . . yes!" She opened a drawer to reveal a slithery pile of black one-pieces, with sizing tags still attached. "Pick any one you want," she said. "Everything's new. Kip likes to have them on hand, just in case."

"How do you know this guy?"

"Technically, he's my boss." Jenny's smile was hard to read. "He's the one who told me I should be careful about talking to you."

"Why?"

"Who knows," she said, laughing. "He's very paranoid. I told him not to worry, that we go way back."

I changed in a bathroom aglow with snowy white marble. I loved the way I looked in my black one-piece; it was modestly cut yet intensely flattering, reminding me of the first nice dress I'd bought for myself—a black Audrey Hepburn–esque sheath. Jenny's words echoed in my mind: *We go way back.* I wondered if this could be the beginning of a new stage of our friendship—a more real, grown-up version, one with money and plane tickets. I could visit her on the West Coast; this house could be a regular escape. And she could come east and stay with me. I'd show her around DC, and we'd visit old haunts near Lost Falls. Or else we'd drive to the Eastern Shore, rent a house in kitschy Ocean City. . .

"I'm in here!" Jenny called from the kitchen. I found her standing at an enormous island, assembling a snack tray. She wore her robe unbelted like a duster to reveal her swimsuit, a tropical print splashed with green, yellow, blue, and pink.

"Have a seat." She handed me a glass of white wine. "I turned the hot tub on, but we need to wait for it to warm up. Did the suit fit okay?"

I nodded, sipping the wine. It had a sharp, fresh flavor. "This is really good."

"Isn't it? Kip brought a case of it back from New Zealand. I'll send you home with a bottle."

She was a good host, chatty as she arranged dried figs, seeded crackers, olives, and cheese on a terra-cotta serving platter. The pantry was always well stocked, she explained, because Kip liked his houses to be prepared for unexpected guests. He was a very spontaneous, magnanimous person—and he could afford to be because he was Kip *Fielding*, one of the grandchildren of the founders of Ambar-Fielding, the pharmaceutical company. I hadn't heard Kip's name before, but I knew Ambar-Fielding. I'd been briefed on all the significant pharmaceutical companies. Many of them were developing technologies like IRTH2, and we were supposed to be on the lookout for potential collaborations.

"Kip started as my client," Jenny said. "Some tech guy referred him. I figured he was just another corporate person trying to be more productive."

"Do people come to you for that?" I was still trying to figure out how Jenny made any real money from her therapy.

"Absolutely," Jenny said. "Nobody's interested in trees for the sake of trees—except Kip kind of was. When we started talking after my sessions, I found out that he was really into visiting old-growth forests, and he had theories about forest bathing and how companies should encourage their employees to walk outside on their lunch breaks or take day trips to go hiking. He was trying to get Ambar-Fielding to do stuff like that. I felt like he didn't even really need my therapy, but I gave him some advice, and then we got coffee. This was when I was feeling really burned out. I ended up telling him everything—how I'd finally gotten the attention I wanted when I was trying to be an actor, but now I was miserable and in debt. He was like, 'Karma's a bitch.' But then he offered to fly me to New Zealand to see the forests there. He said there were no strings attached, and that I could stay in his apartment in Wellington, which was just sitting there, empty. Nobody was living there—he had bought it when he was building a house on the coast and never gave it up."

"So you just dropped everything?" I asked, knowing the answer but taking vicarious pleasure in Jenny's story. I'd never allowed myself such freedom, even before I had Rose. The one risky thing I'd done in my life was to search out Hecate's Key for my mother.

"It was definitely a weird offer," Jenny said, smearing goat cheese on a cracker, "but it came at the right time. And I ended up staying for six weeks, just hiking and barely talking to anybody. One day toward the end of my trip, I went on a more challenging climb with a tourist group, and one of the men on the hike died of a heart attack—which was awful, obviously. But it was also kind of moving because the guides wrapped him in blankets, said a prayer, and carried him back down the mountain. They shut down the trail for two days, out of respect. I thought how they'd never do that in America, how they would cover up the death and make it a secret, and how annoyed people would be if a trail was unexpectedly closed. I felt like, from far away, I could finally see how sick our country was, how afraid of death, how in thrall to comfort. I decided right then and there that I didn't want to spend another minute of my life 'building my brand.' I'd take a steady part-time job like Dorothy had done, just enough to get by, and the rest of my life would be devoted to my therapy and to learning more about plants. I honestly thought I'd figured out the meaning of my life."

Jenny paused to check the time on her phone. "The water's probably warmed up by now—want to take these outside?" she asked, lifting her wine.

I followed Jenny through the pantry and out a side door that opened onto a path of flat, smooth stones that were cool beneath my bare feet. I sipped wine as I walked, feeling decadent.

Steam rose from the tub's purring bath. We hung our robes from hooks on the ledge of the tub and eased in, carefully balancing our glasses on the ledge. It was saltwater, free of chlorine, and the contrast between the cool night air and the hot water was heavenly. I watched bubbles form on the surface, and I fell into a mild reverie as I recalled childhood trips to the beach. As a kid, I loved to swim in the shallow, foamy expanse that appeared just after the waves broke. I called it *mermaid water*.

"You all set?" Jenny asked, and when I nodded, she hit a button that turned off the bathhouse lights. Suddenly the sky seemed like a heavy blanket, pricked with light. I felt like I was dissolving into the water.

"This is amazing," I murmured.

"Now do you see why I was willing to drive all the way up here on a random weeknight? You probably thought I was crazy."

"I never thought you were crazy." I didn't mean just that day. I was talking about Jenny's high school dreams of becoming an actor, and even her ideas about talking to trees. I could feel the presence of the centuries-old cedars standing nearby, regarding us with the calm of their species. Beneath us, stretching for miles—perhaps endlessly, in one magnificent embrace of the Earth—was a dense net of mycelial strands, cradling us, knotted and ancient.

"So, where was I?" Jenny asked, sinking down into the water.

"You had just figured out the meaning of your life."

"Right," Jenny said, laughing softly in the dark. "So, after my revelation, near the end of my trip, Kip called to say that he was in New Zealand, and that I should come visit him at his country house. He sent a car to pick me up. His house was beautiful, of course—like this one, but bigger. Too big, honestly. It had kind of a bunker vibe. There was a pool and a theater and a gym—and a squash court. Who was he going to play squash with? He told me he had built it in case he needed to expatriate himself from the US. I said I thought that was a ridiculously expensive way to ease anxiety, and he said the funny thing was that it hadn't given him any comfort, but the protocol I had shared with him, my very basic regimen of taking a half-hour walk and touching and documenting all the different trees and plants he saw, *had* helped him. And then he confessed that when he first met me, he hadn't really come for a treatment. He had come as research for Ambar-Fielding."

"What kind of research?"

Jenny raised her eyebrows. "They want to develop longevity treatments—or that's what they're calling it. It's more like preventative care. They think that the future of medicine is going to be totally online, and they want to build a platform that can assess people and give individualized stress-reducing techniques, like the ones I teach."

"Do you know what the platform is? Is it a website, or more like an app?" I couldn't help thinking of the report I would eventually have to write about Jenny. If I could salvage an interesting tidbit, maybe that would make up for the fact that I used a work trip to hang out with an old high school buddy.

"I don't know. Kip doesn't actually care. He just uses this as an excuse to hire people like me to work for him. He tells his family that he's working on a digital nature portal, a place where you can go to hear soothing soundscapes or to interact with virtual plants and animals or something. It could all be bullshit. Some of the things he's told me sound absurd. Like, he just hired this girl out of college who says she's writing an algorithm that can transcribe plant vibrations."

"That sounds interesting."

"It's ridiculous," Jenny said flatly. "And I *believe* in plant vibrations. I just don't think you can translate them into code or whatever this girl is doing. Her name is Lily. Apparently she goes to Stanford. She's probably just some cutie he met in a coffee shop. He's employed all kinds of wackadoos—including me."

"What are you doing for him? Consulting?"

"No, he bought my whole business. Hire and acquire. He convinced me that nothing would change, except I would be paid well. And I would share details about my patients with Ambar-Fielding's research division—not their names, but what kind of people they are, demographically, and what kind of problems they have."

"The kind of thing I was asking."

"Exactly," she said. "Kip was very suspicious that I knew you. He wanted me to record our encounter. I said, *No way*. He has trust issues. His family is totally dysfunctional, and his coping mechanism is to be really controlling. He's awful to work for. I wish I could quit."

"Why can't you?" I asked uneasily. I had an idea of what she was going through. But whenever I thought about leaving, I remembered that I'd already burned my professional bridges and destroyed my marriage. The military was my last remaining institution.

"The terms were that I would stay with the company until 2020. Which isn't that long. Just four more years. Sometimes I think I'm stupid to complain. This is the first time in my life I've had a steady income—and the perks are good, obviously. It's a golden-handcuffs situation, I guess." Jenny twisted her hair into a bun on top of her head. "It's good to talk to you. I can't tell anyone I know that I'm working with a pharmaceutical company."

"I'm not supposed to talk about what I do, either," I said, helplessly copying her as I gathered my hair into a loose knot behind my neck.

"You don't have to say," Jenny said. "I've already decided you're in the CIA."

I laughed. "It's not that bad. But close."

"The FBI?"

"No, but they did recruit me." I looked up at the night sky, dark and protecting. I felt the benevolence of the nearby cedars. I decided then that I was going to tell her everything.

9.

I started off sharing things that felt personal but safe—how I met Carter, how I decided to become a law librarian—but pretty soon the subject of my mother's illness came up. Usually, when I talked about my mother, it was with people who'd never known her, so I tended to gloss over the details and change the subject. Some part of me agreed with my father: it was better not to tarnish her reputation. With Jenny, I knew she would appreciate the truth; in fact, I thought she might even know about Hecate's Key already. But when I mentioned it, she seemed confused.

"Maybe Dorothy told me about that once," she said uncertainly.

"Did your dad ever say anything about it to you?"

"No, I don't think so," Jenny said. "Why? Did you tell him about it?"

I was surprised; it seemed Jenny had nothing to do with the mushroom, had never spoken about it with her father or come across it in her work.

"Is it a magic mushroom?" Jenny asked. "Like psylocibin?"

"It's kind of like that," I said. "But it's a different species. It only grows in certain northern forests."

"How did you find it?"

"It was right under my nose. At my office, of all places."

Jenny reached for the wine bottle, balanced on the ledge, and refreshed our glasses. Then I sank a little deeper in the water and let the rest of the story spill out.

At my law firm there was a woman, Marika, whose job it was to care for all the indoor office plants. There were many potted plants, at least one in each attorney's office, and several among the secretarial cubicles—green sentinels that stood perched on broad ledges of partitions, next to nameplates and outboxes. These were species that had learned to thrive under fluorescent bulbs. We had sunlight-loving ones in the library, too, positioned near the tall windows on the southern side.

Marika was Greek, and her English wasn't fluent. At first, I thought that was the reason she took the quiet job of watering plants. But over time, I realized she was a serious gardener. She took her time with each potted specimen—watering it, pruning it, and moving it to a different location if it didn't seem to be thriving. She never seemed to be in a rush or even on a particular schedule, though she explained to me once that she worked in several downtown office buildings.

I'd heard an odd rumor about Marika, and it came back to me after my father told me about Hecate's Key. In addition to plant care, people claimed that Marika supplied amphetamines and other illicit substances to lawyers in need. The story was that she would deliver the pills on her watering rounds, leaving baggies of treats in the foliage or the saucers beneath the plants. Initially, it struck me as ridiculous, but I'd seen Marika walking into the building in her zip-up sweater and comfortable clogs, carrying plastic pots and bags of fertilizer, and security just waved her on by. And it wouldn't be suspicious for her to go into anyone's office because there were plants everywhere that needed tending.

I was friendly with a second-year associate, Jason Slater, who I knew from my paralegal days, and who I saw frequently outside of the building, nurturing his smoking habit. I found him one cold November morning, sheltered by a cement column. I asked him what he knew about the rumors about Marika.

"What are you looking for?"

"Nothing, I'm just curious."

"Bullshit, Glenn." He'd started calling me by my new surname shortly after I got married.

"It's something for my mom."

He looked away; we were close enough that he knew she was sick.

"It's true, as far as I know. I'm not an Adderall person, though."

"Okay. Thanks, Jace."

"Let me know how it works out."

I spoke to Marika that afternoon when she came into the library. I stood nervously reshelving some books near the spider plant, waiting for her to water it. Finally, she came over to where I was standing. Outside, the sky was overcast, a gray sheet of paper. I could see the rooftops of nearby buildings. I whispered, which would have been odd if we weren't in a library. "Marika, can I ask you a question?"

"Please, go ahead."

"I don't know how to put this, and I don't mean to offend you, but I've heard that in addition to taking care of the plants, you also deliver . . . things?"

She glanced over her shoulder before nodding.

I was so relieved that I blurted everything out in a speedy whisper. When I was finished, she said calmly, "Write the mushroom name, and I will ask Ossi. You know Ossi?"

"In Word Processing?"

Marika nodded. "She's in charge. Go to her on Monday."

I had never met Ossi, but I had seen her in the cafeteria. She was hard to miss: a tall broad-shouldered woman who favored jewel-toned blazers and wore her long gray hair in a Dutch crown braid.

I went to see Ossi first thing the next morning. Her basement office was nicely decorated, with a large jade plant and framed black-and-white photographs of mountains. There were several orchids on her desk that had been clipped back, and I nervously asked if she'd ever gotten them to bloom again.

"Marika does," she said. "I hear she sent you down here."

Ossi was clearly not happy about the new business. "Look, I don't know you from Adam. The lawyers are on deadlines, and they're stressed out. I know I can trust them. I don't know what's motivating you."

"My mother's dying."

She stood up and closed the blinds on the interior windows that looked out to the hallway.

"How did you hear about Hecate's Key?" she asked.

I explained as quickly as I could—about my dad and the New Age shop and my mother, who was being eaten up by despair. I said she had never been depressed like this, not ever. My father thought the mushroom could help her. He needed it as much as she did.

"Okay," Ossi said. "I believe you. But I don't know much about this mushroom. When Marika gave me your note, I had no idea what you were talking about. I had to ask my ex—she's a chef, and she likes to cook with mushrooms that no one has ever heard of." Ossi's gaze softened. "Have you heard of Butter Caps? Emmy used to make this amazing risotto with them."

I shook my head.

"Well, they were delicious. I'd get them whenever they were on the menu. But then the mushroom disappeared. The woman who was foraging for Emmy couldn't find it anymore. Emmy stayed in touch with her, just in case. Her name is Astrid, and she lives in Ontario, in the forest. She's old. Emmy asked her about your Hecate's Key. And she said she found some recently and has been waiting for someone to call for them." Ossi raised her eyebrows. "I guess you're that person."

"You really think so?"

"No!" Ossi laughed. "But Astrid does. Her belief is that mushrooms don't appear without a reason—which you can take with whatever size grain of salt you want."

I decided that day to believe Astrid's theory, if only for the confidence boost.

"I have to meet Astrid in person to get it," Ossi said. "She won't give it to me otherwise. This is risky. I'll be transporting what is technically a Schedule 1 drug across an international border."

"You won't do it?"

"I'll do it. But it's going to be expensive. There are ten doses per mushroom, but you can't buy just one dose, you have to buy the whole mushroom. That's how she sells it. Then there's travel expenses. I'll need a car rental, and maybe a night in a hotel—plus my fee, which includes Marika's."

"Okay, whatever you need. We can pay."

Ossi gave me a wistful smile. "You're a very trusting person. You must have had a good childhood."

I just nodded. If I spoke, I'd start crying.

"There's one more thing," Ossi said. "You can't be with your mother when she eats this mushroom. Astrid was very clear about that. It won't work. A mother can't face death with her child in the room. It should just be her and your father—or a close friend, if your parents don't get along."

"They get along," I managed.

"Marika will give you messages from now on. Don't call me, don't email me, and don't come down here again. If you need to speak to me, I'm in the cafeteria every morning at 7:40."

"Okay, thank you. Thank you so much."

I left her office feeling like something momentous had happened all too simply. I also felt paranoid. I knew I shouldn't email my father, but I wasn't sure about calling from my cell phone, and my office phone was obviously not an option. I don't know what possessed me—maybe it was Ossi's stern demeanor, maybe it was a premonition of my life to come—but I decided I needed a burner phone. On my lunch break that day, I used cash to buy a prepaid cell phone from Rite-Aid. Then I called my dad.

My father, of course, did not pick up when I called him from my new, unrecognizable number. I left him a message saying that I'd figured out how to get Hecate's Key. When he called back a few minutes later, he was even happier than I expected.

"Let's be careful with this," he said. "Don't mention it to anyone else, okay? Not even Carter—unless you've already told him."

"I haven't."

"Good. I mean, you can tell him if you want, but it might be easier not to."

After I got off the phone, I silenced the ringer and zipped it into the hidden pocket of my purse, the one I used to smuggle candy into the movie theater. I pretended it was as innocent as that, just a bag of Peanut M&M's. Insofar as I chose to justify my secrecy, I told myself I wouldn't want Carter implicated if something went wrong.

A couple of days after I spoke to Ossi, Marika came into the library with her watering can. On her way out, she stopped by my desk with a Delaware manual and told me it needed to be reshelved.

After she left, I opened the book. There was a sticky note on the inside cover that told me where to wire $1,500. If the money went through by the end of the week, the mushroom would be delivered on November 26—right before Thanksgiving.

Carter and I usually took off the day before Thanksgiving to visit both sets of parents. We'd start with mine, driving up to Lost Falls Wednesday night to have a vegetarian dinner. We called it Pre-Thanksgiving. The next morning we'd wake up early for a flight to Savannah, where we'd arrive just in time for cocktail hour. Thanksgiving dinner at the Glenns was a festival of animal fats and colorfully named pies. I loved it. But this year I wanted to deliver Hecate's Key to my mother as soon as I could. I couldn't figure out how to explain why I needed to stay at work on Wednesday without telling Carter the whole story.

I ended up picking a fight with him, something along the lines of, *Why do we always do the big Thanksgiving at your family's? Do you think your family is better than mine?* Which hit a nerve because Carter *did* think his family was better than mine, and this secret snobbery was one of the unspoken truths of our marriage. He thought my parents were at best socially awkward, and at worst mentally unbalanced. They did tend to talk too much, and for too long. Carter's parents always spoke to you for just the right amount of time. Carter's mother, Deborah, put on makeup first thing in the morning, before she'd even had coffee. She told me once, "I don't feel like myself until I put my face on." I wanted to dislike her for that, but I couldn't help wishing I had a simple ritual to make me feel as though I had a stable self. I always felt I was a disappointment to Deborah. I was pessimistic, introverted, and I had no idea how to cook, prepare, or barbecue meat, especially beef, which, thanks to my parents, I can't even look at without thinking of land scraped bare of trees. I think she worried I wouldn't want to have children, and then, when I became a mother, that I wouldn't provide the right comfort that a child needs.

I knew that in some dark corner of his heart which he's never examined, and never will for fear of discovering that he's a slightly awful person like all the rest of us, Carter resented my mother's illness for the way it stopped our steady march toward settled adulthood. That resentment was in the air when we fought about Thanksgiving—that and the secret I was keeping from him. He got so angry, going on about the tickets we'd already bought. I said I would call for a refund, and he yelled, *They won't give you a refund until your mother is dead.* And that pretty much ended the fight. We decided to go our separate ways for the holiday.

My father prepared for the mushroom's arrival, purchasing eyeshades and choice snacks, and making playlists of favorite songs. My mother, for her part, enjoyed the waiting period; for the first time in many months, she had something to look forward to. I had the cruel thought that we should just tell her that Hecate's Key was delayed and let her die in happy anticipation. I admit I was afraid of what the mushroom would do to her mind, what curtain it might pull back, what peace she might find. For her to be at peace with death was to be at peace with saying goodbye to me.

I could barely sleep the night before the delivery. I woke up early, without an alarm. I was alone; Carter was already in Savannah, having changed to an earlier flight. My commute was easier than usual, the crowds already thinned by the upcoming holiday.

In the elevator, two partners discussed how a certain big holding company had to write down a billion-and-a-half of debt. I thought *write down debt* sounded poetic; in those days dispatches from the real world had a dreamy quality. I was living with one foot in the world of the dying, and I couldn't decide if my mother, father, and I were the only ones in touch with reality, or if everyone else was making their way through the grimy day-to-day and I was in a fog.

I waited all day for Marika. I didn't get lunch because I was scared I would miss her. To stave off my hunger, I drank milky cups of coffee and ate bags of salted cashews from the snack machine. At two p.m., the other librarian on duty asked if I would mind if he left for the day, and I practically pushed him onto the elevator.

When Marika finally arrived around a quarter after four, the library was dense with silence. It was just me. She could have done the handoff out in the open, but she gave the same little wave as always. Nothing in her demeanor revealed an iota of conspiracy, so much so that I began to worry. After about ten minutes, she headed toward the door, stopping by my desk to let me know that I should check on the orchid before I left to make sure it had drained properly. "Just lift up the pot," she said.

I sat there until five thirty p.m. on the dot. Then, with my jacket already on and my handbag over my shoulder, I walked to the back worktable where the orchid arrangement was displayed. I lifted the pot and, sure enough, beneath it was a very small envelope, about two inches square. I slipped it into my coat pocket and left the building. Outside, I called my father with news of my success, and he put my mother on the phone.

"You're my brave girl," she said. "Come on home now."

10.

Jenny and I were both starting to get too hot, so we took a break and sat on the edge of the tub with our feet dangling into the bubbling water. The cool air tickled our bare shoulders.

I told Jenny how I'd stayed away when my mother ate the mushroom, obeying Astrid's warning. My mother didn't want me to be alone on Thanksgiving, so we had dinner together—not a Thanksgiving dinner, because she was supposed to eat lightly in case the mushroom upset her stomach. Then I went to a hotel for the night, while my mother drank her tea and donned eyeshades—to help her look inward—and sat in her favorite chair in the living room, listening to her favorite music. Apparently, she started with Bach violin concertos but quickly switched to music she'd grown up with. My father said they listened to "In My Life" and "A Case of You" over and over and over. My mother cried, but my father said the tears were happy, and my mother said she was walking through the songs, that each note was a room, and each room was beautiful. My mother talked about her religious upbringing, the verse "in my father's house there are many rooms," and how she'd always thought that was about the beauty of Earth, not heaven. Then they went outside, bundled up against the November chill, and walked around the gardens, dormant in winter, and my mother started laughing uncontrollably, saying she didn't know why she'd ever worried about anything—least of all, death. And then they went back inside, and they must have talked about a lot of other things, because they didn't fall asleep until dawn.

During all that time, I was sleeping in a Marriott Garden. I'd brought a bottle of wine to drink the night away, but when I got to the hotel, I took a hot shower instead and slipped into the cool sheets. When I woke up, I couldn't remember anything I'd dreamed, but I had the sense of a world receding, certain wisdom lost.

I spent the morning in a shopping mall, waiting for my parents to call and say I could come back. I knew they were probably asleep, but I still felt anxious when I didn't hear from them. It was Black Friday and the stores were crowded. Everyone looked tired and busy and dazed. I tried to shop, but everything I picked up seemed like it was made of ashes. I gave up, got a peppermint mocha, and sat by an indoor fountain. Kids nearby were throwing coins, so I threw in the contents of my change pocket. I was going to wish for my parents to text me—a desire that felt in proportion with the synthetic, silly pond—but when the coins plinked the water, I found myself hoping for a baby. I thought, When I see Carter again I'll apologize, and we'll put on sultry music and make a baby and I'll have a baby and everything will be fine. And I was sort of right about that. At least for a while.

At last, my mother called. I could hear in her voice that something was different. I hurried home, and she was waiting for me on the front porch, all wrapped up in blankets with a knit hat pulled down to her eyebrows. She looked calm and tired, as if she'd finished a long hike. I sat down next to her, and we talked for an hour or so. For the first time since her diagnosis, she wasn't distracted. I hadn't realized how distant she had been, and now that she was close again, it was such a comfort. Whatever demonic fear of death that had been consuming her was gone. Now she was taking tea with angels. I tried to get her to articulate her revelations.

"I was the breath of God," she said.

I wondered what God meant to Sylvia Bowers, a woman who had always wanted to look down to the earth instead of up to the heavens. I asked her as much.

She didn't really answer and instead took my face in her hands like she used to when I was little: "Leigh, I am so sorry for all the worry I caused you. I'm sorry I was so sad—"

"You don't need to apologize. You have cancer, of course you feel bad."

"I mean before I was sick. When I was just your mom, dumping all my angst on you, all my fears about the fate of this planet, all my grief. I shouldn't have put that on you."

"You didn't put anything on me. You told me the truth."

"I know, sweetheart. I didn't lie. But I didn't make things easier for you, either."

"It's okay."

"It's okay if it wasn't." She wiped a tear from my cheek. "I wonder what it must be like to be you. The world I grew up in was so different. My parents were so different. They were always trying to be good, but in a way that I couldn't relate to. They wanted to trust authority, to follow the rules, to agree with other people. I fought with them so desperately. With you, I tried to be the parent I wanted, but maybe you needed something else."

"No, no. I never did," I said unsteadily. I couldn't decide if I was happy or sad.

"Not even when your friends came over and had to eat my weird vegetarian meals?"

"Well, maybe a little then."

My mother laughed. Her cheeks and the tip of her nose were lightly pink from the chilly air.

"You really seem a lot better," I said.

"I am. That mushroom, it took me down low, but in a good way. It was like I was under the pulse of the world. I saw how everything is connected, how there's no beginning or end, how we're all in this together." She closed her eyes. "That sounds so banal. I can't really describe it. All I can say is I have no regrets. My whole life is icing on the cake."

The next morning, Teresa came to check in with us. Right away she saw the difference.

"Sylvia, you're in a good mood today! Did you have a nice Thanksgiving?"

"I did. Steve made pie from squash from our garden. There's extra if you'd like some."

"So, your appetite is back? That's great. You're sleeping well?"

"I sleep like a baby—a good baby, the kind that sleeps. Like Leigh. You were a good baby."

Teresa asked me to help her carry some supplies from her car and then stopped me in the driveway.

"What did you give her?"

I wasn't sure if I could trust Teresa with the truth. Yes, she had told me to try weed, but marijuana was commonplace. Hecate's Key was borderline witchy.

"We got her some pot, like you said."

"She didn't smoke pot. And I never said that."

We stared at each other in the cold.

"I can't tell you," I finally said. "It's for the best if I don't."

My mother lived for four and a half more months. Her cancer teetered at stage IV, not growing, but also not subsiding, mystifying her doctors. My father thought she was being sustained by all the REM sleep restored to her. I think she was waiting for spring.

Her final weeks were joyful. She had physical pain, but her mind was at ease. She took painkillers and ate ice cream every night. She listened to music, and my father read to her. Friends and family came to visit every few days. I talked to her on the phone every night and visited most weekends, sometimes with Carter, sometimes without. She told me she had never been happier, though in the evenings, when the pain came on, she grimaced. The mushroom didn't solve everything, but it took away her bitterness, and in her last days, she was content as she sat on the front porch watching for spring's arrival.

One night, she fell asleep and didn't wake up, crossing into another world in her dreams.

Teresa confirmed her death, and her body was removed from the house, cremated, and returned to the garden my mother had planned and helped plant. It all happened so quickly. The weeks before she died were slow and detailed, like the molasses time of childhood, and the weeks after were cleaning, sorting, deleting, deciding, and writing checks. At some point I realized the hurry was about hiding death from everyone, and making it disappear. I let go then, and just sat on the porch where my mother had spent so much time.

I was sitting in her rocking chair when Teresa pulled into our driveway in her blue Toyota Camry. It must have been a week, maybe ten days, after my mother's memorial. Teresa was wearing a peacoat, skinny jeans, and suede sneakers. Her hair was down. I'd never seen her in anything but a nursing smock and clogs, with her hair in a tight bun.

"Leigh," she said, "I was hoping to find you here. Is your dad around?"

"He's at the store."

"Okay, good."

I knew then what she was going to ask me.

"I've been wondering something." She awkwardly sat down on the chair facing me. "I know it's none of my business, but how did your mom manage to . . . relax so much? If you know what I mean? She was just so happy. And I just want to know what you did, if she took something? Or went somewhere?"

"She didn't go anywhere."

"So she took something?"

I shrugged.

"Your mother, she had such a good death." Teresa lowered her voice. "I've seen a lot of them, and they don't usually go that way. If you could tell me—you don't have to be specific, but if you could point me in the right direction?"

She was still sitting at the edge of the chair because I'd never invited her to make herself comfortable, and I felt terrible, because we were peers, and I was being so rude, and she was being so brave, and all for the sake of people who were going to die anyway.

"Hecate's Key," I blurted.

"I'm sorry?"

"She took a mushroom called Hecate's Key. It takes away the fear of death."

Teresa took out her phone and I got nervous.

"You won't find it online," I said. "It's not legal in this country. Please don't write it in an email."

Teresa took a small notepad from her inside coat pocket. "Can you spell it for me?"

I watched as she carefully wrote it down in block letters. I realized that I had never put the mushroom's name on paper; it was like she was making the whole thing real for me.

"Is it a psychedelic?" she asked.

"I guess, yeah."

"Is it safe?"

"As long as you're not alone. You need someone to sit with you— but it can't be your child. My dad was with my mom."

"He told you about it?"

"He didn't tell me much about the trip, just a few things. I mean, it was a long time, like ten hours or something."

"No, I mean the mushroom. Did he tell you he was going to give it to her so you would know why she changed?"

"Well, it was his idea, but I got it for him."

"*You* got it? Can you get more?"

"I don't know if the person I got it from has more."

"Could you ask your person? I'm working with this guy who's just like your mom was. He can't stop crying, he can't sleep, he's miserable—and he's young. Forty-eight."

"I don't know . . ."

"Please, Leigh. Think of how much better your mother got."

I felt like I had to decide in the moment, even though, in ret-rospect, I could have said, "Give me a few days to think about it." Or, "This is a big decision, it's going to turn my life upside down." Or, "Look, you have the wrong idea about me. I'm not the kind of person who obtains psychedelic mushrooms—that was the exception to the rule. Look at the job I chose! Look at the guy I married! Look at my bank account! I'm saving for a nice house, with two and a half bathrooms, a dishwasher, laundry room, and an extra freezer in the basement."

I could have said any of those things, but instead I remembered that Ossi had purchased an entire mushroom, ten full doses, and I'd only used one. There were nine left. Technically, I'd paid for them.

I thought I could just get the remaining nine doses and give them to Teresa, but Ossi didn't see it as such a simple transaction. She made me meet her at a run-down Starbucks far away from the office, where we could talk privately.

"Leigh," she said, "did you ever wonder why I just didn't give you all ten doses?"

I shook my head.

"Of course you didn't." She sighed. "Do you know anything about Hecate?"

"She helped Demeter find Persephone in Hades."

"That's right. She went to hell and back. Whoever named this mushroom chose Hecate. You have to ask yourself why." Ossi leaned forward. "This is not a mushroom to take for recreational purposes."

"I don't want to take Hecate's Key," I said. "I want to give it to a hospice nurse. I don't see a lot of risk there. She's only going to use them clinically, with her terminal patients."

"I don't think you understand what you're getting into," Ossi said. "Let's look at the best-case scenario: the mushroom works wonders on all these hospice patients. Then your nurse friend is going to want more."

"She'd have to have nine different families who would want it," I said. "That could take years. Most people aren't going to want a mushroom."

"People are more open-minded than you think—especially when they're out of options. If it works, your nurse will want to use it again. And if she tells any other hospice nurses about it, they'll want it, too. Those doses will be gone in no time. Then she's going to come to you for more, and she's going to want them cheap. You'll end up the middleman in some poorly run nonprofit operation."

"What are you saying? We shouldn't give it to her?"

"I'm saying I don't want to get into the business of mythical mushrooms. I made an exception for you. It was a one-off thing. You can tell your nurse that. She can get it from someone else."

"You know she can't. It's not an easy thing to find."

"That's not your problem, Leigh. You did what you needed to for your mother, and now it's over."

We sat in silence for a few minutes, sipping our coffees. I felt a desperate twinge of guilt for using a disposable cup when I had a ceramic travel mug, one I'd been too lazy to wash. Beneath that was a slow-moving tsunami of regret for all the careless habits I'd adopted over the years away from my parents' home, as well as an irrational feeling that this carelessness had somehow contributed to my mother's death. Wasn't there a theory that cancer rates were rising because of pollution, because of chemicals leaching into the soil, because of the spiraling gyre of trash in the North Atlantic? Wasn't the heedlessness of oblivious middle-class consumers like me killing us all?

"Ossi," I said, "what if I sold her the remaining doses at a good price, and I gave you a cut? And then, if there were more orders, you could introduce me to Astrid—I mean, if you *really* don't want to sell it. I'm not trying to take business from you."

"Do you need money? Is that what this is about?"

"No, I'm fine. I'm not worried about that."

"Then what is it?"

What was it? It was my mother. She had stopped appearing in my dreams. In the months after her death, she had visited often. She would talk to me about my father, about the yard. She was concerned there was a little tree in the yard that needed to be fenced, otherwise the deer would strip the bark. She wanted to make sure I knew where the wool sweaters were stored and that there were pickled beets in the basement, and chutney, too. I had the sense she was tying up loose ends. I liked her quotidian worries. They were nice, they were comforting. But eventually she retreated, and I was left with just her voice in my head. It wasn't always a kind voice. Sometimes it was chiding. Sometimes it was depressive.

"I don't know," I said to Ossi. "I think it's just knowing that there are nine doses left. That's *nine* good deaths. Nine families left in a much better place. The psychic ripple effect of that is huge. And if I went up there, I could get a bunch of mushrooms and bring them all back, and the price wouldn't be so high because there'd be economies of scale, you know?" My voice was getting higher, but when I tried to modulate my tone, I only got more emotional. "I need something like this in my life right now."

Ossi reached across the table and took my hand, the one that was gripping my sinful paper cup with its plastic cap. The kind of cup my mother never would have used.

"Okay," she said. "I'll give you what's left of the mushroom. But I'm just getting you started. We're not going into business together. I'll introduce you to Astrid and that's it. Got it?"

Teresa became my first client. Ossi was true to her word and set up a meeting with Astrid, which meant going to Astrid's cabin in rural Ontario. Her ex, Emmy, wanted to come along, so the three of us road-tripped together. I told Carter I was going to my dad's for the weekend. It was one of many lies that could have undone me but didn't. The way I got found out was the way I least expected. But I guess that's typical.

11.

Hecate's Key appears in late spring and blooms all summer long in the forests just north of the Saint Lawrence River. Ossi rented a boat so we wouldn't have to worry about going through customs—though, in truth, large amounts of dried Hecate's Key can easily be mailed, which was how Astrid got them to me after our initial meeting.

It took a day for us to drive up to the Saint Lawrence. We spent the night in a state park cabin on Wellesley Island, and then took our rented boat to meet Astrid at a small private marina on the Canadian side of the river. Astrid was petite, with thinning white hair, tufty eyebrows, and deep creases on her forehead and cheeks. Her eyes were a grayish blue that seemed inherited from the river. She offered us coffee from a thermos, presweetened with cream and sugar.

"I'm afraid we have a long drive ahead," she said. "I brought some snacks—and this."

Astrid reached into her vest pocket and pulled out a knotted bandanna. It all felt so clandestine that I half expected her to blindfold me, but she untied it to reveal a pale-yellow mushroom with a long, shaggy stem and an oblong cap. Bits of soil clung to the bottom of the stem.

"Hecate's Key," she said. "I thought you'd like to see it fresh. I spotted it this morning when I was out with Luna."

"You still have Luna?" Emmy said.

"She's getting on in years, but her nose is as good as it ever was." Astrid turned the cap of the mushroom up so that we could see the purplish gills. "That's how you know it's from Hecate—the lavender. This mushroom is the fruit of a fungus that associates with the lavender birch and the cirrus pine, which always grows near the lavender birch." She turned to me. "Why are you drawn to Hecate's Key?"

I stammered, talking about my mother, about wanting to ease the suffering of others. I talked about a culture that doesn't acknowledge death, and doctors who can't even say the word. Finally, I said I had fallen into it. Circumstances beyond my control, etcetera.

She said, "No one falls into anything. Why do you like mushrooms?"

"I don't know that I like mushrooms in particular. It could have been a flower and I'd feel the same way."

"I don't think you would," Astrid said. "Flowers are plant life, they feed from the sun. They're celebratory. Mushrooms are different. They're connected to an underground place that we can't see."

Astrid looked from me to Ossi to Emmy and back again. For a moment I thought she was going to tell us to turn around and go home. But all she did was wrap the mushroom back up in the bandanna.

"Okay," she said. "Let's go."

She took us deep into the woods, the roads getting narrower until finally we were on an unpaved one-lane fire road that still had piles of snow at the edges. It was early May, and the forest was waking up, the leaves in their first pale green and the understory coming back to life. It was so different from the May I'd left behind in DC where everything was in noisy bloom, with crushed petals underfoot and café tables dragged out to the sidewalks.

As soon as I saw Astrid's cabin, I thought: *My mother would love this place.* It was built so closely among the trees that it was as if it had grown up out of the woods. On the eastern side of the cottage, there was a screened-in porch that was actually built around a large hemlock, with a hole cut in the floor and ceiling to let the tree grow up through it. Vivid green moss surrounded the little house and stretched deep into the forest. It was the kind of landscape that made you understand why people told stories about fairies and elves.

We went on a foraging walk in the surrounding woods, stepping gingerly on the cushiony moss. We hoped to find more Hecate's Key, but we had no luck. Astrid told us not to worry, she knew a spot farther north where there was a grove of lavender birch. I purchased Astrid's entire stash of dried Hecate's Key that day, about four hundred doses, and we made a plan to get in touch in October after she'd dried the summer harvest. She said that she could mail me the next batch, now that she'd met me.

"What I gave you should get you through the next few months," Astrid said.

It did, but just barely. When I got back to DC, I alerted Teresa to my new supply, and I guess she'd been talking it up, because all of a sudden my phone was full of texts. My career as a mushroom smuggler had begun.

It was an exhilarating time. There was the adrenaline-fueled risk of it all, paired with the heightened intimacy and feeling of responsibility because you're placing your trust in other people and vice versa. I was surprised to find that I liked the administrative complexity. In a year's time, I had a client base of around twenty people who included hospice nurses, doulas, therapists, social workers, two Unitarian ministers, and a rabbi. I would usually give them the doses in person, at a Metro stop or a park near my office. Often, I went out on my lunch break—or else I'd leave early for work. It didn't feel that risky, and no one suspected me.

During this period, my marriage flourished. Carter and I were back on the same busy page. I was glowing with my secret success, and I can't remember a time when he was more attracted to me, even in the early days of dating. At the end of that first summer of selling, I was pregnant with Rose. I worried about the effect of pregnancy on my business. I thought clients would perceive me as vulnerable. I didn't realize that people inherently trust a pregnant woman, and want to help her—especially a white, well-to-do mother-to-be with a security pass to one of the city's most prestigious law firms. Pregnancy also gave me flexibility at work, allowing more time for my side hustle. I took longer lunch breaks, claiming that I was at the doctor. I even skipped a few real appointments with my OB in order to meet contacts.

After Rose was born, I got a burst of energy and confidence. The postpartum hormones were like a love elixir, and I couldn't stop touching Rose's soft skin and kissing the top of her head. Carter and I spent a week just staring at her and sleeping in with her between us. Then Carter had to go back to work. I pretended to be annoyed but was secretly glad. It meant I could easily coordinate sales of Hecate's Key from home. I took six months' leave and devoted most of that time to growing my network, nursing Rose while I made calls. She was a sleepy, calm baby, and the first months of her life were unexpectedly relaxing. When it was time for deliveries, I just strapped her into my Ergo and we were off. Things got more complicated when I was back at work and she was in daycare. Carter wasn't good about picking up the slack, and I couldn't explain to him why I was so frazzled. Still, he was never suspicious. The money I was making might have tipped him off, but I set the price so that my profits were small, and I would sell at cost, or even below cost, if someone couldn't afford it. I was distributing thirty to forty doses a month in the DC/Virginia/Maryland area. Whatever I managed to pocket, I used to pay off my library school debt. But the real reason the extra cash didn't register is that Carter and I had good salaries. The recession wasn't touching us. We bought a starter home and even called it that: *a starter home.* Then we bought a second car—another whole car! We were spewing carbon dioxide into the atmosphere, but I felt it was okay because I was spreading peace via Hecate's Key.

Then one day, near the fourth anniversary of my mother's death, my old friend Peanut Chews showed up in the law library. Although he'd stopped hiding out in the stacks, he still paid visits every now and then to trade gossip. I'd tell him about the interoffice dramas among the support staff, and he'd fill me in on the drunken behavior of associates at after-hours dinners. He usually came by on Fridays, late afternoon.

So when he showed up on a Tuesday morning and headed straight for my desk, I was immediately wary.

"Leigh, I need some help with this title." He handed me a slip of paper that said, *My father is terminally ill. Jason Slater said you could help.*

"I think that one might be in the basement," I said, slowly putting the note in my back pocket, as if nothing were amiss. He followed me out the door and into an empty conference room.

"He can't sleep," Peanut Chews whispered. "He's in agony, a hell on earth. He can't enjoy his grandchildren, a game on TV, nothing. All he thinks about is dying. Jason said you might know of something to make it easier, some alternative treatment. Please, I need to know."

I shouldn't have helped him. I could have said that Jason was mistaken or that my mother had smoked weed, end of story. It would have been so easy to lie. But Peanut Chews was just one of those innocent grown men you want to protect. And I liked the idea of someone like him opening his mind to a mushroom like Hecate's Key. So I told him about it. I described what it had done for my mother. I explained what the hospice nurse said. I cited recent scientific studies about psilocybin mushrooms. The only thing I didn't tell him was that I supplied these mushrooms to hospice nurses throughout the tristate region. Instead, I made it sound like it was something I could get from a wacky family friend.

He wanted it, he paid for it, and I gave it to him. I even personally delivered it, which in retrospect, was stupid. Because he wasn't working with a nurse, I advised him to find a trip guide, and gave him the number of a New Age center in Frederick that could help him. Barring a guide, I said, his mother or a close friend could administer the mushroom, but I warned him not to be with his father when he went on his trip. I wrote down that instruction: *Children of the hospice patient should not be present when the mushroom is in effect.*

You would think that a lawyer, of all people, would respect the written word, but he didn't. He stayed with his father while he took Hecate's Key. To this day, I don't know if his father had a bad experience because

Peanut Chews was there or if Peanut Chews had a bad experience because he saw what he shouldn't, or if it was some unholy Freudian nightmarish mix of the two. All I know is that Jason was waiting for me in the library the Monday after and told me that if I was smart, I would turn around and head back home. I was worried enough to dump my burner phone on the way out—choosing the often-emptied trash can outside of the cafeteria—but I was still shocked when my ID badge set off an alarm when I tried to exit the building. Suddenly it seemed like all the partners were in the lobby and Peanut Chews was pointing. He was on the verge of tears as he yelled at me, "He almost died! Because of you, he almost died in the most awful way."

They fired me that morning, bringing me up to the formal conference room to lecture and intimidate me. They wanted to know if anyone else in the firm was involved with selling mushrooms, and I was glad that I could honestly say it was just me. They kept pushing, threatening to launch a police investigation. They told me that the only reason they weren't pressing charges was that they knew my husband and his firm and wouldn't want to embarrass them. As soon as they said that, I realized they were worried about their own reputation. They would be humiliated if it got out that a librarian was arrested for selling mushrooms from their offices. It was too juicy a story for the press to ignore. They would look like fools, and they couldn't afford that, not when they were still recovering clients after the financial crash.

I knew I would avoid the worst of it, but I had to tell Carter everything. His first reaction was bewilderment. Then he got angry. I tried to explain my motives, but he didn't care. He got stuck on the fact that everything I had done was illegal. That I had put myself and our family at risk. He couldn't believe that I'd decided to get pregnant, been pregnant, and had a baby while *committing a felony*—that's how he put it. He described everything in legal terms.

There's a relief in getting caught, and a burst of energy; you feel as if the world can finally see you, truly. Carter couldn't understand why I wasn't drowning in shame. He insisted that I retain a lawyer in case my firm was building a case against me. I thought he was being paranoid. Then he served me divorce papers. He wanted full custody of Rose, who had only just turned three, and he probably would have gotten it if my firm had actually pressed charges. Instead, I was leaving my lawyer's office when an FBI agent stepped in my path and said she wanted to talk to me. At first, I thought Carter had been right, and that I was about to be arrested, but she quickly told me that she only wanted to ask a few questions. It helped that she was close to my age and was dressed casually in jeans and a sweater. She wore stylish, clear-framed glasses. After showing me her badge, she asked me to walk with her toward the National Mall. In the manner of a doctor explaining a complicated prognosis, she told me that my activities had come to the attention of a team of researchers at the DOD, and they were interested in hiring me.

By then we had reached the wide, pebbled walkways that traverse the lawn. We were heading toward the Washington Monument, passing school groups who were no doubt learning about the mismatched marble made from two different Maryland quarries with a stripe from Massachusetts in the middle. Once, the marbles had all been the same pearly gray, but the weather had affected each one differently, and they had changed over time, becoming more like the places they were from, just as people do. I stared at that ill-conceived obelisk as the agent continued with her pitch. If I was amenable, she said, she would interview me for possible employment.

I didn't feel like I had much of a choice. She was from the FBI, she knew some pretty damning things about me, and I was newly divorced, without a steady income and references to call on. So I followed her to a nearby bench and sat down next to her. I tried to act normal.

"What was the job?" Jenny asked, settling into her seat in the tub. We had both gotten cold and were back in the water.

"She didn't tell me right away. It is, hands down, the weirdest job interview I've ever had. The first question was: What is the meaning of life?"

"No, it wasn't!" Jenny said, laughing. "What did you tell her?"

"I said I didn't know. She insisted I give her *something*, so I said the first thing that came to my head: to take care of things. She liked that, I think. Then she asked me, Do you believe in the soul? I said I believe in consciousness. Then I just . . . went off on Hecate's Key. I told her how a mushroom is the bloom of a large underground network that is possibly the brain of the earth. I said who even knows if consciousness is individual, maybe it's this large, branching intelligence that all living things tap into. Then she told me I was hired. She said that the DOD was looking for people who could help them discover alternative healers, people they might not come across through their normal networks. She said it was a good position, excellent benefits, and not dangerous."

"So you said yes, right then and there?" Jenny asked.

"I tried to put her off. I said I needed to think about it. But she basically just laughed. She was like, *Do you have a lot of other job offers coming in?* Then she asked me what I was going to do about Rose. Which freaked me out. Because I hadn't told her Rose's name. She knew all this stuff about me. She said it wasn't going to look good for me during the custody hearing if I was still unemployed. She also said the federal government had plenty of evidence that I'd been selling a Schedule 1 drug for several years, and they could make an example of me if they wanted. She said it would be to our *mutual benefit* if I took the job."

"Oh my god," Jenny said. "That's so creepy."

"It was," I agreed, though that time in my life felt very far away—the whole world felt far away at the moment. I had a pleasant feeling of displacement, floating for so long in the warm water.

"Wait, am I on some government list?" Jenny asked. "Is that why you wanted to interview me?"

"Sort of," I said, sitting up. "My boss looks for people who do nature-based healing. He thinks it's probably the best thing for PTSD. He's also worried about Climate Anxiety—do you know what that is?"

"You mean, the sinking feeling that we're all frogs in a boiling pot?" Jenny laughed lightly. "Yeah, I'm familiar."

I nodded, feeling glum. The light was rising, morning was coming soon. I would have to go back to my real life in a few hours.

"Sometimes, I think I should just see as much of the world as I can," Jenny said. "Enjoy it while it lasts. Other times I feel guilty because I'm not staging daily protests in front of the White House."

"I'm right there with you." There was some relief in hearing someone say these things out loud.

"But you have a child," Jenny said. "So you *have* to care about the future."

"You don't?"

Jenny shrugged. "I don't want to be nihilistic, but sometimes I think the sooner we humans go extinct, the better. Leave it to the plants and animals."

"And the mushrooms," I said. "They actually do quite well after extinction events. There's evidence that they covered the earth after the dinosaurs died out."

"There you go," Jenny said. "Let the mushrooms take over." She glanced up at the house, its windows looking like burnished mirrors in the dawn light. "We should probably get back, huh?"

"Yeah, I guess so." My limbs felt heavy as I climbed out of the tub. I couldn't believe that in just a few hours, I would be flying through the sky I'd been gazing at all night.

12.

I avoided my reflection as I changed back into my tight jeans and sweater. After my youthful evening, I looked decidedly not young. I rubbed tinted moisturizer over my puffy, blotchy skin, but it didn't do much to revive me. I had a headache from the wine, a certain fuzzy feeling at the back of my skull. The last thing I wanted to do was board a plane. I wished I could sleep in a guest room and wake up at noon. I wished I could drive to the sea with Jenny and jump in. I wished I could stay in California for the rest of the week—maybe the rest of my life. Why not? If I didn't have Rose, I would do all those things and more.

But I did have Rose—as Jenny had pointed out. She was the organizing principle of my life, after my mother. Or maybe before my mother. I wasn't sure, anymore, if I was a mother or daughter first. I felt very unsettled after confessing everything to Jenny, as if I'd revived dormant memories that were best left undisturbed.

My black bathing suit was in a ball on the floor. I rinsed it in the sink and hung it over the metal towel rack, a black shadow in a gleaming white room.

There was a coffee waiting for me when I returned to the kitchen, served in a pale-green glazed mug. The Pavlovian smell was faintly cheering, and I tried to rally for Jenny's sake. She had changed into fresh clothing and was wearing a mint-green hoodie, jeans, and Birkenstocks. She didn't even seem tired. She seemed wired, actually.

"So," she said playfully, "what are you going to tell the Pentagon about me?"

"I have no idea," I said, rubbing my forehead. The prospect of trying to fit my experience with Jenny into a bureaucratic memo filled me with dread. "I guess I'll write something about the way you use plants as an intermediary."

"They're not an *intermediary*," Jenny said, mock-offended. She continued sincerely: "They listen, they listen better than me. And then people listen to them. I don't understand how it works, but I think it's natural for people to communicate with plants and animals. I think it's innate. Don't you?"

I nodded, too exhausted to say much else—though I did agree with her.

"They could send soldiers out into the woods, and it would probably work wonders," Jenny said. "They could have them do restorative work, like planting native species or making compost."

"I love that you think the military would have a composting initiative," I said with genuine affection. In Jenny's idealism, I saw my own efforts to smuggle ecological ideas into the DOD.

"It just seems like a missed opportunity . . ." Jenny paused to sip her coffee. "I'm surprised that they aren't doing more with Hecate's Key. You'd think that would be good for like, going into battle."

"I thought that's why they recruited me, at first—because they wanted access to it. But they already knew all about it. They studied Hecate's Key back in the seventies. They did a bunch of trials and found out that it's not good for soldiers to lose their fear of death. It doesn't make you any braver. Fear of death is actually a good thing, in general. It gives you an edge."

As I spoke, I thought of the terrible phrase *enhances soldier lethality*.

"Why not prescribe it for other things?" Jenny asked. "Wouldn't it be good for anxiety? Or PTSD?"

"They probably would if they could cultivate it. But it only grows in the wild," I said, recalling the bits of leaves and dirt that I would sometimes find in Astrid's packages. "Sometimes I miss selling it. I never questioned what I was doing. I knew I was helping people."

"So why not try to sell it again?"

"No way!" I said with a laugh. "I think it got me in enough trouble the first time."

"But what if you did it again, and this time, you had someone like *me* helping you?" Jenny said, pointing to herself in a comical way.

"Jenny, if you want to sell Hecate's Key, you're welcome to take the idea and run with it, but I don't know how it would work on the West Coast . . ." I paused, uncertain of how seriously to take her. She jumped in, assuring me that she wasn't trying to take on a new side hustle. What she was proposing was bigger than that. She wanted us to go into business together. It wouldn't just be Hecate's Key, it would be tree therapy *and* Hecate's Key and whatever other mushrooms we could scrounge up or even cultivate: Lion's Mane. Chaga. Chanterelles. It was the right moment for mushrooms, they were trending, she could feel it. Together, we would have an amazing network of contacts.

"There are so many people who need Hecate's Key," she said, pitching me the same way I had once pitched Ossi. I had the sense her idea had been brewing since I'd first described the mushroom to her. She wasn't just talking off the top of her head. "We could sell it across the country."

"But Astrid is my only source." I wondered if Jenny understood how small my operation had been, how little money I made.

"We'll develop new sources. There has to be at least one other place where they grow. And it's not like we need to have a huge business. We won't have shareholders to please or big marketing campaigns that we need to fund. It will just be a simple, vital service. Two women selling mushrooms. That's it."

"What about your tree therapy?"

"I don't see it as a separate thing. Mushrooms and trees work together in nature, why shouldn't we sell them together?"

"You're serious about this," I said, surprised by the enthusiasm in her voice. I'd hoped, since I'd arrived on her doorstep, that we would become friends again, but my fantasy had only extended to occasional visits, email updates about our separate lives. I'd never dreamed that she would want to collaborate with me.

"Leigh, this is the universe sending us a message. Do you really think it's a coincidence that you, who sells mushrooms, should reconnect with me, who works with trees? It makes sense. We grew up together, in the same soil."

I didn't think then about how we'd only been in the same place for one year. Honestly, I don't remember what I thought, exactly. I was dazed, sleep deprived, and melancholy—no match for Jenny's manic enthusiasm.

Driving to the airport, Jenny detailed her plan. It occurs to me now that maybe she was high on something. For someone who spent years selling mushrooms, I can be innocent about drug use. I never suspect it. Still, I don't think Jenny was under the influence of anything but her imagination. I believed in her then, and I still do in a way. What I mean is, I think people should nurture the soft, fanciful parts of themselves that wish to see faces in flowers and love between two trees growing closely together. I don't think Jenny was wrong about any of that. You really can talk to a tree. It will listen.

Jenny thought we should move to Ontario, in the same region as Astrid. We could become Canadian citizens and set up a new life there. She understood it would take time. Her tentative plan was that I would stay at the DOD for another year while she went back and forth to Canada, meeting with Astrid, and getting to know the trees in the area. Back in DC, I would discreetly contact my old crew and introduce them to Jenny. Then, when I was ready, I would move to Canada. Start fresh.

"What about Rose?" I asked.

"She would come with you, of course! It would be such an amazing way to grow up. Better than suburban DC. Trust me, I went to those schools. It's not good. How do you think I ended up in Lost Falls?"

I'd always thought Jenny had come to Lost Falls because she and her mother weren't getting along, but I vaguely remembered that she'd also been pigeonholed unfairly at her old high school. Bad grades, maybe. Or a bad boyfriend? In that moment, I should have realized how little I knew about her. But I was too carried away by the idea that Jenny and I would remain friends.

Carter once said that I sold Hecate's Key because I had survivor's guilt. I never liked that interpretation, but over the years I've come to see that our actions have many branching causes. It's the work of a lifetime to appreciate our entanglements.

Jenny walked me to security.

"I know what I'm saying is bananas," she said as she hugged me goodbye. "I was just thinking about how we're both feeling so compromised, so *stuck,* and I thought, maybe we could get ourselves unstuck, you know?"

"I know," I said. And I did. I wouldn't have flown to California to meet her if I hadn't been feeling so restless.

"Just think about it," Jenny said. "And stay in touch."

"I will," I promised.

After I boarded my flight, I fell asleep almost immediately. When I woke up, we were landing at Dulles.

The terminal was crowded and noisy and smelled like fast food. I was hungry, but nothing looked good to eat. My neck hurt from sleeping while sitting up, and there was something wrong with one of the wheels on my carry-on suitcase. I felt grumpy and not at all well rested, but I had to pick up Rose and pretend I was in good spirits—or, at the very least, not take my bad mood out on her.

Long-term parking was a desert of parked vehicles, not a tree in sight. When I finally made it to my car, its interior was hot and stale. I felt defeated as I waited for the AC to kick in.

13.

Carter dropped Rose off at my place on Wednesday morning and didn't even come up to the front porch. He just nodded at me, like he would at a babysitter, and drove off. Actually, he would have been a lot nicer to a babysitter.

"Did you enjoy your days off with Daddy?" Carter and I had arranged to take time off from work for her spring break, rather than enrolling her at some kind of "vacation week" camp. If we were still a couple, we might have gone on a real vacation, but I tried not to think about that alternate reality.

"It was okay," Rose said. "He had to work every morning, so I got to watch a movie after breakfast. Yesterday we went to the fancy mall. Then we got Shake Shack."

Movies and the mall. I wasn't philosophically opposed to either, but I was annoyed that she hadn't been outdoors. Jenny's plan flickered in the back of my mind: a vision of a cabin like Astrid's, deep in the woods. There would be misty mornings and crackling fires in the evening. It was a mirage, but it gave me comfort.

I'd hoped to squeeze a little work in during my Rose staycation, but after hearing about her time with Carter, I resolved to be the more involved parent. And I was, for the first two days. I took her to the C&O Canal, where she could ride her scooter, and then we went out to lunch, dining al fresco. On Thursday, I arranged to meet a friend of hers on the playground, and I chatted with the other mother about normal things, like schools and childcare and TV shows. When she commented on the warm weather—how nice it was to finally leave jackets at home—I didn't share how the pleasant temperatures made me nervous, because every year it seemed to get a little warmer, a little earlier.

My honeymoon period with Rose ended on Friday, when we went to the zoo. I have never really liked zoos, even as a little kid. Growing up near farms and woods, I saw plenty of animals. I couldn't see the point of driving to look at them in cages. But, maybe because Rose was more of a suburban child, she loved going to the National Zoo. So I took her whenever she asked. As far as animal prisons go, it's one of the prettier ones, beautifully landscaped with lots of shady spots to take breaks.

At first, it was marvelous: my anxiety about the warming weather dissolved when I found myself in a crowd of delighted children. To them, spring meant only one thing: summer was coming! The parents seemed happier, too. Scarves were loosened, necks bared. Ice cream was consumed before lunch.

Rose and I wound our way through the park, eventually arriving at our favorite area: the elephants. The baby was out in the yard, getting bathed by his mother, who used her long trunk to spray him with water. The little elephant shuddered with each shower, prancing around his mother, wanting more attention, more fun. He stamped his feet in the nearby puddles that were forming, swished his tail, swung his long trunk. His thick, gray, wrinkled skin was spattered with mud and water that rapidly disappeared in the sun.

Rose and I sat and watched them for a half hour or so. Then I made the mistake of looking up "decline in elephant population" on my phone. I knew it would be bad, but I wasn't expecting to learn that one-third of all the elephants had disappeared in seven years' time. If 30 percent of the human species were killed, that would be 2.46 billion people dead and buried. I looked that up on my phone, too, along with some other statistics about the devastation of the planet. I basically fell into the internet. Rose got annoyed, and I was just about to put my phone away when I got a text from Jenny. It was a link to an article about how mushrooms were predicted to be the next big thing in health care. Hey! Hope you're having fun with Rose. Saw this and thought of you and our crazy plan. Maybe not so crazy? xJ

For the rest of our zoo outing, I surreptitiously texted Jenny, ignoring side-eye from Rose. Jenny was surprisingly knowledgeable about the alternative health market and already had some clients in mind who might want to buy mushrooms in bulk. She also had ideas about how to handle the financial side and where we might live. It had apparently been her dream, for some time, to build a cabin off the grid. I could see her pulling it off. I was surprised to find that I was actually tempted to join her. If Jenny had suggested that we start some mail-order business where I'd be working out of DC and she'd be in LA, I'd have said hell no, I couldn't take that chance with Rose, not with Carter just waiting for me to mess up. But she was giving me permission to imagine a new life, a way of living that would allow me to do work I knew was good, and to live in a place with easy access to the outdoors. I didn't like that I was raising Rose in a car-bound suburb, always shuttling her from place to place. She had no wild places to roam, just a patch of lawn, with one scraggly tree in the middle.

Jenny kept texting me—all weekend. Email, too. It was a bit overwhelming, but at the same time, a much-needed hit of adult conversation after so many days of solo parenting. After Rose went to bed, I read the articles Jenny sent about mushroom cultivation and the deep intelligence of forests. I made a "mystic mushroom mix" playlist—a mashup of songs that spanned pop genres across the decades and shared mystical undertones—and listened to it while I scrolled Reddit forums about fungi forays and perused cabin listings in the region where Astrid lived, gathering details to embroider my fantasy of woodland life: Rose would go out every morning to gather kindling, and I would accompany Astrid on her foraging trips, carrying a handmade straw basket. I'd learn the names of mushrooms and which trees they associated with, which ones were safe to eat. I'd become a wonderful cook, and people would talk about my subtle, nourishing soups. Meanwhile, Jenny would receive visitors in her cabin, which would be just down the road from mine, or maybe we'd live in a sweet little village, where Jenny could have a shop and I'd have an office. We'd have good internet and all the other comforts of modern life—TV, hot water, coffee beans, chocolate—but none of the noise. Rose would attend the local grade school, or maybe she'd be unschooled, picking up the survival skills that children in her generation should be learning anyway, like how to grow and prepare food, how to collect and filter water, how to build and repair, how to live on less. She'd be prepared for what was to come in ways public school education could never afford her. Even if, when she grew up, Rose decided to move to the nearest big city, she would have the emerald memory of a childhood among mushrooms and moss. It would be her spiritual inheritance.

I loved my vision—except when I remembered Carter. I couldn't take Rose from him, but I could never leave her behind. He would have to agree to let her live with me up north, to limit his visits to summer. But why would he do that? Jenny thought Carter might settle nearby, in Toronto. She didn't seem to give any thought to work visas or moving so far away from his parents. She actually wrote, **Toronto is a very cosmopolitan city**, and I sent her a crying-laughing emoji because what did "cosmopolitan" even mean after globalization, when there were really just tiers? There was the upper one: an elite nation of photogenic tableaux, paraben-free moisturizers, fair weather, and vegan ice cream; and then the many lower tiers of cracked phone screens, unpaid parking tickets, dead batteries, second jobs, third jobs, side hustles, and insurance that won't cover damage caused by flooding, wildfires, or other Acts of God that were actually Acts of Men.

On Sunday morning, it was time to send Rose back to Carter. I had to get her dressed for church because Carter had returned to his Presbyterian roots after we split up. Carter had packed a dress for her that was new to me, a pale-pink confection with a tulle skirt; it was pretty in a sophisticated way that made me think that Megan must have picked it out. I said nothing until Rose took a small lavender compact from a pocket in her bag and told me she needed to put on lip gloss and eye shadow, that all the other little girls wore it.

"Where did you get that?" I asked, thinking to myself, *Megan.*

"It was in the goody bag," Rose said. "At Layla's birthday."

Goody bags. You didn't want to be *that mom* complaining about all the plastic crap, especially when you might be handing it out yourself a few months later. I opened the little case to find two small bars of gooey petroleum by-product, shiny as an oil slick. If I threw it away, it was just another piece of garbage. If I let her wear it, I was training her for a lifetime of chemical enhancement. Or maybe I wasn't. Maybe it was just a fad, like the jelly shoes of my childhood.

"You can't wear this to church or school," I said. "Only for dress-up."

"But I want to wear it for *real life!*" Rose said, her voice quickly become helium shrill.

"This isn't real life." I snapped the compact shut. "It's just plastic junk."

"Daddy says plastic is very useful, he says doctors use it to save people from heart attacks."

"I'm not saying plastic isn't useful. I'm saying it's *overused.*"

"Give it back, it's my present!"

Carter pulled into the driveway then, and I felt a wave of shame. All weekend long, Rose and I had barely disagreed, and now he would see her flushed cheeks and know we'd been fighting.

I handed her the makeup. "It's yours," I said. "Just save it for dress-up, okay?"

Rose took it without saying anything and put it back into her bag. She wouldn't make eye contact as she walked toward the door, but then at the last minute, she turned and ran to me.

"I'll miss you," I said as I embraced her.

"You always say that."

"It's always true."

And it was. My chest tightened as I watched Carter buckle her into her booster seat. It had been two years, and I still wasn't used to the push-pull of shared custody. I badly needed a break, but it didn't need to be three whole days.

Inside, the condo smelled like stale coffee and laundry detergent. I picked up a few of Rose's toys left on the carpet and contemplated going to a yoga class. I knew group exercise was the kind of thing I should seek out when I was feeling down. But I also had work. I needed to get started on my report about Jennifer Hex.

I procrastinated by researching Jenny's boss, Kip Fielding. At first I had trouble finding him, but then I remembered that Kip was a nickname. His proper name was Emmett, and his title was Innovation Director. He didn't seem to have a lot of power within the company; maybe that was why he was lording it over Jenny. The most interesting thing I discovered was that he had an ex-wife, Monica Walker-Fielding. She was involved with a nonprofit that protected Arctic wolves, and had been photographed at numerous charitable events, looking svelte in column gowns. She favored wolfish colors—gray, silver, ice blue.

The field report template remained empty for a long time. An honest account would describe Jenny's shiny green car, the night falling as we drove, the road pulling us along with its own energy. It would include the winding path down to the whirlpool, the smooth stones beneath bare feet, the wind shushing the cedars above, releasing their sweet, sharp fragrance. It would include the past, all the memories swirling around us.

To give a truly exhaustive report, I would also have to describe the unlikely future that I was shaping, this vision of a greener life where

I'd be directly in touch with the mushroom that had already changed my trajectory once. I wondered if I was deluding myself, if I would really be happier in the woods. I had, after all, been just as enchanted by the creature comforts Jenny offered me—the wine, the snacks, the soft towels and stylish swimsuit—as I had by her ideas of tree therapy. I wondered if I was losing my grip on reality or if I was finally coming to terms with it. The fact was, I didn't really like my job; I just found ways to enjoy it because it was all I had. Lately, it felt like I was just going through the motions for the few days a week I got to spend with Rose.

I glanced out the window at Walter, my tree friend. I went outside to see him, in penance. There, on his branches, were the tiny green dots of new buds! I thought of the Larkin poem my mother loved, and the cross-stitch my father made for her, hanging by our front door, the one I read almost every morning of my teenage years while waiting for my mother to gather her things and drive us to school. *The trees are coming into leaf / like something almost being said.* Walter's buds were so fantastically bright—nearly fluorescent—that I wondered if that was what Jenny meant by Divine Green.

"Walter," I said, "am I crazy to even indulge her?"

Walter said nothing. Or if he did, I couldn't hear him.

FIELD REPORT

IRTH2: Spiritual Readiness Initiative
April 4, 2016

    Agent: Leigh Bowers Glenn

    Practitioner: Jennifer Marie Heck a.k.a. Jennifer Hex

SUMMARY

I visited the practitioner, Jennifer Marie Heck (JMH), on March 28, 2016, at her home office in Los Angeles. There, I received treatments for intermittent depression and anxiety. I was diagnosed with this condition by JMH after a 45-minute interview.

JMH's treatment contained the following elements: *Intake Interview, Intellectual Stimulation, and Stress Reduction Ritual.* No medicines or physical therapies were administered as part of her treatment.

JMH's therapy is a combination of common stress-relieving techniques: meditation, deep breathing, and physical movement.

JMH inspires confidence through both her online and IRL persona. She is successful in convincing subjects to practice a daily ritual. Both the preinterview writing exercises and postinterview protocols emphasize mindfulness, spiritual awareness (the interconnectedness of all living things), and increase a subject's exposure to natural light. Her practices also increase sociability and feelings of well-being associated with active social lives as patients learn to feel a connection to the natural world.

TREATMENT ELEMENTS

Intake Interview

Before my in-person interview with JMH, I completed two online forms. The first form asked about medical history, vital statistics, and diet and exercise habits (Attachment A). The second form explored my "relationship to nature," time I spend outdoors, the number of plants in my house, the area where I grew up, and the types of trees and plants I could identify from memory (Attachment B).

JMH read and interpreted the forms in advance of our meeting. She was an attentive, spontaneous, and warm interviewer. She established trust through leaning forward, pausing to think about things that I said, mirroring body language, and repeating information I shared with her. She asked follow-up questions and took notes.

Intellectual Stimulation

JMH reminded me of the basic facts of plant biology. She showed me some of her favorite plants and taught me the names of plants that I did not know. She shared with me her theory that human beings are happier and healthier when they feel appreciation for their natural environment. She helped me identify ways that I could spend more time in nature.

Her knowledge of plants does not seem to be extensive, nor does it exceed information already included in Dr. Duke's database at the USDA. However, her presentation of the information is appealing and personal and is enhanced by the long interview process, which incorporates aspects of talk therapy.

Stress Reduction Ritual

For her clients, JMH will devise a personalized daily protocol that incorporates meditation, journaling, and cognitive reframing. She will exchange daily texts with clients to help keep them on track.

EVALUATION

PROS

- Inexpensive: the therapy does not require special equipment, nor does it require physical or sensory data from Soldier, e.g., weight, heart rate, REM cycling, etc.
- Accessible: plants and trees are a readily available spiritual resource
- Adaptable: therapy can be incorporated into a variety of religious beliefs and faith-based disciplines
- Self-directed: Soldiers can undertake therapy on their own time without supervision

CONS

- Self-directed: therapies require a high level of imagination and motivation to work effectively
- Unstable outcomes: plant-based knowledge sparks a wide variety of spiritual insights; as with other meditation techniques, it may be detrimental to Soldier lethality and Soldier engagement
- JMH unlikely to collaborate with programmers: JMH is employed by Ambar-Fielding as a consultant, and any collaboration would have to be brokered through them

CONCLUSIONS

JHM's therapies can be incorporated into **Mental Readiness** strategies, including heart rate control, stress control, cognitive reframing, and interpersonal capability, especially nonverbal communication.

JMH's therapies can be incorporated into **Spiritual Readiness** practices of journaling and meditation. JMH's therapies may enhance humility, resilience, moral and ethical reasoning, and productivity and performance. They may also be beneficial as a post-conflict treatment to help Soldiers reestablish a sense of interpersonal connection and to restore the mind-body connection.

JMH's therapies may also be beneficial in **Sleep Readiness** when her meditation exercises are incorporated into a pre-sleep routine.

Finally, JMH's therapies show a high potential for inclusion in the **Climate Anxiety Readiness Pilot**. Her emphasis on the resilience and intelligence of plant life is an example of cognitive reframing that can address feelings of hopelessness. Her mindfulness exercises, which encourage the close observation of nonhuman species, can also restore positive emotions of appreciation and love.

14.

I presented my report on Jenny to our Spiritual Readiness team. There were two other researchers on the team: Sandra, who studied mystical and religious rituals, and Tim, who kept up on self-help trends—a nebulous category that could include anything from productivity gurus to cold-water dipping.

Our team meetings usually consisted of just the three of us, plus Marcos, but every few weeks someone from the IRTH2 development would drop in. Ileana, one of the highest-ranking leaders in Holistic Health, and easily my most intimidating colleague, decided to show up on the day that I presented Jennifer Hex. A former marine, Ileana always wore a perfectly fitting black T-shirt and blazer, with her hair in a tight ponytail. When I stood up to deliver my report, I instantly felt ridiculous in my shirtdress, which I had chosen because it had a botanical print. I'd wanted to channel some of Jenny's energy. Instead, I just looked like I was on vacation. Ileana didn't nod or smile as I spoke; she just stared at me with an intense focus that I imagined all marines must learn. I never had any idea what she was thinking.

Tim was easier to read; he was a wiry, antsy person, a former professional cyclist who'd had a nervous breakdown in his early thirties and then healed himself through meditation and kayaking. Marcos recruited him from a yoga center, where he'd been teaching. He was not impressed with Jenny; I could tell from the way he was taking notes in his bullet journal that he had some points to make. When I finished my report, Tim said that, in his opinion, Jennifer Hex wasn't doing anything beyond unlicensed talk therapy with some environmental psychology thrown in.

"I basically agree," I said, throwing him a bone, "but I don't know how to talk to trees, so maybe there's something going on there that we can't see."

"That sounds faith based," Tim said, glancing at Sandra, who had just given a presentation on prayer-chain apps and was knitting placidly from her designated spot at the end of the conference table. She had seven grandchildren and was always working on a sweater for someone.

"It's good if there's overlap," Marcos said. "Holistic health is all about integration."

"This also dovetails with our virtual reality fitness initiative," Ileana said. "We have a new forest run that is very immersive. Have you tried it, Leigh?"

"I haven't," I admitted. I tended to visit the same parts of the fitness center each week, and I'd been negligent in testing the new equipment. "I don't think Jennifer Hex would advise anyone to take a run through a virtual forest. She wants people to interact with actual plants. Her insight as a healer is that it's the plants *themselves* that are soothing people, and that she's just bringing people into communion with them."

"Studies have shown that looking at a picture or a video of a natural landscape is beneficial," Ileana said. "I think her therapy is applicable in virtual environments."

"I'm sorry, but I don't think that's true," I said, reddening a little. It was nerve-racking to disagree with Ileana. "It's about listening, not looking. You can't communicate with a pixelated image."

"You're saying you want to instruct soldiers to literally go out and speak to plants?" Ileana asked.

"There are guided exercises they can do, but they don't have to talk if they don't want to. It's more about directing your attention to the natural environment so you can get out of the human mindset. It's *spiritual*."

"I'm concerned about the feasibility," Ileana said.

Tim nodded. "Think about where we're deploying people," he said. "Some bases, there's hardly anything growing, let alone a garden."

"It doesn't have to be the most wonderful plants in the world. The point is to connect with what's around you. Get outside."

"That's what the dogs are for," Tim said. "Let the therapy dogs take people for walks in the woods."

I was frustrated by the pushback—and yet not especially surprised. Tim and I often sparred; he thought my nature therapies were too squishy, and I thought his self-help gurus focused too much on productivity.

"Let's not forget that Jennifer Hex is consulting for Ambar-Fielding," Marcos put in. "Leigh tells me that they are working on a wellness app with a virtual reality aspect. Apparently, they hired some Stanford kid who writes algorithms for plant vibrations."

"Do you know who?" Ileana asked me. "Are they in the Comp Sci department?"

"I don't know," I said. "Her name is Lily."

"I wonder if it's Lily Dawson," Marcos said. "Didn't we have her on the shortlist for Project Demeter?"

"Yes, but the budget got cut. I was going to try her for next year."

"What's Project Demeter?" I asked.

"It's one of the experimental AI therapies," Ileana said. Which meant it was classified. She turned to Marcos. "Why don't you reach out to Miss Dawson and see if she's happy at Ambar-Fielding."

"Will do."

I worried that I'd accidentally revealed something that could get Jenny in trouble, so I tried to cover it up, pointing out that Ambar-Fielding was hardly alone in launching VR platforms and health care apps.

"Of course," Ileana said vaguely as she typed notes into her phone. She paused to look at me. "Do the forest run. I think you'll be impressed."

"And don't forget, tonight is Taco Tuesday at Mas Amigos," Marcos added. "Sleep Readiness is hosting."

The meeting broke up. As we all made our way into the hallway, Tim came over to me. "Hey, I'm sorry if I pushed too hard in there," he said. "I wasn't trying to shut you down."

"I didn't think you were, don't worry," I said quickly. I didn't want to talk any more about Jenny; I felt like I'd drawn too much attention to her already.

The H2 fitness center was in a nondescript building a few miles from the Pentagon, across the street from a strip mall. I often went to the Monday-morning boot camp, and I liked the "enhanced" rower, where you could exercise in front of a video of a flowing river. But I rarely visited the VR pods. They just seemed too complicated.

The screen in my pod curved around the hikermill—a large square platform about eight feet across—in a semi-sphere. Behind me was a light-blocking curtain. I wore lightweight smart glasses, ear pods, and a heart rate monitor. Using an app on my phone that synced with the hikermill, I selected a trail of medium difficulty. The hikermill adjusted the grade accordingly. Then the lights went down, as if a movie were about to start, and birdsong filled the pod. A forest appeared in front of me, in three dimensions, startlingly real. Tree branches swayed in a breeze that I could feel in the pod, and one branch seemed to be inches from my face. I reached out to touch it, but there was nothing. For a few moments, I felt something akin to motion sickness. I had tried VR before but nothing as detailed as this. It was like a lucid dream.

"Are you ready for your workout?" a voice asked. "Start jogging when you would like to begin."

The hikermill moved with me, undulating slightly to mimic the uneven ground of the forest. The images on the screen were in sync with my movements, or maybe it was something in my glasses. I couldn't work out how the illusion was maintained—I guessed it was some combination of augmented reality and virtual reality—but it immediately felt as if I were making my way through the forest. When there were rocks in my path, the platform became bumpier. When I looked down, I appeared to be running on a forest trail. I found myself avoiding roots and puddles that seemed to be in my way and looking for trail markers. Birds flitted through the trees, small animals rustled in the underbrush, and I swore I could smell decaying leaves, pine trees, and moss. I was completely absorbed. The only thing that felt amiss was my own self-awareness. In a strange way, I lost track of my body; at one point I felt confused by the sweat on the back of my neck. My heart was beating faster, but I didn't realize how ragged my breathing had become until I stopped to rest. The machine allowed me to slow to a walk; it was impressively in tune with my movements. In the distance, I could make out a large limestone rock. Sunlight glimmered in patches all around me, and a nearby tree trunk was adorned with shelf mushrooms. I found myself worrying about the tree, trying to remember if shelf mushrooms were parasitic. Then I remembered that none of it was real. I started jogging again, toward the limestone in the distance, but before I could get there, the voice announced that my workout was over. The birdsong receded, and the images around me faded away. I took off my glasses and found I was staring at a white, concave screen.

I stepped out of the pod in a daze. "Good workout?" asked the attendant, a muscular man wearing an army T-shirt.

"I'm not sure," I said. "It was surreal."

"Make sure you hydrate."

"That's the plan—I'm heading to happy hour."

He gave me a thumbs-up. I stretched in the shower to save time, and towel-dried my hair, pulling it into a damp ponytail. I'd worked up an appetite from my quasi-hike and was eager to get to the restaurant. I felt like I was back to normal, but when I got outside to the parking lot, the uncanny feeling took over again. It had apparently rained while I was in the fitness center, weather that was at odds with the sunny hike

I'd just experienced indoors. The air was heavy, balmy in a way that reminded me of the humid summer to come.

Mas Amigos was in a different strip mall a few miles away, and was already busy with the after-work crowd when I arrived. It was a casual Tex-Mex place, where you found your own seating at painted picnic tables and Adirondack chairs arranged haphazardly in a large open space. I recognized a few DOD people at a bright turquoise table and was heading toward them when my phone rang: it was Carter. I picked up immediately. "Everything okay with Rose?"

"Rose is fine. She's watching a show before bed. I was calling because—where are you? I can hear voices."

"I'm at a work thing," I said, exiting and going back outside. "What's up? Do you need to switch weekends?"

"No, I just wanted to tell you something. I wanted to tell you before I told Rose—or even Megan."

I knew what he was going to say. I felt the tears gathering, a certain tightening in my cheekbones, and walked a few paces away from the restaurant to a shoe store with heels perched on pedestals of varying heights. Silk cherry blossoms were scattered on the floor beneath the display, a sight that immediately conjured up spring, and walks down the esplanade in new sandals. I'd taken that stroll with Carter many, many times, and I thought of those weekend afternoons as Carter let me know he planned to propose to Megan, who was coming over later. He was doing it that night because it was Megan's birthday. She was turning thirty-five.

"Okay," I said, focusing on the pink blossoms in the display, trying to convince myself they were real. But their pristine beauty gave them away; they weren't browned at the edges or blued with crush marks.

"That's all you're going to say?" Carter asked, disappointment straining his voice.

"Do you want me to give you my congratulations?" I looked toward the darkened parking lot. "Congratulations. I'm happy for you."

"You don't sound happy."

"You need me to sound happy, too?" I wondered what his fantasy of this moment had been, how he'd hoped his ex-wife, the mother of his child, would react.

"I don't know why I bothered calling," Carter said.

"I don't, either." But as soon as I spoke, I realized that he wanted to be thanked.

"I'm just trying to do the right thing," he said. "I wanted to be transparent."

"No," I said. "You wanted to be blameless." Then I hung up. It wasn't the most gracious moment in my existence, but it was among the most self-preserving.

I considered going straight home, but everyone had already seen me, so I went up to the bar and ordered as extravagantly as I could from a fast-casual menu. I was standing there sipping a margarita when Tim came over and invited me to join everyone at the table.

"I'll be over, I'm waiting on food." I wasn't quite ready to be in a big group.

"I'll wait with you," Tim said, signaling the bartender for another round. He smiled at me, curiously. "Your hair's wet," he observed. "Were you at the gym?"

I nodded. "I tried out the hikermill."

"And . . . ? What did you think? Did you commune with the virtual trees?"

"It was trippy, in a good way," I said lightly, sensing I was in for a ribbing.

"How did it compare with Jennifer Hex's therapy?" Tim asked with an amused smile.

"I wouldn't compare them," I said, "because it wasn't real trees, so I wasn't getting any real tree knowledge." I knew Tim would find this illogical, but I wasn't going to pretend there wasn't a mystical element to Jenny's treatment.

"You really fell for this Jennifer Hex person, didn't you?" Tim took a sip of his Pacifico, which the bartender had just delivered. "From what

I know of Ambar-Fielding, it's a family business on its last legs. They're just throwing things at the wall to see what sticks."

"Or they're being open-minded."

"I doubt that," Tim said. "I didn't want to be too dismissive at the meeting, but to me, Jennifer Hex seems like an actress looking to make a little extra money with her tree-pantomime shtick."

"Maybe you're not taking her seriously because she's a woman."

"Oh, I take her seriously," Tim said. "She's an operator. She's the person telling the emperor he looks great when he's butt naked. Except she's telling people that their trees can talk to them and heal them."

"It's deeper than that." I leaned forward, trying to channel Jenny. "She wants you to look at trees and plants in a different way, to see them as having agency and wisdom. She's trying to restore the natural connection we have to other living things."

"I think *that's* real," Tim said. "I'm just not sure Jennifer Hex is the right conduit. The DOD isn't going to pick someone who has people hugging trees."

"That's not what she's doing."

"You know what I mean. The army wants to win. They want people who want to win. If they could just churn through twentysomethings like the NFL, they would."

"That's so depressing." I pictured a scrum of helmeted football players crashing into each other, the sickening clank of helmets. "Why are they bothering with holistic health?"

"Because it's a good idea. If people rest more, they're in better shape. They're saner, more in touch with reality. Climate change is part of that. They know they have a crisis coming. They've known for decades—not that they've done much to stop it."

"How do you square that for yourself?" I asked. "We're trying to help people deal with the spiritual fallout of war and climate disasters, but then we're funding the wars and burning the jet fuel."

"I guess I'm used to it," Tim said. "I come from a family where a lot of people are in the military. I almost enlisted after 9/11."

"Why didn't you?"

"I just didn't feel right about it. Also, I was *really* into cycling. That was probably the bigger factor. I didn't have that mentality of wanting to serve my country. I was more into, What does *Tim* want to do?"

I nodded, remembering my own youth. I hadn't been service oriented, either. "My parents are teachers," I said, eliding the fact of my mother's death. "They aren't big fans of the military."

"They don't have to be," Tim said in a matter-of-fact tone. "It's always going to exist. But it could change. The way I see it, if our country is ever really going to address the climate crisis, it can't be a fringe movement. It has to become mainstream. We have this big, complicated logistical problem that the Pentagon could actually be good at solving."

"Don't you ever feel like the problem is just too big? Like when you read the IPCC reports—"

"I never read those," Tim interrupted. "It's for my own mental health. I need to stay positive."

My food arrived: a black bean quesadilla, guacamole, and a side of elote. I was trying to go back to a vegetarian diet after years of being an omnivore.

"We should probably go join the others," I said.

"We don't have to," Tim said with a funny expression.

I looked at him, suddenly getting that we'd been flirting. I hadn't given any thought to the idea that Tim From Work might be interested in me, and I was flustered by the realization that I might feel the same way. I tried to get the conversation back to work-related issues, but he interrupted to ask if I had weekend plans. When I said that I didn't, he suggested that we meet at the canal to go cycling.

"Do you like to bike?" he asked when I hesitated to reply.

"I do, I just haven't gone in a long time. I'm not even sure where my bike is."

"You can borrow one from me," Tim said. "I have a bunch, and we're about the same height. I could bring it with me, and you could meet me there."

I didn't know why I felt unsure. I loved to bike on the canal. I used to go on the weekends, in my twenties, before I met Carter. It was a simple thing that made me happy.

"I haven't dated anyone in two years," I blurted out. "Since I got divorced."

"Okay," he said uncertainly. "Are you still hung up on your ex?"

"I don't think so. But he just told me he's getting married—like twenty minutes ago."

"Oof," Tim said with real sympathy. "I'm impressed you even came here."

"I was really hungry," I said. "After that weird hikermill."

When I got home a couple of hours later, Tim sent me a photo of three bicycles hanging from a wall in his stairwell. The caption said, Your choice!

Below that was a text from Carter about picking up Rose on Wednesday. It was sent shortly after he'd called me. He was probably engaged now, planning his future with Megan. The kids they would have. The house they would buy. The whole upper-middle-class shebang.

I sat down on the edge of my bed and looked at the photo of the three bikes hanging in the apartment of an attractive man who not only seemed to like me but also appreciated what I did for a living—though maybe he was more conflicted than he let on. I didn't know much about him, really. I imagined sitting in the shade after our bike ride and asking him questions about his past. I imagined sharing a meal, a shower, a bed—a whole day with him. A life, even. Was it absurd to imagine that? He could be a father to Rose, we could have another kid. It was so easy to picture a future with him—or someone like him. I could do what Carter had done and begin my second couplehood. DC would get hotter, the Potomac would flood its banks, and I would cry in despair as the lush, abundant world of my childhood receded. But I would also find a way to forget about it on a regular basis.

I pulled up Jenny's Instagram, and there was a close-up photo of a tree trunk, plush with moss. The caption said, Moss-covered bark is a sign of clean air. Look for the green tree trunks in your neighborhood.

I scrolled through her photos. Green, green, green. Outside my condo was gray, gray, gray. America could have chosen something different, but we went with automobiles and asphalt and empire. I returned to Tim's argument, his idea that the military could facilitate climate solutions. Maybe he was actually more idealistic than I was. Because I couldn't bring myself to believe that the Department of Defense would ever turn its back on fossil fuels. In my lifetime, they had only ever started new wars. I recalled my mother's despair, after 9/11. *Now they're never going to do anything.* That was her refrain for years—until she took Hecate's Key. Then, she had faith—in what, I didn't know.

Rose, I feared, would grow up and ask me why I had never done anything. I could see her, sitting across from me at the kitchen table in the house I lived in somewhere with someone, surrounded by conveniences. She would have long arms and legs, a messy bun high on her head. She would be heading to college but wondering, *Why bother*, disillusioned at age eighteen. I wouldn't know what to say to her except that I'd had the chance to escape, once, but I'd turned it down to give her a more comfortable life.

My phone pinged with a new message from Jenny. Are you ready to do this thing?

Before I could change my mind or really consider what it meant, I replied.

I'm in.

PART TWO

Hecate's Key

15.

That spring, Carter and Megan were engaged, Rose celebrated her sixth birthday, I crowded my windowsills with houseplants, and Jenny and I formed a rough plan for our future as mushroom foragers and distributors. At first, even after I sent that late-night text, I didn't believe that it would happen. It wasn't the same as deciding to sell Hecate's Key before Rose was born. Then, I had already had the product, a willing buyer, and a lot of free time. What Jenny was proposing was basically a midlife crisis—though for her, it wasn't so dramatic. She came from a world of entrepreneurs and entertainers; she was used to spinning professions from whims. To her, mushrooms were the most down-to-earth business she'd ever been involved with.

I talked to Jenny more than anyone else in my life during that time. She texted several times a day, asking for information about my schedule and resources, prying about my contacts, and just checking in to say how excited she was. A normal person with a balanced social life might have found the number of texts a little odd, possibly even intrusive, but I liked the way our conversation threaded the days together. It made the loneliness of that spring easier to bear. With Tara gone, I tried to reach out to some of the mothers from Rose's school, hoping some playdates might turn into adult friendships for me, but people were busy, always busy. I couldn't be sure, but I often felt I was left out because I wasn't part of a couple. Sometimes it seemed like high school all over again, trying to navigate the social dynamics. Jenny's responsiveness was a relief after so many gentle rebuffs. And it was fun to collaborate, to brainstorm names and logos, to think about the other products we might sell: T-shirts, baskets, coffee, chocolates . . . A part of me was skeptical that we would ever really go into business together, but I reasoned that plenty of companies had gotten started on less.

Then a truly weird coincidence occurred, one that made me think that there were cosmic forces at work: Astrid called to check in. We hadn't been in touch since I'd been caught. I wasn't even aware that she had my real phone number.

"I'm sorry to bother you, dear," Astrid said. "But Hecate's Key is back. I felt I should tell you, just in case you needed it."

The mushroom had been absent from the forest for some time but had recently started to reappear. She sent snapshots from a recent hike, and there it was: the elfin cap of gold, peeking out from beneath a layer of pine needle debris. There were also photos of silvery lavender birches, blue lichens stippling crags of limestone, and serene oval puddles reflecting cirrus clouds.

I forwarded them all to Jenny, who immediately wrote back: When can we go??

My initial reply was, I can't, you go without me, but Jenny, who by then knew my summer plans, pointed out that Rose was going to be in Hilton Head with Carter for a week in late June—exactly when Hecate's Key would peak. Ask your boss, what's the worst he can say?

I had already requested time off at the end of August to visit my dad, and in my paranoid accounting, a second summer vacation was suspect. But Marcos encouraged me to take the time off.

"You should always use all your vacation days," he said. "Where are you going?"

I made up a lie on the spot: North Carolina, to visit a college roommate who had moved to Asheville. Marcos remarked that the music scene there was good, and I nodded in agreement, too distracted to feel guilty. For the first time in a long while, I had something to look forward to.

My optimism expressed itself in the purchase of potted plants. I seemed to find one every time I went shopping; they beckoned to me from grocery shelves and hardware store displays, they sat prettily arranged in gift shops and florists. Even the big-box stores had them. I rescued them from IKEA and Target, lining them up on my south-facing window, enjoying the way they foregrounded Walter, whose leaves shone in the same sun. Walter seemed to be healthier, more robust, with brighter and more numerous leaves. Perhaps it was because I talked to him on a regular basis, or maybe I was noticing his vitality for the first time.

With our June foray on the horizon, Jenny was ready to think bigger. She thought that we should buy as many mushrooms as we could when we visited Astrid. One of us could return in the fall to get the second harvest—if there was one. Once we had our stock and had determined pricing, packaging, shipping and/or delivery, we could start our business in earnest. In winter, Jenny would begin selling on the West Coast through her contacts. I would be the administrator who would build out a network of death doulas and trip guides. I would also get in touch with some of the people I'd researched—people like Jenny, who the DOD had ignored but who I thought had merit. Our hope was to connect nature-based healers so that they could share knowledge and possibly combine their treatments. We wanted to bring people back into relationships with their first loves: plants and animals, trees and forests, clouds and puddles, stones and dirt.

Jenny and I wrote to each other often, sharing ecstatic utopian visions: a world where city-dwelling humans lived happily in skyscrapers whose rooftops and balconies teemed with flowers, and where hardy, sun-loving vines climbed latticed solar paneling. A world with free, accessible public transportation, ample parkland, and community gardens galore. A world where it would be stylish to wear your clothes to tatters, to work less, to live simply. People would go outside more, eat fresh food, swim in clean water, and spend more time with their children, their spouses, their pets, their friends, the sky.

Beyond the cities would be a vast and astonishing wilderness. The ecosystems would repair themselves if left alone—like Chernobyl, like Fresh Kills Landfill, like the Korean DMZ. Huge expanses of ocean would be cordoned off, free of boats and war machines. The whales, at last, would be able to hear themselves think. The turtles would hatch undisturbed.

I hadn't allowed myself this kind of idealism before Jenny came back into my life. I'd been too focused on worst-case scenarios: food shortages, a threatened water supply, animal-borne pandemic diseases. But Jenny wasn't doom and gloom. She thought that the answers were out there in nature, we just had to pay attention.

At work, I had never been so on the ball, so *insightful*. This was, in part, because I was spending so much time in my own archives searching for potential contacts for me and Jenny. But I was also doing well because I was happier. My head felt clear; I was no longer distracted by thoughts of Carter and regrets about the past. I dreamed of morning fog caught in the branches of centenarian pines, of mushrooms drying on a tree stump, of spiderwebs glinting with dew. In the back of my mind, I was wandering through the woods, and I interviewed healers with fresh curiosity.

My efforts did not go unnoticed. On a Friday in early June, Marcos called me into his office and told me I was overdue for a promotion.

"Once you're approved, you'll get a salary bump and a higher security clearance," he said. "Which means you'll be hands on with the device and its users. I know you've wanted that. I've wanted it, too. I think you're going to be excited when you see some of the projects you've been contributing to."

I was so surprised that I couldn't think of much to say beyond a thank-you. I'd gotten my job under such bizarre circumstances that it hadn't occurred to me that I could rise in the ranks.

Walking back to my office, I recklessly took out the burner phone I used to text with Jenny, and wrote to her: I think I'm going to be promoted?!

Jenny texted back right away: It's just like when I was acting. They always want you when you have one foot out the door.

I slipped my phone back into my pocket as I headed into the break room to microwave my lunch—leftovers from the night before. Tim was there, sitting at the round linoleum table and eating what looked to be a chicken sandwich.

"Okay if I join you?" I asked.

"Sure," he said—friendly, but slightly reserved. Ever since I'd turned down his biking date, he'd refrained from initiating anything one-on-one.

"I'm trying to go vegan," I said, feeling that my messy plate of lentils, tofu, and brown rice needed explanation. It didn't taste as bad as it looked.

"I see you're in the brown mush phase. You should try sweet potatoes with black beans and avocado. Better color contrast."

"Are you vegan?"

"Ish." Tim waved his hand in the air. "Today I'm vegetarian, according to my grandmother."

"I don't think vegans allow for *ish*." I waggled my hand the way he had done.

"They definitely have a bit of a puritanical streak. Though I wouldn't say that's unique to vegans." Tim took a sip of his seltzer. "You know what's really good? If you freeze bananas, then put them in the blender, they taste just like ice cream, you don't even have to add anything."

"I'm still eating regular ice cream," I admitted. "I can't give it up."

"Do you know about the ice cream paradox?" Tim asked. "It's this finding that keeps popping up in nutrition studies. It doesn't make any sense, but it turns out that if you eat a little bit of ice cream every day, you're healthier all around. Even people with high cholesterol who aren't supposed to have high-fat dairy. They can't figure it out."

"Doesn't it just make people happier?"

"That's what I think," Tim said. "It's obvious, right?"

"Should we try to get that into the field manual? Daily ice cream rations?"

"I have enough goofy stuff I'm trying to Trojan-horse in there." Tim paused, putting down his sandwich. "Leigh, I know it's none of my business, but did you . . . meet someone? You seem really, I don't know, upbeat lately."

"I'm just feeling better about work," I said. "I'm getting promoted, actually."

"Congratulations." Tim seemed genuinely pleased. "I meant to say to you, before, we all get down about this job, from time to time. I'm glad you found a way out of it."

16.

Rose was wandering around the front yard while I packed up the car. I scanned the trunk to make sure I had remembered everything for her trip to Hilton Head. It was the morning of her kindergarten graduation, and Carter was taking her directly to Georgia afterward.

"Mommy! Come here! There are worms eating your favorite tree!" Rose was holding one of Walter's lower branches. The leaves were covered by a mass of white threadlike material. Underneath the threads was a roiling pile of green-and-black caterpillars. She was right. Walter was being eaten alive.

I stood back to assess the damage and noticed that three other branches were entombed. Many of the leaves were discolored, with reddish-brown lines effacing their shiny green surface.

"This doesn't look good," I said. "I have a friend who knows about trees. Let me text her."

"That one has them too," Rose said, pointing to the tree in the yard of the condo next door, which was still unoccupied.

I took photos of Walter and sent them to Jenny along with a reminder to text me her flight info. We planned to meet in Upstate New York. From there we would head to Ontario.

At school, Rose hurried off to her classroom while I waited in the auditorium with the other parents. Everyone was on their phones, including me. Jenny, to my surprise, had written back already: Looks like webworm, which can get pretty gnarly. Walter will probably lose all his leaves but then he'll get a second growth in August

I wrote back to ask her what she was doing up so early. It was five thirty on the West Coast.

"Hello, Leigh! Is there room here?"

It was Carter and Megan, bearing flowers. The creaky fold-down seats squeaked loudly as I scooted over to make room for them, as if voicing my own discomfort at the sight of Megan's and Carter's fingers intertwined. I'd recently received a "Save the Date" email for their wedding, planned for June 14, 2017. I couldn't decide if this was generous, cruel, or psychotically polite. Most likely, it was Rose's idea. When I got it, I took a screenshot and sent it to Jenny, who wrote back: We should save that date for a girls' trip.

I glanced at my phone to read Jenny's reply to my latest text: Trying to reset my circadian rhythm. I get really bad jet lag otherwise.

"Trying to squeeze in a little more work?" Megan asked sympathetically.

"No," I said. And left it at that.

Fortunately, the possibility of chitchat between the three of us was cut short by the arrival of the children onstage, wearing paper sashes that said "Class of '28"—the year, I realized in horror, they would graduate from high school. It took all my willpower not to look up projected temperatures on my phone. I could see Rose searching for us amid all the waving parents. When she saw us sitting together, her smile was so sincere that I wished I could bottle its sweetness and give it back to her, later in life.

A musical program began with the kids singing about getting along with people from all over the world. Then they performed "Shenandoah," and even though the melody came out seasick, they nonetheless captured some of its mournfulness. Half the parents sitting near me wiped their eyes. The rest were holding up cell phones, trying to virtually capture the moment, missing it while they blocked my view. I felt grumpy and old and out of step.

After the concert, there was a reception for the families in the cafeteria, where folding tables were covered with disposable tablecloths and laden with a variety of baked goods and fruits cut into bite-size pieces. I filled a paper plate with mini muffins and hothouse strawberries, and brought them over to Rose, Carter, and Megan, who sliced a muffin in half with a delicate gesture that I tried not to dislike. Her tidiness irked me—and yet there was a part of me that recognized that, at some point, I would have to become friends with her. We were already raising Rose together, albeit in different households. And if I really did move to Canada, I wanted her to be on my side. Maybe she would even convince Carter that living farther apart was for the best, that we would all get along better if I was in another country entirely.

Believe me, I know this was not the most mature train of thought. I would never argue for my maturity, especially during this period of my life.

Megan thanked me for including her in Rose's graduation, remarking that it had been a really touching ceremony.

"It would have been a lot nicer if people had put their phones away," I groused.

"You sound like your father," Carter said.

"My father would say they're getting cancer from their phones. It's a completely different flavor of Luddite."

"Some schools have cell phone bans." Megan jumped in, trying to smooth things over. "The teachers take a video and send it to everyone."

"That's a good idea," I conceded. I glanced at Rose, who was scowling at her graduation certificate. "What's the matter?"

"They put glasses on the owl." She pointed to a cartoon owl in the corner of the laminated card, decked out in spectacles and a mortarboard. "A bird of prey would never wear glasses. They have excellent vision."

Carter laughed. "You're so funny, Rosie."

She glared at her father; she wasn't trying to be funny. "Why is he wearing glasses if he doesn't need them?"

"Maybe it's to prevent bugs from flying into his eyes," I said.

"Maybe he's in disguise, maybe he's a spy," Carter said. He turned to me, subliminally or not, and asked how work was going.

"I got promoted," I said, forgetting, for a moment, that he was under the impression that I was a librarian. I hoped he didn't have any follow-up questions.

"When can I see *Jurassic World*?" Rose asked, apropos of whatever stream of childhood thought led her from owls to dinosaurs.

Carter and I spoke at the same time. I said eight, he said ten. Rose didn't seem to process the difference. To her, all that mattered was that she couldn't watch it over the weekend.

"It's too scary?" she asked.

"Yes, my love." I gave Rose a hug and a kiss. "I have to get to work. Call me before you leave for vacation with Daddy, okay?"

"What about when I'm nine?" Rose said. "Can I watch it then?"

I wanted to say "Sure," because in my increasingly realistic fantasy, she'd be living with me in Canada when she was nine, and it wouldn't matter what Carter thought. But I just gave her another hug and told her how I proud I was that she'd graduated from kindergarten.

17.

It was raining when I arrived at Syracuse Hancock International Airport. Jenny had instructed me to meet her in temporary parking, but I kept wondering if I should go into the airport. People were coming into the lot, and they weren't her, and I was worried she'd missed the flight. Our plans felt so tenuous; I'd been up since dawn, and we still had to drive another four hours to the Saint Lawrence, where Astrid would pick us up in her boat and drive us even farther.

I was getting the map from my glove compartment when I saw Jenny striding toward me, clad in a dark-green hooded raincoat, jeans, and hiking boots. She carried a rolling suitcase behind her, topped with a sleeping bag. Her long hair, which had been tucked into her hood, was falling in front of her face, a few strands sticking to her wet cheeks.

"Leigh!" she called out. "This is perfect mushroom weather, right?"

In the car, she took off her raincoat and threw it in the back seat. Her face was bare of makeup, and her complexion was rosy from the rain. She looked great for someone who had just gotten off a red-eye.

"I can take the wheel if you want," she said. "I slept the whole flight, and then I had coffee, so I'm wired."

"You don't have to drive," I said. "I can do it."

"I don't mind," she said. "Really, I'd be happy to."

I had the sense she was trying to win me over, and I was flattered. We switched seats, and Jenny put on some mellow music for napping. I resisted for a few minutes, trying to get a conversation going, but as soon as we got on the highway, sleep descended, and I succumbed. *It is so nice,* I thought as I fell asleep, *to be driven, so nice to take turns, nice to share, nice to have company.* It reminded me of the best parts of my marriage.

When I woke up, we were pulling into the Thousand Island Marina parking lot. The sky was a cleared-up blue, with the clouds huddled at the horizon, blown by the wind that was making the river choppy. It was a wide, deep body of water with a strong current, a corridor for ships as well as pleasure boats. There were hundreds, if not literally, thousands, of islands, many of them privately owned and built up with cottages, houses, and the occasional mansion. Although it had its ritzy elements, it wasn't the Gilded Age playground it had once been.

"I've never been up here before," Jenny said admiringly. She stretched her arms above her head. "Want to get something to eat?"

We walked up the steep embankment to a pavilion where there was a concession stand. We got a meal Rose would have loved: french fries, ice cream, and fountain sodas, and ate it at a weathered picnic table near a stand of pine trees. I watched the boats coming and going, feeling relaxed and well rested. Jenny kept checking her phone. It looked like she had a lot of missed calls from someone.

"Are you getting a signal up here?" she asked.

"I turned mine off." I didn't want my phone to have a record of my location.

"Don't you need to check in with Rose?"

"She's fine, she's with her father," I said lightly, pretending to be more relaxed about it than I was. My own childhood summers had been gloriously unplugged, with my parents out of reach for long stretches of time, but things were different now. There was the feeling that you were supposed to be on call, vigilant—in case of, what? Who knew, really. If something truly tragic happened to Rose, there was little I could do from the other end of a cell phone. Sometimes I felt like digital technology just provided an illusion of control—that was the whole appeal.

"I should turn *my* phone off," Jenny said. "Kip keeps calling me, he's driving me crazy. This is the kind of stuff he does."

"I'm sorry," I said, feeling her distress. She wanted a new job as badly as I did.

We went down to the docks to watch for Astrid's boat. Water sloshed beneath us, lightly splashing the edge of the decking. The smell of gasoline wafted over from a filling station, mixing with exhaust and fried food.

"Next time we should rent our own boat. Kip had a little one he used to let me use." Jenny shaded her eyes with her hands as she looked out at the water. "Is that her?"

"I'm not sure." There was a skiff headed toward us with five people on board. As it got closer, I recognized Astrid. Her hair was the same white as the crests in the water, and she wore a lightweight red jacket. She was sitting next to a young man whose arm was draped over the shoulder of the young woman sitting next to him. A man in a baseball cap was driving the boat.

"That's Astrid," I said, "but I don't know the others."

"They look fun," Jenny said, and I had to agree with her split-second appraisal. They seemed happy and windblown and free.

We met them at the side of the pier, where Astrid greeted us both with quick hugs. She introduced us to the couple, who were getting off to go to work in a nearby restaurant. The driver, Clay, was staying. It was his boat.

"Clay's my point man for deliveries," Astrid said. "He's coming back with us to my place to take my latest harvest. But first we're going to pick up Emmy at Blackbird Island. Do you remember her?"

"Ossi's friend?" I asked. "The chef?"

"Yes! I convinced her to cook dinner for us on her night off. I found a bunch of Butter Caps this week. She's making her legendary risotto. Clay's had it—haven't you?"

"That I have," said Clay. "I would not attempt to describe it with mere words."

"I thought it would be fun to have a little dinner party," Astrid said. "You're not too tired, are you?"

"Not in the least!" Jenny said, glancing at me with a look of surprised delight. Even though I'd planned none of it, I felt a sense of pride.

It was twenty minutes to Blackbird Island. Astrid filled us in on her latest ventures. Mushrooms and other foraged ingredients were becoming popular in local resorts—especially those with fine-dining options—and so she had found a new niche in the culinary world.

"Restaurants love me now," Astrid said. "It wasn't like this before. It used to be the occasional chef or home cook. But now mushrooms are the thing, and I have all these young people coming into my life. Which is good, at my age. Young people keep you young."

"I'm not that young," Clay said, from the bow. "Neither is Emmy."

Astrid just laughed.

Emmy was Executive Chef at the Blackbird, a hotel remodeled from the bones of a nineteenth-century robber baron's estate. She waited for us on the hotel's private dock, adjacent to a stately boathouse. She wore cutoff jeans, a denim shirt, pink Crocs, and a white bandanna to hold back her short hair. She carried a large backpack that made a clanging noise when she hoisted it into the boat.

"You know I have silverware, right?" Astrid said.

"I've seen your kitchen," Emmy said wryly. She glanced at me and Jenny. "Have you been to her place?"

"I have, once," I said. "I came up with Ossi?"

"Oh, right! Of course, you're here for Hecate's Key. Astrid said they're coming back—along with my Butter Caps." She smiled at Jenny. "You look familiar. Have we met already, too?"

"Maybe you saw me in a commercial for protein bars. In another life, I was an actor." Jenny had a self-deprecating tone I'd never heard her use before, one that struck me as a little bit fake, like she was trying to say what she thought would please these new people. It left me feeling uneasy, but I couldn't say why.

We arrived at the marina a few minutes later. Clay's truck was parked nearby, and he and Emmy went together, leaving me and Jenny to ride with Astrid in her small car. I was up front with Astrid and felt irrationally nervous about the border crossing, but it was over and done in a few minutes. I wondered what it would be like if I tried to get across with Rose, then quickly put the thought out of my mind. It was too complicated to think about how she'd get there, too painful to consider what Carter would say if I asked his permission—and what he would do if I didn't. If we'd never had a child, it would be so easy to leave him behind, but without Rose I wasn't sure I'd feel such a desire to escape. I wanted to set an example for her, the way my mother had done for me.

The towns close to the Saint Lawrence were touristy, with souvenir shops and places to rent kayaks, paddleboards, and canoes. Handmade wooden signs advertised firewood and fishing bait. I couldn't help feeling like I was on vacation, especially when we stopped at a big grocery store and bought a week's worth of food, mostly items that were amenable to camping. Astrid said we should prepare for an overnight trip to visit the best spots for Hecate's Key.

Civilization fell away as we headed north. The highway was a gray stripe cut through a kingdom of trees. Occasionally there would be a clearing where a group of houses stood, the false start to a small town, but they would slip away before making an impression. The sky was a huge blue canvas, with the clouds piled up like scoops of ice cream, lusciously detailed. We were headed toward Blue Lake, the village closest to Astrid's cabin. Its banal name concealed the stunning natural beauty of the area.

"How close is your cabin to where the mushrooms are growing?" Jenny asked from the back seat. "Do we need to drive more tomorrow?"

"Most of the mushrooms I forage are close to where I live," Astrid said. "Hecate's Key is a little different. There's a map in the pocket behind my seat, if you want to see where we should go."

Jenny unfolded an ancient-seeming road guide to Ontario, with creases that had been repaired with tape. It showed the locations of campsites as well as gas stations. Little white smudges of typing fluid dotted the forested sections of the map, each marked with a symbol and a date.

"Look for the Ks," Astrid said.

"It looks like we should head northwest," Jenny said. "Where there's some kind of wilderness preserve?"

"Yes, that's right. That's where the lavender birch and cirrus pine grow most prominently, though things may have changed. The trees are on the move these days, it's hard to keep up."

"You've been doing this a long time," Jenny observed, examining the dates on the white dots. "Some of these go back to the eighties."

"And that's just when I started using that map," Astrid said.

As we sped down the empty roads, Astrid told us that she first learned about mushrooms from a gardener at her parents' country club. Her parents played golf every weekend, and she would wander the grounds after her swimming lesson while she waited for her parents to finish their game. She became friendly with the gardener, Sara, a woman who, unlike her mother and unlike any woman she knew, wore dungarees and men's work boots. One of Sara's jobs was to remove the mushrooms that popped up on the golf course, and she would take Astrid with her on her rounds, gathering the puffballs and honey mushrooms that were considered unsightly and detrimental to the game. On one of those walks, Sara shared a fact that stuck with Astrid for the rest of her life: all the mushrooms were connected underground, via a network of white fibers that were something like phone lines. They had their own way of communicating that had nothing to do with us, and they held secrets in the ground that humans could never understand.

"Is that when you started studying mycology?" Jenny asked.

"Unfortunately, no," Astrid said. "I didn't move to the woods full-time until I was twenty-six. My husband built my cabin for me. He was trying to save our marriage, I think. I wasn't happy in Toronto; I didn't like being the wife of a young executive. Throwing parties and all that. He thought if I had this escape in the summer, maybe that would make it tolerable."

"But it didn't?" Jenny asked.

Astrid shook her head. "It just made it easier for me to leave him. Maybe he knew that. I should give him that credit. He wasn't a bad guy, we just never should have gotten married. It was the last thing I did to please my parents."

"I can't remember the last time I tried to please my family," Jenny said. "What about you, Leigh?"

I shrugged. My parents had raised me to become a poet, or an activist, and instead I was a DOD worker bee, developing questionable technologies. "I guess when I got Hecate's Key that first time," I said. "As soon as my dad told me about it, I knew I would try to find it."

"And now it's calling you back," Astrid said.

When we arrived at Astrid's cabin, Clay and Emmy were already there, preparing dinner. The smell of garlic, onion, and butter pervaded the small cabin, which was dingier than I remembered. In my mind's eye, it was artfully disheveled, but now it struck me that the place needed actual repair. There were some yellowish stains on the ceilings, suggesting unaddressed leaks, and flaked paint on the windowsills. Silver-gray rectangles of duct tape were a leitmotif throughout the room, holding together torn screens and band-aiding small appliances. Still, there was a mishmash coziness that I loved: quilts and blankets draped over the backs of chairs and thick braided rugs covering the wood floors. Clay and Emmy had set the table with colorful napkins and handmade pottery. Clay poured us mugs of wine from a ceramic pitcher, and we sat on the screened-in porch and toasted the sunset. When dinner was ready, Emmy lit candles. Her famous risotto soothed me to my bones.

I glanced at Jenny throughout the meal, wanting to make sure she was having a good time. I worried, given all the lavish places she'd stayed in the past, that she wouldn't be impressed. But she seemed happy, laughing at Emmy's stories about unruly guests and Clay's sideline as a sailing instructor. They both made their living off summer people, and Clay went south in the winter to catch a second tourist season in Florida.

"I used to chase tourists, but now I make enough off private clients to get by," Emmy said. "Plus, I don't have a boat to pay for."

"Maybe I should start charging you for rides," Clay teased.

"You might want to get a boat if you move here," Emmy said, turning to me and Jenny. "Especially if you're going to do your own deliveries."

Jenny and I had told Emmy and Clay about our plan to work with Astrid and possibly relocate, and I was pleased that they entertained it as a real possibility. Lots of people were coming north, they said. It was cheap and no one bothered you. When Emmy wasn't on Blackbird Island, she lived in a tiny house just outside of Marion, a nearby town that she thought I would like. It had a cute little school with grades K–6 in one building. Rose could go there.

"If I were you, I'd hold on to that house in California," Clay said to Jenny. "You're going to want to escape this place around March or April. Summer doesn't really start here until late June."

"Summer starts earlier than it used to," Emmy said. "The world's changing fast."

"Let's not go down doomsday road." Clay stood up. "I'm going out for a smoke."

"I'll join you," Jenny said.

Clay held open the screen door.

I felt left out, even though I hadn't touched cigarettes since the Prosecco years of my early twenties. I busied myself in the kitchen, cleaning up, while Emmy and Astrid went out to walk Luna, their flashlight dancing ahead of them. Jenny's laughter drifted through the open window; Clay's voice was too low to make out. I missed Rose, the ritual of putting her to bed, of lying down with her in the semidarkness, slowing my breath to match hers.

My loneliness shifted into solitude as I filled the sink with hot water. I was at the end of a long day; I was possibly at the beginning of a new phase of my life. Or maybe this was just a strange interlude. I couldn't tell. When I put the leftovers in the refrigerator, I noticed there was a snapshot taped to the door: a young woman posing in front of a car and smiling tentatively. She wore a light-blue sheath with a matching bolero jacket, hat, and gloves. Red lipstick and high heels complemented the look. I was staring at it when Astrid and Luna, back from their walk, came into the kitchen.

"That's me," Astrid said, "if you can believe it."

"You look so glamourous," I said. "Like Elizabeth Taylor."

"I found it in one of my mother's books a few months ago. According to the date on the back, I'm eighteen years old. I don't even remember that dress. I probably had a dozen just like it."

"You were rich," I said without thinking.

"Yes." She nodded. "My father gave me this land as a wedding present. I never wanted for anything."

"That's nice," I said uncertainly.

"It's funny to me," Astrid said, looking at the photo. "When I was younger, I thought I was radical to leave all those dresses and shoes behind." She put the photo back on the refrigerator. "I was just lucky to have the means to escape."

In the morning, Clay and Emmy left after breakfast, taking a crate of mushrooms and fresh herbs with them. Jenny, Astrid, and I set out soon after, in a light rain that we couldn't feel once we were in the forest. It drizzled all day, and the canopy became luminous, with all the June leaves shining and the mosses glowing chartreuse. Birds chirped and called to one another, their bright voices accompanying the soft patter of the rain. I thought to myself—smugly, perhaps—that the DOD's hikermill could never approximate the rich palette of smells and sounds and sensations as we made our way through the woods. We saw dozens of mushrooms: Lion's Mane, Coxcomb, Yellow Chalice, Widow's Hat, Candelabra Coral, Pink-Staining Stinkhorns, and of course, the Common Wood Sprites that grow closely together, looking like jostling commuters with umbrellas. The fungi were so abundant that I didn't really notice that we weren't seeing any Hecate's Key.

We did not locate Hecate's Key on the first day, the second day, or even the third day. On the second day, I started to feel nervous; on the third day, embarrassment crept in. I feared that I'd taken Jenny from her work for no reason, and that I'd exaggerated my past. Perhaps I'd made it sound as if I were helming a lucrative underworld business, when really I had just been naive and lucky, an accidental link in the psychedelic supply chain. I'd never made any real money on it, never tried to rely on anything as capricious as a mushroom for an income stream.

I wasn't like Clay and Emmy, who on the one hand showed me that a life up here was possible, while on the other, revealed that it could only work if you had a certain scrappiness. I didn't see myself as scrappy. I wasn't even sure, anymore, if I was outdoorsy. I had forgotten how much I disliked sleeping on the ground, in a tent. I remembered only the most vivid, poetic experiences from my childhood trips: embers dancing in the night air, the smell of smoke from a campfire, the stars like spilled sugar, and the soft, peachy sunrise every morning, waking you from a deep, cozy sleeping bag. In reality, those rare moments were dependent on good weather and my parents' considerable efforts.

Astrid, Jenny, and I had neither clear skies nor loving parents to attend to our needs. It was overcast and intermittently rainy. We spent our days circling birches and pines with our eyes toward the ground, focusing every particle of our attention on the places where Hecate's Key might be hiding. Gently and patiently, we lifted branches and pieces of bark to peer underneath. We rolled logs and lugged stones. We combed through leaf debris. Astrid didn't like for us to talk or even hum to ourselves; she said it would ruin our concentration—and hers. She was looking for other mushrooms, and as we walked, she managed to fill her basket with specimens. But ours remained empty.

At the end of the first night, Astrid said, "Don't worry, we're seeing lots of lavender birch and cirrus pine, so we know we're in the right place."

At the end of the second night, Astrid said, "If worse comes to worst, we can extend our trip by another night."

At the end of the third night, after a lean dinner of baked potatoes, turkey jerky, and apples, Astrid said, "Girls, I think we need to call it. We'll turn back tomorrow. If we're lucky, we'll find some on the way back."

"What if we don't?" I asked, hating how childish I sounded but unable to use another register. We were sitting around a small, dying campfire, and in the damp, smoky darkness I couldn't imagine anything but a dreary hike back to Astrid's house and a stressful drive home.

Astrid reached over to squeeze my hand. "These things always work out. You just need to trust the mushrooms. They have their own way of doing things."

I waited until Astrid was out walking Luna to talk with Jenny.

"I'm really sorry," I said. "I thought this was more of a sure thing."

"I'm not worried about it," Jenny said, leaning back on her palms. "We'll still have the ones Astrid got near her cabin. And the dried ones."

"That won't be enough to get started."

"Sure it will. We can cultivate them from the spores."

I looked at Jenny, surprised that she seemed sincere in this belief. "There's no way to grow Hecate's Key. You heard Astrid."

"She doesn't have access to like, labs and high-tech equipment," Jenny said. "I'm sure there's a way to do it. Maybe it's more like distilling them to their essence."

I reminded Jenny that the Pentagon had already researched Hecate's Key, and found, along with its other defects, that it wasn't possible to replicate it chemically.

"Well, that was in the eighties," Jenny said dismissively. "A lot has changed since then."

"And a lot hasn't," I said, poking at the embers of the fire with a stick. I felt like Jenny was being willfully delusional.

"All right," Jenny said, standing up. "Come on, you need to try something. Have you ever done ancestral walking?"

"A.k.a. walking barefoot?" I'd first learned the term from one of my early interview subjects: NoShoesNoBlues, a YouTuber who claimed that going barefoot for a year had cured his depression.

"I used to do it in my early classes," Jenny said, ignoring my sarcasm. She kneeled to untie her boots. "It's like a shortcut to meditation. Go ahead, take off your boots."

I did as I was told, tugging off my hiking shoes and wool socks, and stepping barefoot on the packed dirt near the fire.

"It's almost like a dance technique." Jenny demonstrated how to walk in the cleared area near our tents. The goal was to move without making a sound. You did this by testing the ground with the *blade* of your foot before putting your full weight on the *ball* of your foot. If you felt something pointy or sharp, then you would find a different place to put your foot down.

"I know it sounds obvious," Jenny said, "but most people have lost the ability to move quietly through a landscape after a lifetime in sneakers and sandals. They walk mindlessly because their soles are so thick."

"I didn't know you were so anti-shoe." It was amusing to see Jenny go into teacher mode.

"Just try it," Jenny said.

I took a few tentative steps. Jenny immediately told me to slow down.

"It might help to bend your knees a little," she said. "Good, that's good. Now, stop for a minute and close your eyes. Just listen for a minute. I want you to try to hear the moss breathing."

I laughed nervously.

"I'm serious," Jenny said. "You won't be able to, but *try*. And notice how things smell, too. You want to see what you can notice without your eyes, without putting words to it."

I knew what she meant. As a child, I loved a certain stand of white pines that stood at the edge of a field near my house. I would go there and sit for a while, doing nothing. I didn't make any important observations. I just liked the carpet of dried, orange needles that were surprisingly soft, almost smooth to the touch. The sun would illuminate the green needles above. Life was shady and easy under those pines.

"Okay," Jenny whispered. "You can open your eyes. Let's keep walking."

We headed beyond our campsite, and the ground quickly became mysterious, with poky twigs and sharp, hidden stones and decomposing leaves that were disconcertingly spongy. Ahead of me, Jenny seemed to be gliding.

"Hey," I whispered. "Do you remember going to Lost Falls after closing night?"

"I'll never forget it," she said with a soft laugh. "I got in so much trouble. My dad was like, 'You could have been attacked by perverts!'"

"My mom lost her mind. It was worth it, though."

"Most people would have thought it was weird I wanted to skip the party," Jenny said. "I knew you wouldn't judge me."

It had never occurred to me that Jenny would worry about the opinion of anyone in our high school. I figured she had thought of herself as above us all, because that's how I saw her. But maybe I had just wanted to cast her as iconoclastic. It seemed clear to me later that I never really understood what motivated her.

Jenny stopped walking and put her hand on my shoulder, bidding me to look ahead of us. I followed her gaze to a small grove of birch trees. The white trunks were so ethereal they appeared to be blue, or maybe a faint purple. Lavender birch, I realized. They were ringed by tall, scraggly pines that pointed like arrows toward the night sky. Cirrus pines.

We walked stealthily toward the trees as if they were deer that might startle. I wanted to run, but I didn't want to break the spell of our slow walk. It was as if we were playing a piece of music to the end.

We saw the mushrooms as soon as we got to the edge of the clearing. Long-stemmed and golden, they were like strange night flowers drinking the light of the stars. They grew in clusters a few feet from each tree, in seeming bouquets. There were dozens of them. I gaped at the bounty. It was as if Hecate herself had scattered them. The closer we got, the more golden their color seemed. Their stems curved in a way that was swanlike, as if the mushrooms were regarding each other and the forest that they'd sprung from. I honestly felt that if we were quiet enough, we might hear them whispering or laughing.

I knelt and gently plucked one from the ground. Its stem broke easily, and when I turned it over, the gills were violet. Its cap was smooth and springy, like the top of a cooled cake.

Jenny and I hadn't brought our baskets. I took off my hooded sweatshirt and turned it into a makeshift sack, and Jenny did the same with her long-sleeve T-shirt. She had on a white tank top underneath, and—as she squatted to gather the mushrooms, reaching with her long arms and moving awkwardly to keep hold of her shirt—I was reminded of the gawky girl she'd been. With her hair pulled back into a ponytail and the moonlight softening her features, it was almost as if Jenny was under a spell and had become younger.

Carefully, we picked Hecate's Keys, taking as many as we could carry.

"Let's come back with the baskets," Jenny whispered—and then we both laughed, because why were we whispering?

We walked back to the campsite as quickly as we could with bare feet. I was surprised by how close we were.

Astrid and Luna were back from their walk and sitting by the fire, which Astrid had coaxed back to life. She stood up when she saw us. "You found them, too!" She reached into her pocket to show us a perfect specimen of Hecate's Key.

"There's more," Jenny said. "There's a grove of birches over there."

"I found mine in the opposite direction," Astrid said. "They must be coming up tonight."

Going into the woods, we had hiked slowly with the plan of returning more quickly, but we kept finding Hecate's Key on the way back, so we stretched our camping supplies to last one more day. We were running out of places to store the mushrooms we harvested. They weren't heavy or bulky, but there were so many. Astrid said Hecate's Key typically arrived suddenly and in great abundance.

By the time we got back to the cabin, it was the evening before Jenny and I were supposed to go home. As we unpacked the mushrooms, I felt a last-day-of-vacation sadness, tinged with guilt. Jenny and I were leaving Astrid with a lot to do: the mushrooms would have to be cleaned and prepared for drying, and then packaged for sale. I wished I could stay; it would be much more enjoyable to work outside than to return to hot, sticky DC to sit in front of a computer and write reports.

"As long as you girls don't mind, I think I'll ask Emmy to help me clean these," Astrid said, as she sorted through the culinary mushrooms.

"I could stick around," Jenny said. "If there were three of us, it would go faster. And if you need me to, I can run errands—or whatever you wanted."

"I won't say no to that," Astrid said.

"Could you really stay?" I was relieved, but also envious of her freedom. Rose was flying back from Hilton Head the next day, and I'd promised to pick her up from Carter's in the early evening.

"It's no problem," Jenny said. "It will be fun. Emmy will come over—maybe Clay, too."

"I can help out before I go," I said. "Should we start cleaning some of them now?"

"That can wait," Jenny said. "We should celebrate. This is your last night."

"There's some ice cream in the freezer," Astrid said.

Jenny went into the kitchen, and I sat down on Astrid's thread-bare sofa. Sunlight came through the window, illuminating the golden mushrooms that had already begun to fade to a buttery yellow. Dust motes floated in a bar of light on the floor. When Rose was a baby, she used to bat at them. I really missed her. I wished I could teleport her to Astrid's cabin and she could stay with me while we sorted the mushrooms. I wanted her to see this place. I knew it was all going to feel like a dream when I got back.

Jenny ferried me to the marina the next morning, leaving Astrid on the other side of the river to shop in town. It was a ridiculously gorgeous day, the kind astronauts dream of when they're missing life on Earth. The river was full of pleasure boats and water skiers, and I couldn't bring myself to feel sad, even when I said goodbye to Jenny. The weather was just too perfect. *This is the problem with being human,* I thought. *The sun inspires helpless optimism.*

Then I got to my car, and there was a ticket on the windshield like a middle finger from civilization. I'd been fined for using temporary parking instead of long-term.

I shoved the notice into the glove compartment and drove with the windows down for as long as I could, playing music I'd listened to in high school. I didn't turn on the news for one minute, didn't try to gain any insights from podcasts, didn't listen to an audiobook. I only stopped once, for gasoline and candy. When I finally got back to DC, eight hours later, it was evening and the sky was dark—or what counts for darkness in cities.

18.

Rose was back from Hilton Head, sporting a tan, white shorts with a scalloped hem, and a T-shirt featuring a large, sparkly pink shell. She looked like a slightly different little girl in this outfit—one I never would have picked out—and I couldn't stop touching her, as if it to make sure she was really my Rose. She'd picked up some new expressions, too: "Epic!" and "Oh my lord in heaven!"

We were eating breakfast on the back deck, taking advantage of the relative cool of morning. Next door, workers were gutting large plastic bags of soil and raking the contents across the bald yard. For months, the adjoining condo had been empty, but it seemed someone was making a push to sell it, because they'd hung a sign from the porch railing advertising viewing hours. Meanwhile, the landscapers conjured up a lawn, unrolling squares of sod topped with Crayola-green grass that did not match the local bleached vegetation.

Jenny had advised me to reseed my lawn with native species, but all I'd really done was encourage Rose to blow dandelion seeds across the yard. I hadn't heard from Jenny in a few days. Her most recent text said that she'd be out of reach because she and Astrid were about to head out on another overnight foraging trip.

"What are we going to do today, Mommy?" Rose asked, carefully patting her mouth with a napkin—this was new, too.

"I was thinking we'd go to a movie. It's going to be in the high nineties, and there's an air-quality warning. I don't think we can do anything outside."

"Do you want to play real estate?"

"Um, sure." I took a sip of coffee. "How do you play?"

"You pretend like you want to live here. Stand outside the front door. You knock and I'll let you in and show you around. You have to ask questions."

"Okay, got it."

"Wait a little bit so I can set up."

Outside on the front porch, I gazed at poor web-covered Walter. His case of worms had gotten more severe, and now more than half of his branches were wrapped in gauze. I didn't know how he was feeding himself with so few leaves to take in sunlight, unless he was getting secret energy from his roots.

"Mommy!" Rose called from inside.

I knocked and she let me in. She had one of my notebooks and asked me to sign in. On the coffee table, she had arranged a carton of lemonade, two glasses, and an assortment of granola bars.

"There are snacks if you're hungry."

"I just had breakfast, thanks."

"Okay, before we start, can you get a loam?"

"What do you mean?"

"You know, from the bank?"

"Oh, a *loan*. Yes, I think so."

"Great! Let's start here. This is the family room . . ."

She took me on an admirably detailed tour, pointing out features that a Realtor would highlight, like the closets and the half bathroom, but also remarking on things that were of special interest to her, such as the light inside the oven, and the slanted ceiling in her bedroom. Then she led me to the walk-in closet in my bedroom.

"This looks like a closet," she said. "But it's *actually* a time machine. You say where you want to go and then knock three times. Then you open the door and you're there."

"Wow, that's an amazing thing to have in your house."

"Do you want to try it?"

"Sure. Can we see some dinosaurs?"

We said "Cretaceous period" and knocked three times. We found ourselves in a prehistoric forest, where we hid behind some swamp grasses and saw dinosaurs that reminded us of large tropical birds with their brightly colored feathers. After that, we went to the land of fairy tales and walked around a castle with pink marble columns and floors. We saw a king and a queen sitting at a table bearing gold plates and goblets and an incredible amount of delicious food. Then Rose wanted to go back to the day she was born, so we traveled to the hospital where I'd had her, and I held a bundle of my own clothing in my arms and cooed and sang and said what a beautiful baby I'd had.

"Where's Daddy?"

"He's getting me a snack—I was so hungry after you were born! And so thirsty, I must have drunk a gallon of water in a half hour. My body had to make milk."

"I'll be Daddy, I'll get you a snack."

"You don't have to—" I started to say, but she was already out of the room. She returned with a granola bar and a glass of water.

"Thank you."

"Remember, I'm Daddy."

"I know, that's why I didn't say Rose."

Rose watched me drink the water and then cuddle my clothes-baby.

"I wish Daddy was here to be Daddy," she said.

"I know." I knew she wanted things to be simple again, for our happy little family to come back. She'd had to give up that fantasy at such a young age.

"Do you think Daddy will ever be here to be Daddy?"

"You mean, with me?"

Rose nodded.

"No, I don't think so. But he's still Daddy without me."

"I know, but it's different." Rose lifted her shoulders up and down rapidly, the confused shrugging gesture she'd made ever since she was a toddler. I didn't know what to say, and I didn't know if what I said would even matter, so I just cooed to my clothes-baby.

"Let's go back," Rose said.

We crawled out of the closet, and Rose wanted to watch trailers on the iPad to decide what movie we would see. As the busy part of my brain tried to identify the celebrity voice of an animated dog, a thought arrived from the back of my mind, and all at once I knew where Rose's game—and her confused shrug—had come from.

"Hey," I said, pausing the trailer. "When you and Daddy and Megan were in Hilton Head, did you look at houses with a real estate agent?"

"Mommy, put it back on!"

"Just tell me."

"We looked at houses but not in Hilton Head. In Savannah. Near where Grammy lives."

I put the trailer back on and told Rose she could watch an episode of her favorite show if she wanted. Then I went outside and called Carter. He picked up right away.

"Everything okay with Rose?"

"Rose is fine. When were you going to tell me that you and Megan are moving to Savannah?"

"What?"

"Rose just told me you guys were looking at houses—and that you took her."

"Oh, yeah. There were some open houses. The broker is a friend of my mother's. It wasn't a big deal. I just thought, if we are going to move, I want Rose's input."

"What about my input? You need to tell me this stuff. You can't spring it on me, via Rose." I was incensed that he was considering moving. True, so was I, but he was setting off in the wrong direction and for the wrong reasons. Also, why was he telling Rose? It would only upset her. I wasn't asking for her opinion about my mushroom dreams.

"I didn't know she was going to say anything about it."

"Nobody knows what a kid's going to say," I said, annoyed that he was pinning this on Rose. "Just tell me what's going on. Are you guys moving there?"

"We're thinking about it. It wouldn't be until after the wedding. And we could figure out a new custody arrangement if you don't want to move."

"I *don't* want to move."

"You don't have to. Rose could stay with you in the summers."

"And you'd have her the rest of the year? You can't be serious." He was talking about it so lightly, as if he were discussing changing up the weekdays and not putting a nine-hour drive between me and Rose.

"You're getting really upset about a hypothetical situation."

He was right. I was projecting some of my own guilty feelings onto him, my sense that I shouldn't take Rose from him, even though I truly believed it would be better for her to get away from subtropical DC. A recent headline proclaimed: Hottest Summer on Record Is the Coolest of the Rest of Our Lives.

"What else are you planning?" I asked. "You probably have some private school down there you want to put her in—maybe the school you went to."

The silence on the other end of the line let me know I was onto something.

"I don't know what to say to you," Carter said after a pause. "When I tell you things ahead of time, you get mad, and when I don't, you get mad. I feel like I can't win with you."

"What are you trying to win?" I asked.

"Nothing!" Carter said, exasperated. "I just want what's best for Rose."

As soon as our call ended, I got my burner and texted Jenny. Hey are you there?? Just found out Carter is going behind my back and planning some huge move down south & he wants to take Rose with him and have her full time!! What is he thinking?? Please call if you can. I'm losing it. Hope all is going well up north. Wish I was there.

19.

Jenny didn't respond to my distress text. I called a few days later, in case she wasn't receiving messages, but she didn't answer. When I tried Astrid's landline, no one picked up. I figured she and Astrid had gone on another trip, but after a week passed and two more texts went unanswered, I started to feel unmoored. I obsessively refreshed Jenny's Instagram feed, and it kept showing me the same stand of spruce trees in the murky light of dawn. Jenny had posted it the day I left with the caption: Returning from a truly magical foraging expedition. There were no new photos, and when I checked her other social media feeds, I didn't see any updates. Under normal circumstances, Jenny posted once or twice a week, at most. She was probably just busy. She and Astrid had a lot to do.

Midway through the second week, I tried to reach Astrid again, except this time I called over and over, as though I was trying to get a hold of my father. Right before Astrid's answering machine took over, I would hang up and start over. I did this for at least twenty minutes, maybe longer, and got nothing. Finally, I left a voicemail. I couldn't decide if I should be worried or irritated by the lack of communication. Astrid's absence from her cabin might not have anything to do with me or Jenny or Hecate's Key. It was also possible that Jenny had lost her cell phone and hadn't had a chance to replace it. And it was just as likely that Jenny and Astrid had given in to the decadence of summer, the long afternoons, the warm nights that seemed almost like hidden days, the sunshine that sapped all sense of urgency. I could imagine them losing track of time, the way children do.

When a third week passed without hearing from them, I finally allowed myself to feel angry. It just made no sense. Jenny and I had been in touch daily since March. Now it was late July. Jenny was gone, Tara was gone, and Walter looked like he was decorated for Halloween with cotton drugstore spiderwebs. Maybe Jenny was wrong; maybe he was too young a tree to withstand such an attack. Maybe caterpillars combined with drought meant it was curtains for Walter. I was going to feel really sorry for myself if Walter shriveled up and died in my front yard.

Even my divorce lawyer was unavailable. Like the rest of DC, he was on vacation. A few days after my fight with Carter, I got a long-winded legalese email from him that reiterated the terms of our custody agreement: If either one of us wanted to relocate with Rose, we had to prove it was in her best interest. If we couldn't agree, then family court would decide the situation that was best for Rose. Carter was betting that a judge would prioritize moving a child closer to her extended family and loving grandmother. Even though I knew he was just trying to scare me, I felt there might be some truth to his words. A judge would like the idea of Rose being in a classic nuclear family, close to Grandma. There was no matriarch on my side of the equation, no hometown; I was just a bizarre, halfhearted vegan who talked to decorative trees. And what if Carter played dirty and mentioned Hecate's Key? It couldn't legally be used against me, but it wouldn't matter; it would be in the room with us, and I wasn't confident that I would come across as the more stable parent.

I wanted to crumple up Carter's email in disgust, but all I could do was forward it to my lawyer and then read his boomerang out-of-office message: I will be in a remote location with only intermittent access to email . . .

Day after day, the weather was oppressively sultry. At day camp pickup, one of the moms said it was the kind of heat that made you want to get right with God. Rose looked like a lost ghost, her face made pale by the natural sunscreen I insisted on using because it didn't destroy the coral reefs, though probably it killed something else. Every time I smeared it onto her forehead, I thought of Jenny saying that trees were the real natural sunscreen. When we were children, no one cared about sunblock, we played in the shade when it got too hot. I remembered cold sandwiches and sliced, salted tomatoes for dinner, lukewarm showers before bedtime. Those were our coping strategies for heat waves, passed down from grandparents who constructed houses with sleeping porches and thick walls. They weren't going to be enough for Rose's generation.

Astrid finally called me back on the very last day of July. I was on my lunch break, sitting on a bench in the open-air food court, deciding whether to indulge in a mint chocolate chip ice-cream cone, when my burner started buzzing. I grabbed it out of my bag, fumbling as I tried to open it as quickly as possible.

"I'm so sorry, dear," Astrid said. "I would have called sooner. I didn't notice the light blinking on the machine until just now."

"Is Jenny there with you?"

"No, didn't she tell you? She had to go."

"What? Where did she go?" Astrid's tone was confusingly casual, and for a moment I wondered if I'd missed some crucial communication from Jenny.

"She said she had to be in California to deal with some emergency client."

"When did she leave?" The people eating nearby laughed loudly, and I had to cup my hand over my ear to hear Astrid's reply.

"A few days after you left. She said she was sorry, she couldn't stay as long as she'd hoped. But it's all right, it was very sunny after you left, and we dried the harvest enough for her to take back with her."

A few days after I left was almost a month ago. I couldn't believe Jenny had been stateside for that long without telling me; all the excuses I'd concocted for her had to do with being lost in Canada, not busy in California with a massive haul of dried mushrooms.

"Did she pay for them?" Of all the questions flooding my mind, this was the only concrete one I could think to ask.

"No, but we took inventory. There's no rush, my dear. We can work it out at the end of the summer. I know you're good for it."

"I'll pay you before then, I'm so sorry about this."

"It's fine," she said. "You sound upset. Is everything okay?"

My instinct was to press Astrid for more details, but I didn't want to alarm her, this person who had never been anything but kind and generous to me. I told her I was just out of sorts, and that I would call her again soon. As we said our goodbyes, I imagined her hanging up her clamshell phone in her cool, shaded kitchen. Meanwhile, I was trapped in a food court, irritated by hot air suffused with the smell of frying oil. Around me, men in suits, with their ties thrown over their shoulders, sat on concrete benches as they ate their sandwiches. Women poked at salads with plastic forks they would throw away after a half hour's use, utensils that would continue to exist for hundreds of years, slowly disintegrating and reincarnating as they journeyed through the rectal canals of small animals and marine creatures, perhaps becoming wise and attaining nirvana.

I took a deep breath. Then I texted Jenny: Hey are you there? I just talked to Astrid and heard that you're back in CA? Is everything ok?

This time, Jenny wrote back right away: hiiii I am so sorry, I know I've been MIA, things have just been so crazy. Right after you left, I got this slew of angry texts from Kip. He was pissed that I took a leave of absence without clearing it through him. I called and told him what was up and he threatened to sue for breach of contract and stealing his IP and pretty much anything else he could think of. I flew back to CA and have been doing damage control. I think it's going to be OK, maybe it could even work out for the best because he's interested in figuring out how to make medicines from HK

You told him about HK?

Don't worry, nothing specific. But he's into it, he says
mushrooms are on trend

I don't want to work for Ambar-Fielding

We wouldn't. Kip would just be someone we could
consult with

I don't want to partner with someone in pharma in ANY way

There was a long pause, and I felt guilty for my shouty caps. I
waited. Finally, after what felt like ten minutes of flickering dots, her
message appeared: Sorry I shouldn't have told him, but we do have to
consider down the road we might need to make a synthetic version of
HK. Foraging isn't going to be sustainable long term. We can't count on
random camping trips

The word "random" pricked me. It was a ditsy word, not one I
would ever apply to the night we spent gathering Hecate's Key.

I think it will be fine. Look at truffle hunters. Their harvest is
unpredictable and they do fine. If our network doesn't get too
big and we stay underground we should be ok too

Maybe but I think we need to have a strategy in
place

I stared at the text. Usually it was me who worried about long-term
planning. I couldn't figure out what was going on with Jenny, and I
was suspicious that she'd told Kip more than she'd let on. "Strategy"
sounded like a word from his world. I wasn't opposed to planning, but
I wanted to keep things small. The bigger we got, the more complicated
things would get, and the more complicated things got, the more we'd
have to organize ourselves. Before we knew it, we'd be hiring people

and opening bank accounts and sending email blasts. I was trying to get away from bureaucracy and convention. I wasn't going to turn my life upside down just to replicate it in a woodsy setting.

I hit the call button because our conversation was becoming too complex for text, but she didn't pick up. Which was maddening. I knew she was there. I texted: Hey just calling because it's too much to type on a flip phone. Long term plan sounds good. Short term we need to figure out how to compensate Astrid for HK

No reply. I squinted at the little screen that glinted in the midday sun. I hit the call button again. And again. And again.

My thoughts began to spin as I tried to guess why she didn't want to talk it through. I wondered if she was angry, or if Kip was eavesdropping. I didn't even know if she was still in California.

I don't know how long I would have sat there if Marcos hadn't waved to me from across the courtyard. I quickly dropped my phone back into my bag.

"Leigh," he said, "I'm glad I spotted you. I have some good news. You're approved to visit our facilities at Camp David. Tara Barnes put in a special request."

"That's great!" I put on my best go-getter smile.

"I'm going to come with you, so send me some dates that would work for you, and we'll coordinate."

"Will do." I could hear my phone buzz in my bag, and I was dying to pick up.

He excused himself, and as soon as he left the courtyard, I opened my phone. The little screen glowed with a new message from Jenny: sry cant talk now

20.

As Marcos and I drove northwest to Camp David, he caught me up on Tara's project, CATI. They'd had success in a Canine Sleep Readiness Pilot that trained service dogs to respond to feedback from IRTH2 when its wearer was experiencing night terrors and in need of soothing. Now, the programmers were trying to teach IRTH2 to read neural feedback from *the dogs*, who often had special insight and awareness into the humans they were paired with. If a service dog noticed that their person was feeling stressed or anxious, then the device could incorporate the dog's observations into a diagnosis or treatment recommendations.

"We're tinkering with an idea to make it seem as if therapy is coming from the dog itself," Marcos said. "We put a collar on the dogs that's voice activated, and it has a voice of its own, too. So you can talk to the dog, and a voice will talk back to you. It's supposed to bring a personal connection. Otherwise, people are just looking at words on a screen, and that's not enough."

"Is the idea that every soldier is going to have a dog paired with their IRTH2?"

"It might be a good option for soldiers who need intensive care for several months. We need to do a lot more testing. After you try it, you can tell me what you think."

The landscape quickly became rural when we exited the highway. After a strip of chain restaurants and gas stations, we were in farmland. Soon we came to a wooded area, where houses were crouched at the edge of cleared lots and posters taped in windows advertised home businesses: ESSENTIAL OILS 4 SALE, HAIRCUTS, HANDMADE JEWELRY. I couldn't help remarking on the number of campaign signs even though I knew Marcos made it a point not to discuss the election.

"I can't wait until it's over," Marcos said. "Nobody wants to make any budgeting decisions until the next administration gets in."

The houses thinned out, and then there were dense woods on either side of the road, hardwoods that towered over an understory of slender maples whose bright-green leaves caught scraps of light from above.

"Can you get the directions from the glove compartment?" Marcos asked. "We have to get off the main road in a few minutes, and GPS doesn't map it."

The directions took us onto narrow service roads that were pale and oddly pristine, like antique toys that have never been played with. Each time, we were stopped at two separate checkpoints that seemed to come out of nowhere. Finally, I saw a clearing and a large gate ahead, which opened after two soldiers checked our IDs for a third time. We were instructed to park near the skeet shooting range, where Tara would be waiting for us.

Our parking lot was an unpaved clearing of short, scorched grass. I braced myself for the heat when we got out of the air-conditioned car, forgetting how much cooler it is in the mountains. The cicada song was louder than it was in the city, seeming to fill in the spaces between the trees. I felt as if we had arrived in the heart of summer.

Tara came out to meet us. She was in her casual uniform—camouflage pants and hat, an olive-green T-shirt, and a canvas waist pack. We greeted each other with a quick, professional hug, but I felt the vibrations of our friendship in the air. It was so good to see her familiar, crooked-toothed smile. She was tanned, with freckles scattered across the bridge of her nose.

"I'm so glad you made it," she said. "Did Officer Castillo tell you about the plan for us to start working together?"

I looked at Marcos. "Not yet."

"I wanted you to see CATI first," Marcos said.

"Are you ready to try it now?" Tara asked.

"I think so?" I glanced at Marcos, who gave us the thumbs-up.

Tara took us on a short walk past an athletic center and a couple of small outbuildings. We bypassed the skeet shooting area and arrived at an open field, where there were three dogs playing together, chasing each other like kids at recess. When Tara blew her whistle, they came running over and sat in a row in front of her—three German shepherds with kindly eyes and soft fur.

"Only one of them is outfitted with CATI, which you'll figure out pretty quickly." Tara turned to the dogs, gesturing to me. "This is Agent Glenn, a colleague of Officer Castillo, who you already know. Agent Glenn, this is Homer, Ajax, and Asa."

All three looked right at me with alert expressions, their big ears pointing straight up, taking in acres of sound. The one on the end, Asa, said, "Hello, Agent Glenn! It's great to meet you."

I was thrown, even though I knew a voice would be coming from one of their collars. It was just so uncanny, especially the way the other two dogs turned to Asa, as if she were speaking. The voice was female, and her accent was American, with a tinge of the Midwest.

"It's nice to meet you," Asa repeated, looking right at me. "I've heard a lot about you from Sergeant Barnes."

"You can refer to me as Tara with her," Tara said to Asa. "We're friends."

"How wonderful," Asa said, in her weird, disembodied voice. "You know Tara already. She may have told you that I'm wearing a collar that allows me to speak to you. My voice can be adjusted to suit your preferences. But I am not just a voice. I am CATI, a diagnostic, therapeutic intelligence that can be paired with dogs. I can also be used in consultation with human health care workers. But I work best if I have a canine companion, because Asa helps me to understand what you are feeling. Dogs are very attuned to human emotion and body language."

"It's kind of awkward at first," Tara said apologetically. "But CATI is an AI that incorporates Asa's point of view. Did you see how she was able to sense your confusion right away? That comes from Asa's emotional intelligence."

"Look behind my right ear," Asa said.

"Here, I'll show you." Marcos gently stroked behind Asa's ear to show me a small metal square. "This is CATI. It can be removed very easily. The collar is just the voice feature, and it's still a little clunky. But CATI itself is as good as a human doctor at making accurate diagnoses, and it's better at prescribing treatment because it can get people to follow through with Asa's help."

"So CATI uses Asa? Or does Asa become CATI?"

"It's more like CATI takes in sensorial information from Asa," Tara said. "CATI also takes particular insights that Asa has about the humans she's interacting with."

"Is it like CATI borrows the dog's identity?" I glanced at Asa for signs of—what? I didn't know. She was panting softly, keeping her gaze on me.

"That's basically how people perceive it," Tara said. "Obviously they'll know that they're not actually getting advice from a dog. But after you talk to her for a bit, some part of your brain acclimates, and you feel like CATI is the dog."

"Do you want to try working with me?" Asa/CATI asked. "You don't have to share a medical problem. You can tell me what's on your mind. Or you don't need to speak at all. You could take me for a walk."

"Like a dog?" I said, casting an ironic glance in Marcos's direction.

"Like a dog." Asa wagged her tail.

"Just go for a walk with her," Tara said. "Give her a try."

Asa trotted toward an opening in the trees as if she knew I would follow, and I had to move quickly to keep up with her. I glanced back at Tara and Marcos, who made shooing motions like middle-schoolers trying to convince a friend to hit the dance floor.

The woods felt familiar, very much like trails I used to hike with my parents. As I walked with Asa, I remembered a time when my mother and I had run into Everett and Jenny on the Appalachian Trail, which cut through the western corner of our county. This was before I knew Jenny, probably just a few weeks after she showed up at our school. I remembered how casually stylish she looked, wearing a billowing, floral shirt over a pair of cutoffs, her big feet shod in clunky hiking boots, her long arms swinging. My mother knew Everett vaguely, but it was Jenny she was interested in stopping to talk with. Jenny was her new student. As I recall, she was trying to convince Jenny to take AP biology, but Jenny wasn't sure she had the academic chops.

"You're plenty smart. You could do it. All it takes to learn biology is curiosity."

I couldn't remember what Jenny said to my mom, but she did end up taking that class.

"What's on your mind?" Asa asked.

"Nothing in particular." Explaining Jenny felt like too much to get into. I hadn't heard anything from her since our last, slightly combative text exchange. I had texted her several more times, called her, and even left voicemails. I refreshed her social media feeds over and over, only to get the same outdated photos. One night I got so desperate for information that I searched Google Earth for Kip's California house, but I had no idea where to look, except in the mountains north of Los Angeles. I tried to work out how far Jenny and I could have traveled in an estimated hour and forty-five minutes. It was absurd. What would I do when I found the house online, except zoom in?

"It seems like something might be bothering you," Asa said. "Do you want to share it with me?"

"I think I got ghosted," I said. "I mean, I know I did."

"Were you dating someone?"

"No," I said, impressed that Asa knew what ghosting was; Tara had trained her well. "It was a friend, a woman, someone I knew when I was a kid and then we reconnected. We just hit it off, like we did when we were younger. We even went on vacation together. But then she dropped me. Out of nowhere."

"I can hear in your voice that this is very puzzling for you," Asa said.

"It is and it isn't. I don't think I really knew her. I made a lot of assumptions that probably weren't true."

We continued along the wooded path, and Asa began to ask me a series of follow-up questions. I found myself explaining how I'd met Jenny in high school, and the way I'd looked up to her. I told her that Jenny knew my mother, and that she'd given up acting to listen to trees, and how that didn't sound delusional, coming from her, and how she made me feel like there was hope for people, and the world. I told Asa about the ideas we'd had, our visions of green cities with vine-covered apartment buildings and wildflower rooftops; the suburbs abandoned, given over to wolves and migrating birds; the oceans left alone, stripped of cruise ships and fishing boats; the skies clear of airplanes.

"You entered imaginary worlds together," Asa said, looking up at me with her soft brown eyes. Without realizing what I was doing, I stopped walking and knelt to pet her, thinking of all the idealistic visions Jenny and I had shared. All our ideas were impossible, and they weren't even close to enough. Even if we humans managed to clean up our mess, there was still the crushing despair when you realized how much had already been lost.

I don't know how long I stayed there on the path, petting Asa, but after a while she suggested that we head back. When I returned to the field, Marcos and Tara were sitting at a picnic table. They stood up when they saw us.

"It was good?" Tara said.

"Yeah," I admitted. "Does she take you for long walks, too?"

"She's pretty much my therapist," Tara said.

"What are your plans for her?"

"That's what we wanted to talk to you about," Marcos said. "Let's go inside."

The dogs walked with us to a small cabin at the edge of woods, where there was a large fenced-in yard. Tara removed Asa's collar and earpiece before letting her go, and handed the devices to Marcos. When we got inside the cabin, Marcos placed the technology inside a small steel box, which he accessed via fingerprint.

The high-tech steel box contrasted sharply with the rest of the cabin's decor, redolent of the seventies, with wood paneling, shag carpet, and a brown brick fireplace whose mantel held an arrangement of plastic daisies. Everything was very clean and highly polished, with a lingering scent of Lemon Pledge.

We sat down in the chairs by the fireplace, and Marcos brought over some Cokes and a can of Pringles. "Sorry, there's nothing healthier around here."

"So, what do you think?" Tara was looking at me like we were going to dish about CATI now that she was deactivated. "Does she seem real to you? Or should she be more obviously not-real? Is it too uncanny?"

"It definitely messes with my lizard brain when I talk to her," I said. "Do you have any sense of how Asa feels about it?"

"She's used to it now," Tara said. "But it was rough going at first because she couldn't understand where the voice was coming from."

Tara had been tapped to train a dog with CATI, as well as other dogs interacting with a CATI-enabled dog. Now it was time to introduce CATI to human patients to see if she was successful in administering treatments. For the next phase of the study, Tara would take Asa to VA Wellness Centers to test her caregiving abilities. That was where I came in. If I wanted, I could take a break from solo research and travel with Tara to observe and record Asa's work.

"We'll explain what she is," Tara said. "We're going to start with veterans who already have some familiarity with pet therapy. A lot of them live with emotional support animals who remind them to take their medicine or help them with their sleep, so it won't be a huge leap for them to work with CATI."

I glanced at the steel box sitting on the coffee table between us. "I don't understand how we would continue to keep this project secret if you're going out into the public."

"We're not keeping it secret," Marcos said. "The patients can tell whomever they want."

"What about the press?"

"They won't notice. We could put out a press release and they wouldn't care—I've seen it happen with other projects," Marcos said, with a rare look of disgust.

"But if some reporter does get wind of it, aren't you worried about the questions you'll get? I mean, how much did this cost?"

"It could save a lot of money in the long run," Marcos said. "Imagine if we train more dogs like Asa. Imagine if we bring CATIs to VAs all over the country to deal with addiction or to help people manage their chronic diseases."

"It's pretty amazing," Tara said. "It's like this new symbiotic tool."

"That's right," Marcos said. "Asa, and any dog that uses it, will be shaping CATI's programming. It may turn out that this is just a training phase for the AI, a way for it to learn the special things that dogs know."

"Are you going to have the AI learn from other animals?" I asked, trying to get a sense of the scope of their ambitions. "Are you looking at plants? At trees?"

Marcos gave a funny smile. "Who knows?" he said. "But this is where we're at with CATI."

Thunder rumbled outside, startling us. The sky had become overcast with lethargic whitish-gray clouds.

"We'd better leave soon," Marcos said.

We quickly tidied the cabin and headed out to the car. The wind was already picking up, and Homer, Ajax, and Asa were barking with that pre-storm excitement that comes over animals. By the time we'd gone through the first gate, the rain was falling, leaving dark spots on the faded service roads.

Marcos and I missed the worst of the storm, watching as the distant lightning lit the clouds pink. When we were close to the office, I asked him the question that had been nagging me.

"If I worked with Tara, would it be possible for us to work in a different state? Or do we need to stay local?" I was trying to think about my future in a realistic way, for once. I liked the idea of collaborating with Tara, who was reliable, unlike Jenny, but I wanted to know what my options were if Carter did want to go back to Georgia. I felt like I had to be ready for the worst-case scenario.

"You need to be in the tristate area," Marcos said. "Are you thinking of moving?"

"Carter wants to go back to Savannah. With Rose." I kept my eyes on the road, even though I wasn't driving. "That's where he's from, originally. He said I could have her in the summer if he moves there and I stay here."

"The summer?" Marcos looked genuinely stricken, and I appreciated him for that. "Leigh, I'm sorry. That sounds messy."

"It's not your fault. If it weren't for this job, I probably wouldn't be seeing Rose at all."

"Have you ever told him what you're working on?"

"I thought I wasn't supposed to."

"Sometimes people slip up, or spouses figure it out. Do you think he has any inkling?"

I shook my head.

"Maybe you should tell him. You don't need to give him details about what you're doing, but let him know it's something important. CATI's just the tip of the iceberg. There are other things in development that I think you're going to be really excited about. Once your security clearance comes through, I'll be able to show you. I know it's hard to see the gains we've made, but this is a good place for you to be right now."

I really wanted to trust him, but I also wanted to believe Jenny. Underneath all my anger, I still missed her.

By the time I got home, it was evening, and my front yard was soggy from the rainfall. I removed my shoes and socks and walked across my soaked lawn to check on Walter, who looked frail in the waning light. The ground was wet but warm and cushiony. I remembered walking barefoot in the woods with Jenny, kneeling down to look at all the golden mushroom caps nosing their way up, called to the surface by some unseen force, an ephemeral garden. It was hard to believe that my sparse lawn and desiccated sapling were on the same planet. Walter's leaves were almost completely gone, eaten by the webworms who now crawled up and down the railings of my porch indolently, producing dung that looked like poppy seeds. Walter seemed defeated without his green crown. And yet he was still lovely, with water droplets clinging to his twigs, tiny spheres that caught the light.

"Did the rain feel good, at least?" I asked him.

He didn't reply. Crickets chirped in the field behind the condos.

"The caterpillars have run out of things to eat, so how much longer can they stay?" I asked. "You'll be able to grow new leaves soon. You have strong roots. It will be okay."

Walter kept quiet. Maybe he needed an AI collar—a Plant Assisted Therapeutic Intelligence, pronounced like the woman's name, of course. Standing in the company of this quiet, possibly dying tree, I could finally admit my ambivalence about working with CATI. Yes, it was a remarkable technology. Human ingenuity was one of the wonders of the world. But was CATI really so much better than an actual dog? Or a fleet of visiting nurses? Was it better than a society where peace and art and love were centered, rather than war and commerce and resentment? I felt like such a hippie. This was what working for the DOD had done to me.

Maybe it had all started with Hecate's Key.

I went inside, washed my feet in the bathtub, and did something I'd been putting off: I called Astrid. I hadn't spoken to her since she'd told me that Jenny had left. I felt guilty for introducing such a flaky person into Astrid's life, for wasting her time, for inducing her to spill her mushroom secrets, and for absconding with Hecate's Key. I said all this to Astrid, more or less, as I explained what I knew about Jenny's whereabouts. I confessed that, without Jenny, I couldn't really see a way forward for distribution.

"Well, she was hard to read, wasn't she?" Astrid said. "Very gifted, though Luna never liked her very much. I should have paid better attention to that. She's an excellent judge of character. Not all dogs are, I must say."

"Do you have any idea how many mushrooms Jenny took? I want to pay you back, at least."

"You don't owe me anything. It was good to have you girls around. I wouldn't have gone on that trip without you, and I sold all the culinary species I brought back. I'm fine."

"I feel terrible that she took them."

"Don't worry about the mushrooms. They're just the fruit of the fungi, and the fungi know where their fruit should go. Maybe they wanted to go to California."

"I just don't know what to do now." I sat down on my gray sectional and gazed at the vacant eye of my TV monitor. "Jenny and I had a plan. We were going to move there together, and now she's gone. I don't understand, was she going behind my back this whole time?"

"I don't think she's the scheming type," Astrid said. "She seems like someone who goes where the wind blows. Really, she's the opposite of a tree, temperamentally, which is probably why she's drawn to them. For balance."

"I was supposed to build the whole network for selling Hecate's Key with her. I don't know what she's thinking, if she's just going to sell it on her own, or what. She was talking about making a synthetic version."

"She wouldn't be the first to try." Astrid laughed. "Don't worry about her. You can come up here on your own. I'd be happy to have you. Hecate's Key usually has a second showing at the end of the summer. And I still have plenty from when you came. I didn't give them all to Jenny."

"When were you thinking I would come?"

"End of August?" Astrid said. "Early September at the latest."

"I don't know, that's really soon." I stood up to get my laptop so I could look at a map. I couldn't believe that I was considering going back on my own, but I was.

"We can also wait until next year's season—"

"No, I can't wait that long," I said, thinking of Carter's dreams of Georgia. For all I knew, he was putting an offer on a house.

"Then come now," Astrid said. "The summer people are still here, and the river is busy. No one will notice you."

"I *am* supposed to go to my father's next week for vacation."

"There you go," Astrid said. "You already have the time off work. Do you have a passport?"

"I do, but Rose doesn't. And I can't get one for her easily." There was no lie sturdy enough to convince Carter that Rose needed an expedited passport.

"Would your father be able to watch Rose for a few days?" Astrid asked. "That way you could come up here on your own and get the lay of the land. We can ask if anyone's looking to rent their cottage for the off-season. You might have to go back and forth for a while. And you might need to get a temporary work visa. Or something like that, I'm not sure."

"No, *no*," I said, more forcefully than I intended. If I was going to do the thing, I was going to *do* it, I wasn't going to compromise. My life was full of milquetoast choices. That was the whole problem.

"I want to move into the woods," I said. "Like you did. That's the whole thing. And I have to take Rose. I can't leave her with my dad. We hardly get any time together as it is."

"Okay, okay," Astrid said in a soothing voice. "I remember feeling the same way. You're ready to jump in."

"I don't know what I'm going to do with all my houseplants," I said pointlessly, aware that this was the least of my worries. My mind was suddenly buzzing with anxiety as I considered the physical realities of my life: my furniture, my clothes, my pantry with the boxes of granola bars and liquid soap refills . . .

"Just pay your rent and leave your stuff. No one will care."

"Should I pay to the end of the lease?"

"Leigh, you're worrying about the wrong things. You're clinging." Astrid's voice was startlingly calm.

She was right. I didn't even know my landlord; I wrote checks to a real estate holding company. I'd pay out the rest of the lease, and they'd keep my deposit and hire someone to clean out my condo. A new person would move in. Walter would witness it all.

21.

The plan that week was for Carter to drop Rose off on Friday night. I asked him to come alone, without Megan, because I needed to talk with him privately. He agreed with a chilly email reminding me that it would be unwise to discuss future custody arrangements without his lawyer present. I wasn't even looking to discuss his plans to move to Georgia. I wanted to say goodbye to him. But he didn't know that.

I am not sure, honestly, that I was fully aware of what I was doing in the days leading up to my flight. I would get glimmers of it sometimes, while I was packing. I remember folding Rose's cabled tights and fleece-lined leggings, wondering if they would even fit her in four months. The incongruity of my actions: I was so sensible, thinking ahead, trying to avoid a wasteful future purchase; at the same time, I couldn't bear to think of the real costs. The pain Rose would feel when she realized she was leaving her father, her home in DC. The loneliness of starting over. My logic, I guess, was that she was going to lose a parent either way—because I had to go, that was a given. And if I went, I had to take her.

I had always thought that Carter and I would have a child together. When we first started dating, I dreamed that I found a baby in my sock drawer—and when I told Carter, he laughed. After that, I started noticing pregnant women everywhere, and I couldn't walk by a baby stroller without peering inside to see the little creature cocooned within. I dreamed up Rose's name years before I had her, walking home from a dinner party with Carter. It was before we were married. The party was at the very nice apartment of one of his law school friends. I think, at that time, Carter may have been trying to mold us into some version of his very social parents, who hosted dinner parties with other couples. There was nothing wrong with that ideal, except I had no idea how to embody it.

The host, Olivia, had grown up in one of the nicer suburbs of DC, a fact that immediately made me feel intimidated, having been raised in the boondocks of western Maryland, where people like Olivia went for rustic getaways. Her apartment was daunting, too, with its table set for four couples—who had eight place settings at age twenty-six? (They were her grandmother's dishes, she later explained.) She also had a marvelous fashion sense: that night she was wearing a vintage seventies halter sundress, and her thick brown hair was parted down the middle, clean and swingy. I resented and admired her at the same time, an impression I am quite sure she was used to, because she handled me with aplomb, fetching my drink first and giving me a little plate of cheese—checking to see if I was tolerant of dairy—and then introducing me to everyone, announcing that I was just about to begin library school. She said this as if it were a very daring career to embark upon, and I couldn't tell if I was being mocked or if she was just someone who was always on the verge of laughter.

Everyone else was either a journalist or a law student. It went without saying that they all leaned left, except they all said it, all night long. Reagan had just died and they were gleeful. One of Carter's classmates, tipsy on pre-dinner cocktails, raised her glass in a toast, "I'll see you in hell, Reagan!" I asked her if she believed in an afterlife, and she said, "Of course not!" and looked at me like I was probably studying library science because I was too stupid to get into law school.

Later in the party, Olivia announced her intention to never have children and to live to a hundred and fifty, insisting upon extended longevity as a real possibility. "There's going to be warehouses of arms and legs; you'll be able to replenish your body parts."

I thought about Olivia's appendage wholesaler for years after, imagining doll parts in plastic bins and old women with oddly smooth forearms. At the end of the dinner, I felt like a hypocrite. It wasn't as if I were so different from everyone there, as if I didn't have my own high-concept fantasies about the wonders of the future; it wasn't as if I were financially uncomfortable, even if I didn't inherit literal silver spoons. Even if my parents were unconventional, they were also professionals, property owners, and solidly middle class, beneficiaries of all that was bestowed upon white baby boomers. I had benefited, moving up the Candyland ladder and mingling with the power adjacent. It was unnerving, how easily it had all come to me. I felt guilty. I wondered that night what my life would become and how much of it was predetermined by circumstances beyond my control.

On the walk home, I told Carter I hated his new friends, which is the kind of thing you're supposed to wait to say until after you're married.

"How crazy is Olivia, talking about living until a hundred and fifty? What kind of person wants to live that long?"

"I'd like to."

"No, you wouldn't. All your friends would be dead."

"Not if Olivia's still around."

"Okay, you and Olivia can host dinner parties with all the other bionic people."

Carter laughed. "Why didn't you like her?"

"She's just one of those people who doesn't know herself. She should go ahead and have a baby if she's so afraid of dying."

"Didn't you hear her going on about not wanting kids?"

"No one says they *definitely* aren't having kids unless they're struggling with like, some serious existential questions."

"I think you should take people at their word."

"I do, I'm just not holding her to it."

"Do you want to have a baby?" Carter asked.

"Yes."

"Boy or girl?"

"I don't care."

"I think I'd like a girl," Carter said.

"What would we name her?"

That night was warm, bathwater summer air. Carter had taken my hand, and we weren't fighting anymore; he didn't care that I was pessimistic and disdainful—he wanted to have a baby with me. We were passing houses we hoped one day to afford, houses with darkened backyards. I looked at those well-kept gardens, soaked in blue shadows, and thought of how roses were so much stranger and more beautiful when you saw them in a garden, how they lost all meaning in a vase. I remember this because I said to Carter, "I would name a girl Rose." I remember it because, seven years later, when Rose was born, that night came back to me, and I thought really, she was born back then, in those darkened gardens, in the sweet optimism of new love.

But after my mother died, I must have stopped believing in the idea of security; then, after Rose was born, I stopped believing in free will. Maybe I needed a secret. Or maybe Carter just worked a lot, and we didn't spend enough time together. Maybe it was that old story. Or maybe a mushroom winked at me, and the whole world was lit up with mystery. Whatever it was, something inside me changed.

22.

Carter came over alone, as promised, and we stood awkwardly on the porch. Rose hurried inside to watch a show before bedtime. There was no television set at my dad's, so this was her last chance. Carter said she'd spent the whole car ride over debating what she should watch for her *last episode.*

"She made it sound like she was leaving the country for months on end," Carter said.

"That's funny." I was too uneasy to laugh. Strange how Carter could sometimes still know what I was thinking, as if some of our thought tendrils were still helplessly linked, the vestiges of Marriage Mind.

"You all packed?" He nodded in the direction of the car.

"Pretty much." I felt like I had a dead body in the trunk. If he wanted to add something to Rose's suitcase, what excuse would I make for her winter coat and snow boots? There was no way to explain the cash in the glove box and underneath the front seat, or the flip phone and memory cards tucked into one of Rose's old lunch boxes. There was no way to describe my desire to escape. It was like I was trying to outrun dread. I felt like a draft dodger, but the war was something existential my mother had tried to teach me about, and the territory was our daughter's future.

"Sit down a minute," I said, sitting down on the porch steps. "I need to tell you something."

He sat down next to me, close enough that our knees were almost touching. He was still tanned from Hilton Head, and wearing a white shirt that showed it off, though maybe he wasn't aware. I always had trouble gauging his vanity.

"What is it?" he said. "Are you seeing someone?"

"No," I said, surprised by the question and how quickly it tumbled out of him.

"Okay, good," he said. "I mean, it would be okay if you were."

"Yeah, I know." I looked at him. "It's about my job. I talked to my boss, and I can't move to Georgia. I have to stay here in DC."

"Oh." He sighed. "I told you I didn't want to discuss this without my lawyer."

"I have to tell you something that I can't say in front of your lawyer."

"Then you probably shouldn't say it."

"Carter, my job isn't what you think it is. I work at the Pentagon, but I'm not a librarian. I know it probably sounds bizarre."

"I don't understand," Carter said flatly, like he was barely tolerating me. "How are you qualified to do anything but be a librarian?"

"I'm doing research, sort of." I tried to get him to make real eye contact, so he could see that I was telling the truth, even if I couldn't say all of it. "It's a classified project."

"Of course it is," Carter said with a sarcastic smile.

"Why would I make this up?"

"I don't know. I have no idea what you're capable of." He stood up to leave, and I got up, too.

"It has to do with the health of the military, of soldiers, and it's about the climate crisis, too," I said, aware that I sounded a little desperate. "The Pentagon is trying to incorporate holistic health into some new technologies."

"What kind of new technologies?" he asked, looking at me with a mixture of curiosity and suspicion.

"I can't get into specifics."

"Then why are you even telling me about this?"

"I want you to know why I need to stay in DC. And why Rose has to stay."

"Leigh, you know as well as I do that if I want to move to Savannah or California or Idaho or *wherever*, I have every right to do so, especially if I think it's going to be better for Rose."

Down the street, one of my neighbors pulled out of his driveway, and I waved as he drove by, obeying some country instinct from childhood. Carter just stood there with his arms crossed. I felt like it was obvious we were fighting, but I didn't want to go inside where Rose would hear us.

"You're trying to control me," Carter said when my neighbor was out of sight. "That's what the whole mushroom thing was about. It's a way for you to feel like you're in charge of things with your secret life and your secret job doing secret research about the *climate crisis*."

"Why do you say it like that, like it's a joke? Are you a climate denier now?" I knew he wasn't, but his smug tone irked me. "I can't believe I married someone so complacent."

"You know exactly who you married. You wanted to escape your parents' self-righteousness, and now you're taking it on like a mantle. And that's fine. That's your stuff. But I'm not the bad guy here. You're the one who went into a whole other country without telling me when you were pregnant with Rose. You're the one who never thought about the consequences. What if you'd been arrested? What if you'd poisoned someone by accident? You're arrogant, Leigh. You can't see it, but you are."

"Why are you taking her from me?" I asked, my eyes welling up. I felt like, in his mind, I was always going to be a bad person. He'd never seen the value of Hecate's Key, never even tried. "Are you trying to get back at me?"

We both heard the front door open, and there was Rose in her rainbow-striped pajamas that were getting too small. Her wrists and ankles cleared the cuffs by two inches. My overgrown wild Rose.

"My show is over," she announced.

"Okay." I was working hard to hold it together. "Say goodnight to Daddy. Give him a kiss and a hug. You're not going to see him for a while."

I watched as they embraced, and then Carter kissed Rose's neck to tickle her. He used to do it when she was a toddler. Only Carter could make her laugh like that.

I watched them until I couldn't anymore. Then I looked away.

23.

My original plan for vacation was to spend a full week in Lost Falls and take Rose to visit all my favorite childhood spots. We'd go hiking on the Appalachian Trail and eat at Sunny's Breakfast Café. There would be day trips to Harpers Ferry, the Paw Paw Tunnel, and of course, Lost Falls Park. Maybe my dad would take Rose to Lambert one day, or we'd go tubing on the Potomac. I still wanted to do all those things, but I also had to get ready for an extended road trip. I needed food, more cash, clothes, and maybe some basic camping gear, too—and I had to acquire all these things without my dad noticing. I'd already decided I wasn't going to tell him about my move until Rose and I were safe and settled. I didn't want him to know anything if anyone came to question him.

Before we left the condo, I brought out all my houseplants and arranged them on the grass near Walter. Over the last few months, I had gotten so many that they took up half the lawn, like concertgoers in a park.

"Are you doing that so they'll get rained on?" Rose asked.

"Yes," I said. "We'll be gone for a while."

I was jittery at the beginning of the drive, but as the route became more scenic, I relaxed. Rose and I took back roads that swerved playfully around glacial limestone, sloping up and down and never quite leveling out. As we got closer to Lost Falls, I remembered biking certain hills on the weekends, gathering so much speed as I slid down one that

I went halfway up another. On my list of favorite technologies, I would include bicycles—right after recorded music.

My father was waiting for us on his narrow front porch, sitting in the rocking chair. Next to him there was a mound of something brown and black that I at first interpreted to be a pile of blankets. But then it stood up and began to bark.

"Grandpa has a dog?" Rose said.

"I forgot to tell you," I said. "Meet Harold."

Rose unbuckled her seat belt and grabbed her door handle. "Take off the child lock!" she demanded.

Harold's movements were those of an older animal, and his eyes were tired, but they had a fond shine as he sniffed Rose's outstretched hand. My father, meanwhile, started in on a gripe about the terrible state of the neighborhood.

"Did you see Shenker's cows when you were driving in? He's still letting them wade across the stream and get all their crap in the water. Then they push all the dirt from the banks. It's ruining the topsoil. The stream is supposed to be fenced so we don't get *E. coli* poisoning. Our entire country's water supply is being ruined. If it's not shit, it's lead."

"Dad, Rose is listening."

"Sorry, I just have to vent. You know how it is around here. Nobody cares. Even my students are resigned. Half of them think the apocalypse is already upon us and life's just a nonstop party. The other half is trying to make bank—and these are the art students."

"Grandpa, can I go in the backyard with Harold?" Rose was now sitting in the grass next to Harold, petting him, the sun picking up the red in her hair and in Harold's coat.

"Yes, sweetheart. It's nice and shady back there. And there's snap peas in the garden to snack on. You should go with her, Leigh. I'm just going to keep chewing your ear off, and you've heard it all before. So has Harold, poor thing. He probably hoped he was going to be adopted by a sane person. Go on—I'll bring down some iced teas."

I followed Rose and Harold around to the back of the house, stepping over an old garden hose and ducking to avoid a wisteria branch. My dad often says he's going to let the backyard go completely wild just to annoy the neighbors, but the truth is, he likes gardening too much. He practices what he calls lazy horticulture, which involves a lot of walking around and observing what grows easily, and then planting more of that, less of this. He allows weeds like dandelion and purple loosestrife and Queen Anne's lace, but prunes strategically, for beauty. For me, the backyard is my mother's memoir. I see her hand in the phlox, lilies, and peonies, and the honeysuckle and trumpet vine with its vermillion flowers that bring the hummingbirds. The trees are my mother's coauthors; they knew her in her prime.

"Mommy, help!" Rose wasn't quite tall enough to pull herself up into the willow's lowest arm.

I hoisted Rose until she got her footing and began to climb. Harold lay down among the roots to watch. It was a tree that was easy to ascend, with the branches arranged like spiraling stairs.

"The wind sounds so pretty up here," Rose said.

"My mother used to say the wind combs the willow's hair," I said.

"Oh, I like that. I'm going to call this tree Rapunzel."

I think I may have called the willow by the same name when I was her age.

For dinner we had polenta cakes, grilled eggplant and tofu, and a salad of bitter greens. Rose picked at it, which embarrassed me, because I felt it reflected my laziness at the end of workdays, when I just prepared the easiest sure thing: chicken tenders, hot dogs, fish sticks. I'd eaten vegetarian meals when I was her age. But my dad wasn't offended and found fake chicken tenders in the freezer and some penne pasta, which he seasoned with olive oil, salt, and nutritional yeast.

Before bed, Rose wanted to use the composting toilet instead of the regular bathroom, so I took her out to the little shed that was tidy inside, with rolls of toilet paper safely sequestered inside a small cabinet. The wooden seat was smooth from decades of use, and there was a lamp for nighttime visits. I suspected that this was what Rose liked best: turning on the little light and sitting by herself in a small, glowing house.

After I got Rose tucked into my old twin bed, I went downstairs to the kitchen to have a cup of tea with my father. I was prepared to hear more of his grievances, and to perhaps indulge my own doomsayer impulses, but he was sitting in an oddly formal way, his back straight and his mug steaming in front of him. The screened windows were open, letting in the cool air that sometimes arrives in late August, like a whisper of autumn.

"It might need another few minutes to steep," he said.

I had already taken a sip of my tea, which tasted like licorice, with a hint of mint. "It's good now. Do you have any chocolate?"

He went to the cupboard. "I got your favorite."

Ritter Sport, marzipan flavor. I peeled back the red wrapper and snapped off a square. The sweet almond was almost too sweet, which is how I like my candy bars right on the edge of too much.

"Leigh, I have to tell you about a decision I made."

My thoughts started to race. He must be dying, it had to be that. He was dying, and he wasn't going to seek treatment, just like Mom.

"Lambert has offered me early retirement."

"Oh." I remembered to breathe. "Is that a good thing?"

My father shrugged. "It's one of those offers I can't really refuse. They're just going to keep cutting my benefits. If I leave now, I'm likely to have decent health care until Medicare kicks in."

"Why don't they want you to stay? You're such a good teacher. Did something happen?"

"Nothing changed. The problem is I'm getting expensive. They want to hire adjuncts."

"You should stick around just to bug them."

"I was thinking the same thing, but then I got this in the mail."

He turned to get something from the counter behind him. It was a pamphlet with a photo of a small cabin at the edge of a dark wood. Above was a night sky so bright with stars I thought there must be some digital trickery. The caption said, *Still Lake: a profound quiet.* Inside was a map showing a tract of land in West Virginia. Skimming the text, I gathered that it was a place without cell phone service, and there were limits on the use of electricity and lighting at night.

"I don't know what old-man mailing list I'm on, but they definitely have my number," my dad said. "They have cabins for sale at a very reasonable price. I'm thinking of buying one and retiring there."

I perused the listings for cottages of just one or two bedrooms, little houses tucked among spruce and pine. Browned leaves and orange pine needles covered the ground that surrounded them.

"This seems kind of extreme," I said, even as I obviously understood his impulse to leave. But I worried that Still Lake would be filled with paranoid conspiracy theorists, people who thought that retreating from society could cure their maladies. My father was eccentric, but he wasn't out of touch with reality.

"I don't know where else to go," my father said. "It's getting harder and harder for me to stay in this community. It's so noisy. People mow their lawns every weekend, like it's a golf course. In the fall, everyone gets out their leaf blowers. They're going to start new construction on the lots behind us. I saw developers back there with their little flags."

"They've been scouting that for years, Dad. Nothing comes of it."

"It's different now. There's been a bunch of meetings about widening the road. It's going to happen. Everyone wants more development. They want more Amazon and drone deliveries and higher speed limits. When I try to voice my concerns, the vitriol I get is unbelievable. It didn't used to be that way. People were nicer. They at least pretended to listen."

"I'm sorry, Dad." He looked so sad, even the wispy white hairs on top of his head seemed of a piece with his melancholy.

"I can't take it anymore," he said. "I can't stay here and watch it all get destroyed. You know my bird book?"

I nodded.

He got up to retrieve the notebook from the pantry, where it stood on a shelf with cookbooks and foraging guides. Its thick cardboard cover had become fabric-like with age; he opened it to 2001—the year I graduated from college. There was a long list of birds there. Then he started to flip toward 2016. I watched the years go by: my first job, my first apartment, my first date with Carter . . . moving in with Carter, marrying Carter, finding out my mother was sick, finding Hecate's Key, watching my mother die, selling Hecate's Key, getting pregnant with Rose, giving birth to Rose, becoming Rose's mother, selling Hecate's Key, getting caught, getting divorced, getting a job, sharing custody, feeling lost, meeting Jenny, losing Jenny . . .

All the while, the birds in my father's book were dwindling, their penciled-in names decreasing. Each year the list was shorter.

"How much longer can I witness this?" My father closed the notebook and placed his hand on top of it. "I feel like I'm the only one who notices."

"I'm sorry, Dad." I put my hand on top of his. "You sound really burned out. Maybe you just need a break."

"I get a pit in my stomach when I think about the new school year, about doing that commute every day and facing those kids. What am I supposed to tell them? I didn't even become an artist."

"You are an artist, you make things all the time." I gestured broadly to our kitchen, which held many works of art whose creation I could recall: the collage of postage stamps steamed off letters; the bulletin board made from wine corks; the bottle caps glued into trivets; and the garland of rolled-paper beads. On the floor was the hooked rug my father had made at my mother's bedside; hanging by the door was the cross-stitch of "The Trees," the embroidery thread faded from years of morning sun.

"I'm just a teacher," he said, with a derisive glance at his handiwork. "I'm everyone's favorite elective course—and on this road, everyone's favorite punching bag."

"You're being way too hard on yourself."

My father considered this, pausing to sip his tea. "Maybe if I lived in the woods like Everett Heck I wouldn't feel this way. He seems like he's happy, away from it all. I went by his house the other day to pick up Harold's old bed. I've been trying to get him to sleep in his new one for months, and he just won't."

"He probably likes the smell of the old one."

"That's what Everett's daughter, Jenny, said—I mean Jennifer. She goes by Jennifer now. I was trying to remember, was she the same year as you?"

"He was with *Jenny?*" I felt as if I had been prodded awake, the room electrified by the sound of her name.

"Yes, she was visiting for a few days. Apparently, her house—or her boyfriend's house, I wasn't sure—burned down in the California wildfires."

"That's terrible," I said vaguely, disconcerted that Jenny was so close—or had been.

"I know, it's awful. These fires are getting into the residential areas . . ."

My dad descended into a gloomy tangent about fire management strategies, and I lost the thread as I struggled to make sense of Jenny's movements. I decided it had to be Kip's house that burned down. Its disappearance made our night together even more surreal, as if it had never happened, or as if Jenny were erasing it, an extension of her ghosting.

"When did you go to Everett's?" I asked.

"It was last week, maybe the week before? It was kind of odd. Jennifer didn't seem that upset about the house. Maybe she was still in shock. She really looks like Everett, they have that same intense expression, it just draws you in. Do you know what I mean?"

"Yeah," I said. "I do."

I had trouble sleeping that night, and the Wi-Fi was slow at my dad's, so I couldn't obsessively research Jenny on the internet. I decided instead to tackle the box of memorabilia that my father had left in my room for me to go through—detritus from my mom's stuff, which he was still sorting out, seven years on.

I found a newspaper clipping from 1993 about a nationwide veterinarian shortage. My ninth-grade science teacher had given it to me with a note: *I read this and thought of your talents and love for animals.* I couldn't remember receiving this note, or what I'd thought of it, but now I thought it was unbearably sweet that Mrs. Pierce took the time to clip this article for me. It sickened me, when I thought of the number of animals and plants in the world in 1993, and the millions of species that had disappeared since, and how I—a person who supposedly loved animals—had done nothing but go to school and get a job and marry and have a baby, in that order. I had always made the least imaginative choices.

My mother had saved my high school essays. I read a few and winced at what an uptight young person I had been, unaware of my good fortune in the usual way, but also judgmental. I thought some people just had no common sense, that was their big problem in life. I didn't seem to have any spiritual feeling; in my teenage view, people who were religious were deluded, and scientists were more rational than everyone else. It was all black and white to me; I had a terror of being wrong. Yet I was mistaken about so many things.

I wondered if Carter was right, if I was hopelessly arrogant.

I fell asleep in this morass of self-loathing and woke up at ten, disoriented. I could hear Rose laughing from a distance. After a few seconds, I remembered I was home, the window was open, and Rose was out in the yard. How nice for a kid to wake up and just run outdoors.

Soon she would have that every day, she could get the wild upbringing she deserved.

Downstairs there was coffee. I went into the backyard in my pajamas. My dad was puttering in the herb garden, pulling weeds and plucking the blooms off the mint and oregano.

Rose came running to hug me. "You slept in!"

"I'm sorry. It's not that late, though. We can still go to Lost Falls Park. Do you want to come with us, Dad?"

"No, thanks. That place has been overrun by selfie paparazzi. I don't know if someone wrote an article or what, but now there's always a huge crowd."

It was hard to imagine the hordes descending on such a small, subtle location. But it was an easy hike, and the light was probably quite flattering. I was curious to see it for myself.

Also, one way of driving there would take me by the Heck household.

24.

"Mommy, why do you keep slowing down and speeding up?"

"I just want to see if an old high school friend of mine is around—oh, I think this is it."

I slowly drove down the unpaved lane, my wheels crunching the gravel. Jenny's old house, as best as I could recall, was a split-level log cabin at the top of a slight rise, with a large boulder at the end of the driveway. The cabin was smaller than I'd remembered, but the hunk of gray limestone was larger. There were no cars parked outside, the windows were closed, and there weren't any lights on inside the house. I was about to get out, when several dogs came running from behind the house, barking anxiously.

"Are they nice?" Rose asked.

"I don't know. We should probably stay in the car until someone comes out."

"I don't think anyone is there."

"Me neither." We waited another minute or so, and then I slowly backed out of the driveway, too nervous to execute a turn with the dogs jumping around us.

We got to Lost Falls Park fifteen minutes later, and despite my father's warnings, I was surprised when the lot was full. We had to park on the shoulder and walk to the trailhead.

As we headed toward the falls, I heard the talk and laughter of hikers ahead, making their way toward the striking backdrop. I tried not to be cranky, to enjoy the company of other human beings, but I couldn't help it—I didn't like that it had become such a social spot. I wanted to show it to Rose as it was meant to be: a quiet, green jewel.

"Are we there yet?" Rose whined. "My legs hurt."

"It's not even a mile," I said irritably, wishing it were much longer—that way it wouldn't attract so many tourists. I berated myself for sleeping in; if only we had come earlier, we could have beaten the hangover crowd.

"Will you carry me?" Rose asked, still whining.

"No. I did this hike when I was your age." I knelt to pick up a Clif Bar wrapper at the edge of a trail, wondering what kind of poseur influencer needed a protein bar to get through a thirty-minute walk.

"Can we stop and have lunch?"

"No, Rose, we *can't.*"

Tears appeared in Rose's eyes immediately, the drops perching at the ducts, threatening to fall. She pressed her lips together, trying not to cry.

"I'm sorry, honey," I said. "I'm in a bad mood."

"You hurt my feelings!" Now she began to wail, and I hugged her tightly before wiping her tears and pushing her hair out of her face.

"You want me to tell you a true-life story?" Rose always liked to hear about when I was a kid, especially when I got into trouble. "I have a good one about this place. I've never told it to you, but my mom was so mad at me. It was probably the maddest she ever got."

I took her hand, and as we continued along the trail, sometimes pausing to pick up litter, I told her about Jenny. I knew Rose had already had her share of intense friendships—the Sawyers and Avas and Claras of kindergarten—but she couldn't yet understand the desire to separate from me, and to seek out a friend who would help her do that. When I described coming to Lost Falls late at night with Jenny, walking through the dark, navigating by ear toward the sound of the falls, she was astonished that we hadn't had phones with GPS. Or snacks.

"Were you scared to be alone in the woods?" Rose asked.

I shook my head. No, I hadn't been scared, because I had been with Jenny. She brought out the brash side of me. She took me out of orbit.

Before I met Jenny, I was a planet circling the sun of my parents' deep love and expectations.

"Mommy! I think I hear the water!" Rose ran ahead to see the falls. I jogged after her, our water bottles sloshing in my backpack. "Mommy! It's beautiful! Come look!"

It was as magical as I remembered. But there were so many people. Most were in their twenties and had stripped down to bathing suits. They sat with their bare feet in the little pools of water that collected among the rocks near the falls. Piles of clothing, shoes, and backpacks marred the pristine banks. They were taking photos of themselves and their picnics: open-faced sandwiches and fresh fruits, salami and cheese, canned wine and bottled cold brew were arranged on cloth napkins among the colorful mosses. It felt like we were at a party—a fun party, with goofy, warmhearted people, but I hated it with a despair that was pointless to deny. I looked down my nose at all of them, plugging into the collective AI. Every location tag would bring more people here; it was like some new phase of evolution—habitats altered by memes.

Rose was disappointed that we hadn't brought bathing suits, but I wasn't. Oily swirls of sunblock shimmered on standing water that used to be covered by a flowing current. Nearby, a woman sprayed canned Evian on her face to give herself a dewy glow. I decided it would be easier to believe this wasn't actually Lost Falls, but some other place with the same name.

We did not document our lunch of smushed peanut butter and jelly on whole wheat bread, green apples browned at the edges, and Babybel cheese wheels, whose red wax Rose molded into a lumpy heart. I begrudgingly took a few pictures of Rose by the falls, then texted a photo of the crowds to my father with the caption you were right.

He wrote back: Looks like a Ryan McGinley photo shoot.

A second text said: If you see any good farm stands on the way home, can you pick up some tomatoes and corn?

Then, a few minutes later: But don't buy anything from the Shepherds. They mistreat their pigs.

It was around three when we finally returned to the car. I drove directly to Jenny's house, pulling into the driveway as if Rose and I had been invited. This time there was a Honda station wagon parked by the house—but no dogs.

"Hang on," I said. "I'm going to just walk up and ring the bell, okay?"

"Okay," Rose said sleepily.

I knocked loudly and rang the doorbell, but there was no answer. Peering through the narrow panel of windows next to the door, I glimpsed the living room beyond the foyer. It was sparsely decorated with a sofa and several large beanbags—for the dogs, I realized. Everett Heck was probably out walking his brood.

I moved to the side of the house to get a better look into the living room. There was a woodstove and several low shelves holding arrangements of crystals, feathers, rocks, and sticks. I searched for a sign of Jenny's presence—a scarf, a straw hat, an expensive-looking tube of sunscreen. On the wall above the shelves was a large framed painting in bright colors depicting a Gaia-like goddess figure surrounded by animals, plants, clouds, and birds. Tackily sincere, like a lawn ornament. But pretty, too. I wondered if Everett had painted it, or a girlfriend? I stepped away from the window, feeling like a snoop. There was no justification for what I was doing.

Back in the car, Rose had fallen asleep. I drove about a quarter of a mile before I came to a clearing that I recognized and pulled over. Electrical wires buzzed overhead, striping the land down into the valley and over the hills in the distance. I got out of the car to take in the view. This was where people dropped their unwanted pets. *Pet Heaven*, my mother used to call it, ironically. We weren't innocent of it; we had dropped a groundhog here once, a fellow we caught in a Havahart trap. The animal rattled his metal cage the whole way over. When we released him into the field, his body was shaking with fear. Driving home from that ordeal, my mother vowed she'd never do it again. It was too cruel, even for an animal who mauled her flowerbeds.

I heard the dogs before I saw Everett Heck. They yelped when they saw me, an unexpected figure standing on the side of the road. There were about ten of them, of all different sizes, running toward me. My first instinct was to hurry back into my car. Then I saw an old man following behind, calling them back and waving to me. I recognized one of the dogs as the chocolate Lab from Jenny's house, but it still took me a moment to understand that the old guy really was Everett. As he approached, I searched for signs of the man I'd known as a child. His clothes were of the same genre, were perhaps even the same ones he'd worn twenty years ago: a faded purple shirt emblazoned with the silhouette of a wolf, an Orioles baseball cap, and baggy, belted jeans. What made him seem older was the thinness of his wrists and neck, and his posture, which was stooped, especially as he walked uphill toward me.

"Hello there," he said. "Are you having car trouble?"

"No, I'm fine, thanks. I was just stopping for the view. I'm actually from here. You're Mr. Heck, right?"

"Yes, that's right. Do we know each other?"

"I'm Leigh Bowers—Steve's daughter. I went to high school with Jenny."

"Oh yes, he stopped by the other day. He mentioned you were going to visit. He said you have a little girl?"

"Rose. She's asleep in the back seat." I glanced over my shoulder to check that she was still napping. "We went to Lost Falls."

"She's all tuckered out, huh?" Everett said. "Too bad, these guys love to play with kids."

A couple of the dogs barked softly, as if in agreement. They moved around Everett like a strange appendage—an extrasensory organ, maybe, or a second brain.

"You just missed Jennifer," he said. "She made one of her rare visits."

"Oh yeah?" I asked neutrally. "What's she up to these days?"

"Don't ask me," he said. "She's become a Silicon Valley person. Both my children are after money. That's what motivates them—did you know Robert, too?"

"Not really. He didn't go to my high school."

"Right, right, of course you didn't. Robert stayed with Suzanne. Well, Robert does liposuction on women who don't need it, and Jennifer was teaching yoga classes in the woods, or something, and now she's getting married to a tech guy and they're going to make a virtual reality zone where you walk through a forest. Tell me if that's not the most pointless thing you ever heard of."

"It does sound strange." I felt totally disoriented by the news that Jenny and Kip were an item, even though it made sense. Complete and total sense. It was a lot more logical than two women who barely knew each other starting a business based on foraging and talking to trees. I wondered if she had been consulting for Kip all along, if that was the whole basis of our friendship. But if she was a spy, trying to wrest government secrets, she wasn't a very good one. She'd never asked much about the technology the DOD was developing, or even the specifics of the new field manual. Our exchanges were always about the wonderful things that could be, not what actually existed. I wasn't even sure if I'd ever told her about the hikermill.

The black Lab jumped up to Everett's waist; he gently took hold of the dog's front paws and put them on the ground, then knelt to pet the dog's dark fur. His mood seemed to mellow.

"Jennifer has this way of just showing up out of nowhere, and then leaving," Everett said. "I haven't even told her mother that I had a sighting."

"My dad said something about her house in California? He said it was in the fires?"

"Yeah, that's true." Everett seemed annoyed to acknowledge this. "It wasn't her house, it was the tech guy's. Don't feel bad about it. He never should have built up there."

"Still," I said, "it was—I mean, it must have been—a nice house."

"I don't give two shits about nice houses. I only feel bad for any pets that get left behind. They don't ask to live in tinderboxes."

One of the dogs suddenly bolted off toward the woods, and then several others followed.

"I bet he saw a groundhog," Everett said. "People dump their pests here. Or they'll chuck carcasses. If they hunt over the limit, they'll just throw a deer back here. You'll see all the vultures circling." He glanced over his shoulder. "I should follow them. It was nice seeing you. I'd say I'll mention it to Jennifer, but who knows when she'll turn up again."

"Did she say where she was going?" I wanted some clue, a scrap of a motivation.

He laughed. "Everything is on a need-to-know basis with her. Even when she was a little girl. She'd just run out the front door without a word. Children show you who they are right away, like dogs."

He walked across the weedy field with his orphan crew, the tall grass swallowing them up. Pet Heaven. There had been such disappointment in Everett's voice, disappointment edged with bitterness and loss. It reminded me of my mother's despair, before she took Hecate's Key. Her dread of her own demise had always been mixed with her fear that the natural world was dying, too.

I became aware of the crackling of the electrical wires overhead. It was the sound of civilization, the hum of heat and air conditioning, of TV and radio, of toaster ovens and refrigerators, hair dryers and humidifiers, electric blankets, desk lamps, laptops, alarm clocks, coffee makers, waffle irons, microwaves, and routers. It was the sound of cheap toys and expensive video game consoles, of Netflix and YouTube, of noise-canceling machines programmed to play ocean breezes, dolphin songs, and rainstorms. It was the sound of comfort and destruction.

In the back seat, Rose was still lost to the world, her chin tipped up, her chest rising and falling beneath her seat belt. She had been such a beautiful infant. Oh, how I wished my mother could have held her.

I resolved to leave the next morning.

25.

I woke up again to the sound of Rose playing in the backyard. I looked out my window and saw my father crouched in the vegetable garden with his socks pulled over the cuffs of his pants to keep off the ticks. He waved Rose over to show her something, probably a grasshopper, and Rose reciprocated with a kiss to his forehead. I couldn't bear to keep watching, to acknowledge the love and connection I was leaving behind. I ripped a piece of paper from my planner and then sat on my bed for a good twenty minutes, writing and erasing. Finally, I wrote: *Dad, I had to go away. I will be in touch as soon as I can, but everything is okay. I love you.* Then I folded it and left it on my bedside table. I quickly dressed and packed up our suitcases and put them in the trunk of my car. When I was done, I went into the backyard and suggested to Rose that we get breakfast at Sunny's and then go to Gettysburg.

"Why would you want to go there?" my father asked.

I had deliberately chosen a site that my dad would not want to visit. He hated anything to do with war.

"At least you're going during the week when it won't be as busy," he said. "I think I have a National Parks pass that you can use."

While my father packed lunches for us, I went upstairs and flipped through our family album until I found the photo of my mother that I wanted to take with me. She was wearing a plaid shirt, she was smiling, it was autumn. She had eye crinkles, and her teeth were slightly yellowed. She was probably in her early forties, just a few years older than me.

When I returned to the kitchen, my dad handed me a canvas tote with more than enough food for a grown woman with a slowing metabolism and a little girl who had bouts of pickiness. I almost burst into tears.

"Here you go, sweetie. I think I'll grill out for dinner, okay?"

"Sounds good." I hugged him goodbye and told myself that I would find a way to see him in a few months.

One more hug. Then Rose and I were off.

Sunny's wasn't especially busy on a Monday morning, so we were able to get a booth by the window. I ordered eggs, bacon, hash browns, toasted English muffins, and bottomless coffee. Rose got pancakes, breakfast sausage, and orange juice. Outside, the sky was hazy already, a gauzy blue with banks of listless clouds. It was going to be miserably hot.

"Rose," I said. She looked at me over the rim of her orange juice glass. "I have to tell you something. We're not going to Gettysburg. We're going on a much longer drive to a place called Thousand Islands. It's beautiful. It's on the Saint Lawrence River, which is the border between Canada and the United States. There are all these little islands in the river."

"A thousand?" She took a bite of pancake.

"Probably not a thousand, but definitely hundreds. When we get there, a friend of mine is going to take us on a boat ride. Have you ever been on a boat?"

"In Hilton Head, with Daddy." She looked at me uncertainly. "I don't understand why you changed your mind."

"I guess I thought this would be interesting." I gave her a cheerful smile. "But before we do that, we're going to go to the mall! I need to buy some things. And get a haircut."

"Why do you need a haircut?"

Astrid had told me it would be wise to dye my hair brown to match the photo in the passport her friend had procured, but there was no way to explain that to Rose. So I told her I would get her a toy if she was good.

"Anything I want?"

"Sure! It's vacation!"

In the parking lot, Rose took my hand. "Don't tell Daddy," she said, "but vacation with you is more fun."

I used my phone one last time to search for a mall with a Target and a Supercuts, and then I dropped it in a garbage can in the mall's parking lot. A little thrill went through me, a feeling of freedom and terror.

In Target, I bought a road map, that ancient tool of interstate navigation. Then Rose and I powered through the aisles, still shopworn from the weekend rush. With the thought that I might have to keep a low profile for a few months, I stocked up on extra-large bottles of shampoo and conditioner, value packs of bar soap, and, at Rose's insistence, Disney-themed toothbrushes and toothpaste. In the clothing section, I selected underwear, socks, leggings, long johns, rain boots, towels, washcloths, and gardening gloves. I picked out two new sweatshirts for Rose, and four pairs of jeans. In the dry goods aisle, I stocked up on jerky of all flavors, granola bars, trail mix, jelly beans, raisins, rice, beans, and chocolate bars.

I felt like a prepper, high on Reddit threads and hedged bets as I tried desperately to prepare for an unknown future.

Rose chose her toy: a Playmobil set of a wedding, with scenes of a bride in a pink dressing room trying on a white gown, and an outdoor reception that showed a tree strung with lights, a photographer, wedding guests, refreshments, and a white stretch limo that looked to me like a hearse. Normally, I would have urged her to choose a different theme, but I just put it in the cart, along with everything else.

When we checked out, I paid in cash.

Next stop was Supercuts, where I told my stylist—a middle-aged woman named Lisa with a blonde ombre bob—that I wanted my hair cut to the same length as hers and dyed dark brown.

"I don't know if that's going to work with your complexion," Lisa said. "Why not try a light brown? Or I could even do highlights and bring out your blonde?"

"I want to change it up. I want dark brown."

"Can I use a semipermanent dye? That way it will wash out over time, but you'll still have your grays covered."

"Okay, sure."

Rose sat behind me, watching everything. When Lisa toweled off my hair and started combing it out, Rose came over with a serious look on her face. "Did you tell Daddy you're going to do this?"

"Of course not." I glanced at Lisa in the mirror. "We're divorced."

"Oh, this is divorce hair! You should have told me," Lisa said.

"What's divorce hair?" Rose asked.

"That's when you want to show your ex there's another side to you that he'll never get to know." Lisa finished combing my hair and got out the scissors. "Three inches?"

I nodded.

Snips of brown hair fell to the ground. I stole glances at myself in the mirror. Lisa was right; the shade was too dark, overpowering my eyebrows and lashes, and bringing out the spots of acne that always emerged when I was under a lot of stress. I told myself it would be fine; my skin would clear up in my new life. I'd be walking outdoors every day, breathing cleaner air, eating foraged foods.

After the cut and blowout were done, Lisa spun me around and declared I looked like Uma Thurman in *Pulp Fiction*, which I didn't, but I appreciated the compliment as a show of solidarity.

I paid her in cash with a big tip and made one last stop to buy some new makeup. In the car, Rose ate her packed lunch while I put on foundation, blush, noir-black mascara, and lipstick. I reached for my phone to check my reflection but remembered it was in the trash can. Again, I felt a buzz of excitement. I was really doing it, I was leaving.

I pulled down the visor and peered into the little mirror hidden there. Jenny, I realized. I'd made myself up to look like her. I used to paint her face before performances, the two of us sitting on the chorus risers, dipping a sponge into the beige foundation that was thick like tempera paint. There was a dot we used to do on either side of the bridge of the nose, I don't know why. The amount of blush we used was obscene. I remembered running lines with her, listening to poetry that was four hundred years old, verses she made hilarious. I remembered her talent, her unquenchable desire to be seen. And I remembered Suzanne Heck, smoking in the dark, asking what the point of self-awareness was. I felt like I finally understood what she'd meant.

26.

By the time we left the mall, it was after two and we still had about six hours of driving ahead—and that was if we didn't stop. Luckily, the roads north weren't very busy. On a Monday afternoon in August, everyone was either taking shelter in their air-conditioned offices or ensconced in vacationland. The weather appeared mild from inside the car, just an overcast summer's day, but when we stopped for gas, the heat and humidity seemed to fill my lungs. I reached for my phone to check if there were any air quality warnings but realized, once again, that it was gone. The novelty of being untethered was beginning to wear off. I told myself that even if I knew the air was bad, I wouldn't be able to do anything. It would just be another piece of distressing information to absorb.

Rose was bored. I put on NPR, hoping she would fall asleep, but she remained alert. I got the sense she knew something was off and didn't want to miss an important clue. I wasn't sure when, or how, I would tell her the full extent of our road trip.

"You know," I ventured, "this is taking a little longer than I thought. Would you mind if we stayed overnight in a motel?"

"Will there be a pool?"

"Sure, we can stay at a place with a pool."

"Will there be a glass elevator?"

"That's more of a hotel thing."

She considered this and accepted it. "As long as you tell Grandpa."

"I will," I lied. "I'll call him from the motel."

I took an exit into Scranton and drove through the residential streets, looking for a playground to give Rose a break. After a stretch of run-down blocks that took us by an abandoned paper mill advertising bricks for salvage, I spotted a school at the top of a hill. It had brand-new play equipment, a snack bar, and a paved courtyard where a group of families were playing cornhole.

Rose was delighted to have the chance to run around. I bought a bag of Peanut M&M's to calm my nerves, but the chocolate was soft, and I didn't want to finish them. The scent of beer and corn syrup wafted up from the trash can, disturbing some bees. I hurried away, nearly tripping over a plaque commemorating the short life of a child who had died of cancer. Rose called to me to give her a push, and I went, trying to enjoy myself as she pumped her legs and laughed, going higher and higher. In the distance, there was a mountain, half-bald of trees. I forced Rose's swing to a stop.

"Time to go," I said.

"Five more minutes?"

"We're going now," I said sternly, as if it were obvious that I was going to succumb to a mood of existential despair if I stayed at this doomed location for another minute more.

She scraped together some tears and managed to turn them into a tantrum. Nearby adults threw sympathetic glances, giving me the benefit of the doubt because they'd been in my place before or because they'd had a couple of Yuenglings and were inclined to feel generous.

"I'm sorry, honey," I said when we were back in the car. "I just want to get back on the road."

"Can we listen to my playlist?"

"I can't turn on my phone right now," I said, guessing that total disappearance of my phone might alarm her. "But let's find something on the radio, okay?"

She wasn't happy with this, and she pouted and whined, so I gave her a piece of gum. That placated her until the gum lost its taste and then she wanted more, and I said no and she got mad again. And then she fell asleep.

I found a local news station. It was the top of the hour, and they were giving the weather: thunderstorms due late in the day. On the horizon, there was a mass of dark clouds, but the sky was cornflower blue above us, as well as to the northeast, where we were headed. Maybe we'd miss the storm, or just skirt the edge of it.

After about forty-five minutes of occasional raindrops, the cloud bank that had seemed so far away was suddenly upon us, and the rain came down heavily. Rose woke up to its drumming sound.

"What's happening?" she said groggily.

"It's just rain, honey."

"Why is it so dark out?"

"It's late in the day, the storm makes it seem later."

"It's kind of spooky."

"It's passing over us, don't worry."

Just then, lightning lit the sky a freakish ochre. Thunder followed, crashing loudly. It came so quickly it was like the sky had cracked into pieces, a plate dropped on the floor.

I was startled but tried not to show it.

"I don't like this," Rose said.

"It's okay, we're safe in the car." I switched off the radio so I could concentrate on driving.

Another lightning bolt broke the sky, the thunder roaring behind. The cloud bank seemed to be growing larger; it was like a lumbering, restless animal. My wipers were thrashing, trying to keep up with the rainfall. I kept driving, slowing down only slightly.

More lightning, more thunder. The sky was pink, lavender, pink again, purple, gray. Adrenaline wired my body, but I didn't feel scared. The other cars were with me, they were part of the experience, it was like we were driving through an exciting movie.

Suddenly the sky was bright white, and for a split second the landscape was totally illuminated. Thunder crashed like a wave breaking.

"Holy shit!" I yelled. "We must be right in the middle of it!"

Rose was silent in the back seat, awed and terrified.

The lightning and thunder started to taper off, and I thought we had gotten through the worst of it, but then the rain came down even harder. Ahead, the view was blurry, the taillights of other cars just smears of white and red. The sound of the storm was rushing and wild, the water pouring down the window again and again and again, like a bolt of fabric that kept unrolling.

I slowed down; everyone around me slowed down. Now we were all trudging through this storm. Things felt sloppy; I started to worry about getting into an accident. I couldn't get into a wreck, I was driving a car with hundreds of dollars in cash stuffed into the back seat pockets, my hair was dyed a different color, and I was wearing a lipstick called Claret—all en route to pick up forged passports.

I kept thinking, *This has to stop soon*, but the rain kept pummeling us. At some point I realized the sun had gone down, and I felt unnerved, as if I hadn't gotten a proper goodbye.

Ten minutes passed like that, and I noticed there were hardly any cars on the road anymore, everyone had taken exits. I wondered what they knew that I didn't—what their phones had told them. The rain came down at the same ferocious pace.

Rose started to cry in the back seat. "What if it never stops raining?"

"It's going to stop," I promised, but I knew what she meant. I had the feeling that it was just too much water, the road couldn't take it, that the people who'd built it never imagined so much rain would fall, so quickly.

In Ontario, when Jenny and I hiked in rainy forests, searching for Hecate's Key, Jenny explained that you can't feel a heavy rain in a mature forest because the trees absorb it; the water collects on the surface of the leaves and then trickles down the branches and the trunk, gathering in the moss and lichens that grow there. The mosses are sponges that save the water, quenching the thirst of small animals that slake the thirst of even smaller ones, a beautiful chain of dependency.

"How do you know it's going to stop?" Rose asked anxiously.

"It just will," I said uncertainly. On the other side of the highway, I thought I saw a line of stranded cars, but I couldn't be sure, maybe they were just moving slowly.

I concentrated on staying in my lane as I drove through what looked like a large puddle going across the highway. Suddenly, I felt the steering wheel go light in my hands.

"Oh, no, oh no, no, no."

"What is it?" Rose asked.

The car was floating. I took my foot off the gas but wasn't sure if I should brake. What I thought was a puddle seemed to be some kind of flash flood, rising quickly. Then the engine cut out.

Rose began to wail. "Mommy, Mommy, why are we going to the side?"

"It's okay, it's okay," I said, turning the key. Then turning it again. And again. "Shit," I muttered.

"Why shit, why shit?" Rose said. "Is it the water coming in?"

"What water?"

She pointed to the bottom of her door. "It's wet," she said. "Is that normal?"

I couldn't answer, I was too deep in prayer to the higher power I didn't believe in, because why would anyone create a species as foolish as ours. *Please, Divine Being, if you're out there, let my car start, don't let me drift away, I don't know where I am, I don't know how to get out of here, please, I don't want to die, Rose can't be alone in this car.*

I didn't know how long I should keep trying to get the car started. If I got out of the car, what side should I pick, and should I try to carry Rose, and how deep was the water underneath us, and was there a current, and where the hell were we? Was there a river nearby, where was the water trying to go?

After the longest seconds of my life—maybe they were minutes, I don't know—the engine started. A moment later, the tires gripped the road just as the side of the car scraped against the corrugated divider. I gently applied the brakes and steering. My car skidded, ever so slightly, but stayed the course. *Dear God.* The road sloped upward, and in the rearview mirror I could see that the puddle I'd been stuck in was flowing across the lanes and over to the southbound side. Ahead, I saw a highway overpass on a slight rise. Very carefully, I switched lanes and pulled over to the shoulder, parking underneath the bridge with my hazard lights on. Inside the car it was eerily quiet, the rain a distant hush.

Rose had stopped sobbing.

"Is our car okay?"

"The car's fine. It was just too hard to drive. We can wait it out. Do you want to come up front?"

"Am I allowed?"

"It's okay if we're not moving."

She unbuckled her booster seat and crawled up to the passenger seat, where she sat cross-legged. She touched the windshield, tracing a raindrop. We could still see the storm; our headlights illuminated the silver curtain on the other side of the overpass. Occasionally, vehicles passed by us slowly, their headlights briefly shining and receding before they dissolved into the downpour.

"It feels like we're in a different world," Rose said. "A secret world, like Narnia."

We'd read *The Lion, the Witch, and the Wardrobe* recently. It was cozier than I remembered, with several scenes that involved hot tea and baked goods. At first I thought it was too tame, all the animals were so English, so proper and emotionally reticent. Then I got to the ending, when the children tumbled out of the wardrobe. Decades had passed in Narnia; they had become kings and queens, had aged, won battles, grown wise, and then, suddenly, they were children again, back in a relative's country house. As a kid, it's nice to think they've come home again. As an adult, I knew Europe was being blown to bits and that young men, the world over, were being recruited to fight, and that these children were likely orphaned. And I knew that a new weapon was coming, a bomb with the strength of a meteorite, an explosion to end worlds.

As an adult, the children's return to civilization is shockingly sad.

All at once I was overwhelmed by the drive ahead. It would be dark, the roads would be slick, and it would be just me driving, it would always be just me and Rose, and all at once I saw the truth: that wasn't fair to Rose. It wasn't fair to anyone. What was I going to tell her when she was older, living alone in her woodland paradise? That she was the lucky one and everyone else—including her father and grandfather—was stuck in subtropical, storm-ravaged America? I couldn't protect her from destruction, it was coming for all of us, no matter where we lived—even Astrid had said that forests were changing faster than she'd ever expected. I should go alone if I was going to do this risky, selfish thing, but I didn't want to be alone, I wanted to be connected to other people. That was always the allure of Hecate's Key—and of Jenny, too.

A small voice interrupted my spiraling thoughts. "Mommy?"

"Yes?"

"Can I sit in your lap?"

I scooted my seat back and held out my arms. She made herself comfy and reached up to touch the ends of my bob. "When I get home, can I get my hair cut like this?"

"If you want to."

She put her hands on my cheeks, holding my face like it was precious to her. "I want to be like you, Mommy."

I wondered how she could want to turn out like me, a person who had no idea how to live. I started crying. "I'm sorry, I'm so sorry, honey."

"It's okay." She kissed me on the cheek with her soft lips, and I remembered what a sweet baby she was, how she liked falling asleep with her head on my shoulder, and how I could feel her smiling on my bare shoulder—the corner of her baby mouth lifting up—as she drifted off.

"The rain's letting up," Rose said.

"Let's go home."

It was close to dawn when I finally pulled into my dad's driveway. The kitchen lights were on, and I knew he'd been waiting up for me. By the time I got sleeping Rose out of her booster seat and had hoisted her onto my shoulder, he was standing in the driveway.

"Nice hair," he said.

"I can explain."

"You don't have to."

We put Rose to bed, adjusting the fans to blow on her. Then we went downstairs to the kitchen.

"You want coffee?" he asked. "I can make a fresh pot."

"Do you have any beer?"

My dad went to the fridge and got two bottles of Back to Earth, a local brew, and poured them into glasses he kept in the freezer. We sat down across from each other at the kitchen table, where we'd been just a few nights before, drinking tea.

"I'm sorry," I said. "I really am. I didn't mean to make you worry."

"It's okay." He tucked a strand of hair behind my ear. "I think the last time I pulled an all-nighter was when your mother had her talk with Hecate's Key. That was a little more fun for me, I have to admit."

"I'm sorry I kept you up," I said.

"I wasn't looking for another apology, sweetheart. I'm just reminiscing. It was a good night. Your mother couldn't stop laughing. She kept saying, 'These are the best jokes I've ever heard!'"

"What kind of jokes?" My father had never talked very much about my mother's trip. I'd only really heard her version.

"I don't know, exactly. She couldn't explain. I just know now that I live in a world where mushrooms can tell jokes. It's a remarkably sustaining piece of knowledge." He sipped his beer. "Are you still planning to stay for the rest of the week?"

"Yeah, I need a break. I think I'm going a little nuts."

"Well, you come by it honestly."

PART THREE

Project Demeter

27.

I felt emptied out when I got back to DC, the way you feel after a good cry. I dropped Rose at Carter's, and then I went home and filled my cupboards with the nonperishables I'd bought during my millenarian shopping spree. I put all the new clothes in my drawers and took my houseplants back inside, one at a time.

Then I went out and bought a new phone.

It was Labor Day weekend, and I had no plans, no picnics to attend. I drove to Fort Bennett Park and walked aimlessly, eavesdropping compulsively as people described dinners of crispy wontons and recommended CBD tinctures and complained about elderly mothers who wouldn't take a car service even when they should. It was like I was trying to fill myself up with other people's words.

Back at home, I texted Tara to see if she was free to talk, but she was at a cookout. She added: Eager to catch up soon & hear what you're thinking re work. Would be so good to be on the same project together ☺.

I didn't know how to reply, so I just sent the purple crystal-ball emoji, which to me meant: *Who even knows what the future holds, I almost just ditched everything and kidnapped my daughter to start a new life in the forests of Ontario but that's possibly something I will never share with you anyway, but I do like you so much, you are my dear friend, and I don't want to leave you hanging in any way, so here is a whimsical, inoffensive image, love, Leigh.*

Tara sent back a green heart, and then I watched *The Great British Baking Show* for three hours while bookmarking layer cake recipes on my laptop. Maybe I'd make them, probably I wouldn't, but at least winter would come, eventually, and I'd bake something.

Life always just goes on. Sometimes I think of Earth after *homo sapiens*—after the plague and the floods and the fires. When all that's over and it's just Earth, tending her wounds. In that landscape there will be a trash swamp of decaying human-made objects, all that crap we loved to buy and sell and document. And this sludge will be teeming with cockroaches, rats, worms, mushrooms, lichen, moss, and all the micro-creatures we can't see in the warm murky water. I imagine this rich stew, and I feel okay. I feel like we had a good run, us humans— okay, maybe not *good*, and maybe, in the end, not even very significant. But we left our mark. We got on the scene, we made music, and we sailed songs into space on golden discs.

The next morning was Rose's first day of first grade. She was at Carter's, but we'd decided that I'd meet them at the house so we could both be there to put her on the bus. When I pulled into the driveway, Rose was already sitting outside on the front step with Megan. She was wearing her rose-gold metallic sandals and a blue floral dress I had bought for her. Megan was dressed for work, but her hair was still wet from the shower. She smiled and waved me over.

"I like your new color," she said.

"Thanks," I said, touching the ends. I felt silly as I recognized it was now more like Megan's. "It's semipermanent."

"You look like someone ready for first grade," I said, giving Rose a hug. "Do you have your two folders and your lunch?"

She nodded. "Daddy already left."

"He did? Why?"

"He had to get to work early," Megan said. "I'm sorry, I thought he texted you?"

"Maybe he sent it when I was driving." I took out my phone and saw the new messages: Sorry, I can't be there. Had to get the Acela to NYC at the last minute.

As much as I wanted to attribute passive-aggressive motives to his speech bubbles, I believed every word. Carter was a man born to board express trains at the last minute. It was such a relief, I realized, to be divorced from him. To have escaped that version of my life. Godspeed, my ex.

"He works hard," Megan said apologetically. "Here, go sit by Rose so I can take a picture for you."

I obeyed, and she snapped a pic and whooshed it to me via text. I opened the photo immediately, partly to avoid conversation with Megan but mostly to appease Rose, who wanted to see herself. I sometimes worried she'd remember everything aesthetically, according to how she was framed. I hoped she would remember the cool morning air on her ankles, the weight of her backpack, the trees still holding their leaves, the overgrown weeds.

"Lawn needs mowing," Megan said, catching my gaze.

"What is that?" I pointed to a white wrapper, caught in the weeds. I went to pick it up, assuming it had blown out of someone's trash. Then I saw what it was.

"Rose, come look here!" I said. "A mushroom!"

Rose crouched to touch the domed white cap that looked like a hard-boiled egg with bits of shell flaking off. Nearby was a larger one, a full-grown umbrella, its edges like torn paper. There were more, I realized, scattered across the lawn, still in their domed-egg phase.

"Funny how quick they come up after a rain," Megan said. "These weren't here last night."

The school bus appeared, marigold bright. Rose bravely climbed on board and waved to us from the window.

After the bus drove off, Megan turned to me and said, "Carter told me about your job. I don't know if he was supposed to."

"Probably not," I said. "But it's okay."

"I didn't want to stand here and pretend like I didn't know."

"It's good you know. Maybe I make a little more sense now."

She smiled. "I'm not dying to move, by the way. I'm fine with staying in DC if that's where you want to be. I told Carter, let's get a different house, we can start over that way. But you know how he is when he's feeling anxious. He wants to make a big decision, to feel like he's doing something. That gives him a feeling of control, I think?"

"Yeah, that sounds like Carter," I said, though I had never been able to view his behavior with such objectivity. I always took everything he said and did so personally.

I knelt to get another look at the mushrooms, these strange fleshy creatures, neither animal nor vegetable, floral or root. I felt, ridiculously, that they had appeared to greet me. That they had known, all along, that I would come back.

28.

The president began his speech by quoting Proverbs: "Let not steadfast love and faithfulness forsake you. Write them on the tablet of your heart." The sky was sharply blue with a few wispy clouds; summer's humidity had slipped away. It was the perfect September morning, reminiscent of the day being commemorated.

That year, the anniversary fell on a Sunday, and everyone was in church clothes, maybe planning to attend a second service afterward. Marcos was there, with his wife and two daughters. Tara was standing up front, in uniform. Sandra and Tim were somewhere in the crowd. No one on our team had worked at the Pentagon in 2001. I was barely out of college, employed as a paralegal. On the morning of the attacks, I recalled speculating with my coworkers what the other targets might be, all of us staring at the break-room TV in a shock-induced sense of detachment. The Statue of Liberty, we predicted. The Washington Monument. The Golden Gate Bridge. Someone said the Pentagon, and I can't remember if they guessed it ahead of time or if that's when it got hit. We were sent home after that. I tried to call my mother from my cell phone, but I couldn't get through. I had to wait until I was home to use my landline. By then, I already had several messages from her on my machine.

I put on sunglasses to hide my tears and let the sadness wash over me. There was something relieving about it, even grounding. My tears were not disassembling, they were my stability. The woman next to me handed me a Kleenex that smelled faintly of eucalyptus. I thanked her, trying not to cry even harder at her kind gesture. She was standing with a young woman who looked to be in her late teens. I wondered if she'd lost her father, and what she remembered of him. I wondered what Rose would be like at her age, and what the world would look like in 2026, how September would feel, and what speech the president would give on the twenty-fifth anniversary of 9/11. Would we still be at war?

Marcos came over at the end of the service. I said hello to his daughters and to his wife, Shelley, a pretty woman who always carried with her a hint of her youth—today, I saw it in her doubly pierced ears, bearing tiny stud earrings in the shape of hearts and peace signs.

"I'm glad you're here," Marcos said. "I need to talk to you about something."

I figured it must be about CATI, which he had not mentioned since I'd returned from vacation. "Should we get Tara, too?" I asked.

"No," he said. "Shelley, excuse me for a moment?"

We found a random point among the memorial's stone markers. Rose once remarked that they looked like diving boards, and now that was what I saw, too.

"I need to know where you went on your vacation in June," he said.

"My vacation? In June?" I stammered. I felt the heat rising in my cheeks. "That's when I went to Asheville."

"Are you sure that's where you were?"

I stared at Marcos, unable to answer. I couldn't think of any calls or emails I'd made or sent in Canada that would have tipped them off. I'd barely been online. I'd always used cash. I'd been careful.

"Leigh, just tell me the truth." There was a sad, desperate look in his eyes, and I knew I couldn't keep lying.

"Okay," I said. "I didn't go to Asheville. I went to Canada."

"You crossed over the Saint Lawrence?"

"Yes. How did you know?"

He held up his phone to show me a photo of the parking ticket I'd gotten in Thousand Islands Marina. My stomach dropped.

"This got flagged last week when your security clearance was being processed," Marcos said. "They wanted to know why it didn't match your stated itinerary."

"It's not what you think," I said. "I changed my plans."

"That's what I told them. I said you forgot to update your itinerary and that you stayed in Upstate New York. The clearance went through on Friday."

"You vouched for me?" The gravity of what he'd done hit me all at once, and I didn't know what to say. "Why?"

"I like to give people the benefit of the doubt when I can. But I know your history, Leigh. Your old contact is up there."

"I'm sorry," I said. "I can explain everything."

"Not here," Marcos said. "We need to go someplace less busy. Meet me on the C&O Canal at Fletcher's Cove."

Walking back to my car, I couldn't help thinking this was my last chance to get away. But the fantasy didn't seem real anymore; it was just a dead end where I'd end up trapped in a car in the rain at night, terrified of moving forward. Except this time, I'd be alone.

It was always cooler on the canal, where sycamore trees arch over the abandoned towpath that runs parallel to the Potomac. Alongside the trail is the defunct waterway that extends northwest through Maryland and all the way to Cumberland.

Marcos and I met at the cove and headed north, away from the city. For the first quarter mile or so, we indulged in nervous small talk about the weather, our kids' first week of school, and the sights and sounds of the canoeists and boaters on the river. The towpath was busy with weekend runners getting in their miles and couples whizzing by on bicycles, but soon it was relatively quiet, and I was able to explain myself without interruption. I resolved to tell him everything, starting from when I first saw Jenny online, to our extended interview in the hills of California, to our plans to go into business together, to how devastated I was when she broke off contact. I told him how nothing at work felt vital anymore and about Tim saying that the military wasn't really interested in spirituality, that it was all about winning, and how I'd thought—for a few wild weeks—that it would be better if I just left the country with Rose. I admitted how close I'd come to following through. A rainstorm had stopped me, or maybe it was my conscience. I really didn't know.

When I was finished, we had walked over three miles, and the towpath had moved away from the roadway and closer to the Potomac River. Here, the canal was dry and overgrown with poison ivy, jewel plant, ragweed, and fool's wheat, as well as maple and sycamore seedlings.

"I'm sorry," I said to Marcos again. I felt like I couldn't apologize enough. "I like this job, but when I think about the real reason that all these soldiers are hurting, it just seems obvious that it's because we're killing everything, not just other human beings, but the whole planet. Sometimes it's too much to take in. The idea that we're piloting a program to deal with Climate Anxiety—I can't decide if it's absurd or genius. Everything seems so futile. I loved the idea that I could escape it, somehow, that I could protect Rose. Jenny made it seem so real."

"I should have realized you were getting burned out," Marcos said. "It's one of the hazards of the job—Tim and Sandra have both had episodes. I probably should have warned you about it, but you seemed so even-keeled."

"I am, for the most part. I just lose it pretty epically from time to time. I guess. I don't know."

Marcos was walking slowly, with his hands clasped behind him. "I had my own breaking point," he said. "It was a while ago, in the spring of 2005. Shelley was eight months pregnant with Paige. My older daughter, Jesse, was three. It was about a year after I'd been transferred to the DOD. I'd been reading all their projections for the future in terms of the climate. I was mostly looking at the health side, because

I was supposed to work on strategies for soldiers living in places with extreme heat and poor air quality, which was going to be an issue at a lot of bases. It was depressing enough, but for some reason, I wanted to know more, so I requested reports from the EPA on extinction levels. That's when I realized how bad things really were. I couldn't get my head around the numbers, they were so big. And it dawned on me that no one could, that we were just going to keep doing what we were doing until it was too late."

I murmured agreement and kept walking. We were at a part of the trail that was heavily shaded by older trees.

"By then, it was obvious that the wars overseas weren't going to end anytime soon. I knew we wouldn't get the funding we needed to address the climate crisis in even the most basic way." Marcos paused to check a trail marker. "I'm making it sound much more intellectual than it was. Really, it was seeing my wife's belly getting bigger and bigger, and realizing that I was bringing another child into the world. I was already feeling guilty about Jesse. I felt like if I'd known then how bad it was, I wouldn't have had her. Which is a terrible feeling—to regret your own child. And I didn't think I could talk to Shelley about any of this, at least not when she was pregnant.

"One Friday night, I came home and Shelley was already asleep on the couch. Jesse was in bed. I had this awful, restless feeling—I had to get out of the house. There was a sports bar off the highway that I'd been to before. But when I got close, I found myself driving past it. And then, I just kept driving south. I drove all night. I ended up in South Carolina, on the coast, in a little town called Piper's Beach. I checked into a motel, and the next morning when I woke up, there was a *crazy* number of birds outside. I mean, hundreds of birds. Maybe thousands. They were on the concrete balcony outside of my room, they were perched on the railings and the furniture, they were on the walkway leading to the beach, and then when you went down to the water, it was basically a blanket of birds. I didn't know it, but it was migration season. The woman at the front desk told me it happened every year for a few days. She lent me a pair of binoculars and said if I used them to look at the moon, I'd be able to see the birds flying at night. She said they rest and eat during the day and then travel at night, when it's cooler. So I stayed another night to look at the moon. And then it was like magic, you could see the birds flying by, like shadows flickering across. All night long they flew overhead—and I was seeing just a tiny fraction of them. I couldn't believe it."

Marcos looked up at the tree canopy. "There was something about watching those birds at night that let me face how sad I felt. It was like I was seeing the ghosts of the birds that were gone. But I was also in awe of the ones that were still alive. I was amazed by how far they traveled and how much they knew of the world. I couldn't believe my life overlapped with theirs, that they sat on the same plastic chairs outside my motel room, that they stopped in this place called Piper's Beach. It turned my mind around completely. I went home feeling like a different person, but to Shelley I was just a jerk who'd disappeared. She thought I wanted to leave her."

"How did you convince her otherwise?" We'd come to a stop and were standing in the shade. The Potomac glinted through the trees.

"I stuck around." Marcos turned to me. "I know it's hard, and I want you to know, you don't have to keep doing this work if you feel it's too much. We can transfer you to a different department. Or you could go back to the private sector."

"As a librarian?"

"If that's what you wanted." He looked me in the eye. "No one is going to hold your past activities over your head. If you need a recommendation from me, it's yours."

Marcos started walking again, and I fell in step with him. The sun was lower in the sky, and the temperature had dropped, a reminder that autumn was still on its way. Ahead, the canal seemed to tunnel through the trees. I wasn't sure what to do with this sudden gift. I couldn't really imagine going back to being a law librarian. That job had appealed to me when I was craving a soft place to land, but now I wanted something different from my life. I wanted meaning and everything that came with it: uncertainty, doubt, longing, beauty. I didn't mind ambivalence, maybe I even liked it. I wondered when that feeling started and if that was what had broken up my marriage—not Hecate's Key.

"I don't want to quit this job," I said to Marcos. "I thought I did, but I don't."

"I hoped you'd say that," Marcos said. "But if you start having doubts, just tell me—or if you want to be on a different team. You don't have to stay with Spiritual Readiness."

"No, that's what I like doing," I said. "I was just thinking, that feeling of awe you had, when you saw the birds, that's what we want soldiers to feel. But they need to get there without burning out first."

"That's the problem," Marcos said dryly. "Turns out it's hard to program a spiritual breakthrough."

"There might be potential with CATI."

"I've actually been working with Ileana on a new device." Marcos took a small metal box from his pocket that was about the size of a cassette tape. "Now that you have clearance, I can show it to you."

He opened the metal box to reveal green plastic wireless earbuds. Also in the box were two narrow metal wristbands and a black, round object that looked like a polished stone. "This is Project Demeter."

"What does it do?" I asked. "Is it some kind of VR experience?"

"Technically, it's an augmented reality," Marcos said. "But you could just as easily call it a psychedelic trip. I wouldn't use either term because the technology doesn't really add a layer of experience, and it doesn't directly affect your physiology. Do you want to try it?"

"Right now?"

"That's why I wanted to meet here," Marcos said. "It works best if you're near trees and plants."

I picked up the earbuds. They were heavier than I expected. "What happens when you put these in?"

"It helps you to hear better, sort of, but it's not totally auditory. I don't want to say too much. You put on the earbuds and the wristbands.

Then you take the stone and press it to your heart. The heat of your body and the rate of your pulse will activate it."

"How long will it last?"

"As long as you want. It runs on solar power. You don't have to keep holding the stone—it's only for activation."

"Have you tried it?"

"Yes. So has Tara—and Shelley." He looked at me meaningfully, and I registered that Shelley's participation wasn't officially approved. "We've also given it to a few medical professionals and spiritual leaders. Everyone has had a positive experience."

I trusted Marcos, but I was nervous, too. I felt fragile after all the day's moods and emotions. It didn't seem like the best time to experiment with mind-altering technologies. And yet I was curious.

"I can stop at any time?" I asked.

"Yes, just pull out the earplugs," he said, with the controlled eagerness of a parent waiting at the bottom of the sliding board.

"Well, okay . . ." I gingerly placed them in each ear. Marcos helped me with the wristbands and handed me the stonelike activation tool. "When you're ready, hold it to your heart. If you want to walk, you can put the stone in your pocket or give it back to me."

"Okay, I got it." I squeezed the stone and held it to my heart. And then—

29.

The sound poured forth, and it was, I immediately understood, the voices of all the plants and trees on the canal, all the green that surrounded us. I don't know how I knew. It was totally unlike any human sound. In the moment, in the liquid time that followed, they brought joy and the feeling of deep concentration you experience when doing something that occupies every corner of your attention.

I felt as if my entire body were music, as if every cell was listening; it was like swimming in the ocean, or watching the sun disappear at the horizon. Or it was like choral music, maybe Rachmaninoff's "Cherubic Hymn." It was like the tomatoes my mother grew in her garden and the peaches we used to get during two certain weeks in August. It was like the feeling of Rose's petal-soft cheek mixed with the toasty smell of her hair mixed with the high note of the *Hi!* she used to say when she only knew one word—*Hi!*—and would greet the ants that marched through our kitchen every spring. It was like moss beneath bare feet, like snow falling, like mushrooms appearing, like dew collecting; it was the wind showing the silver sides of leaves, it was the shadows of clouds passing over a meadow, it was the moonlight bright as frost. It was holy and refulgent; it was a miracle that made the whole world vibrate with potential, made my pointless life a point of life, made my heart sing, lifted. I was just so happy to be alive. The loneliness of my mother's death, my failed marriage, the hundreds—no, thousands—of wanting social interactions, dissolved like a veil of mist.

At some point, Marcos tapped me on the shoulder and gestured for me to pull the earplugs out. I did, and the rush of sound stopped, like turning off a faucet. I looked up at the trees and heard only a breeze rustling the leaves that were tinged brown at the tips, scorched by the extended summer. But it wasn't only a breeze, it was the wind in conversation with the trees, with each leaf speaking directly to the wind and the wind answering. Literally. It wasn't a metaphor, nothing was a metaphor. We lived in a world populated with intelligent, sentient, calm, wise, tender, fierce, curious green beings. All I wanted to do was thank them.

I knelt onto gravel and pushed aside pebbles to find the sprigs of weeds that were pushing their way through in search of sunlight. These tiny sparks of green were silent now, but I had heard them. Something glimmered at the edge of my vision, and I turned to see chrome, metallic paint, mirrors. I realized I was crouched at the edge of the parking lot. These little plants were singing at the edge of this asphalt field, they always were.

"Are you okay?" Marcos asked.

"I'm wonderful," I said, wiping tears from my eyes. "Did we walk all the way back?"

Marcos laughed. "Yes, you gave me the stone almost immediately."

"How long has it been?"

"Over an hour."

"It feels like there was no time for a while. Maybe I was on plant time—I don't know!" I pulled off the wristbands and handed them to Marcos. "What is this? Where did it come from?"

"We've been trying to develop it for a while." Marcos placed the wristbands back in the box. "Then it took off unexpectedly after you mentioned that post-grad at the meeting, the one who'd written an algorithm for plant vibrations."

"The one Kip hired for his app?"

"Yes, Lily. We got in touch with her because we'd been looking for a way to pair an AI with plants, to take advantage of a plant's healing presence, the same way we do with the dogs. But what we realized is that with dogs, they help people relate to the AI and receive the medical knowledge it can offer. It's the opposite with plants. With plants, the AI is to help you tune in to the plants themselves."

"And Lily showed you how to do that?"

"My understanding is that she was able to take them over the finish line."

"It's incredible," I said. "The way it makes you feel connected to everything is just . . . I don't know what to say. It's like you feel how extraordinary our planet is."

"Everyone who has tried it has said something like that," Marcos said.

"How many are there?" I asked. "Because if you could get lots and lots of people to listen, it would be amazing. You'd have these people who just want to be outside planting things and helping things grow. I mean, this could be the thing that would actually change how people spend their time, and even what motivates them—"

I stopped, realizing where my vision was going. "This doesn't really help with any of the military's objectives. It would definitely undermine soldier lethality."

Marcos carefully slid the metal box into his jacket pocket. "There might be some unintended consequences. I don't think the new administration—whoever it is—will be particularly supportive."

"Are you worried about this being shut down?"

Marcos nodded.

"What's your plan?"

He lowered his voice even though there was no one nearby. "It's two-pronged. First, we've reclassified this as an experimental medication to deal with substance abuse disorder—and I actually think it will be pretty useful in that regard. But our department will continue to track it as treatment for anxiety and grief related to the climate crisis, and possibly as a tool to raise awareness. When the time is right, we will offer this technology to the public on as large a scale as possible, as quickly as possible. In the meantime, though, we need to disseminate it covertly."

"How are you going to do that?"

"*You're* going to do it," Marcos said. "You and Tara and a handful of other agents are going to go around the country and administer it while you work with CATI. She'll be a good cover for you."

"So CATI's just a big distraction? Is that why you made her, as a cover for this?"

Marcos smiled. "We made CATI in all sincerity. I haven't given up on it yet. We don't know where it's going to lead, just like we don't know where Demeter is going to take us."

When I got home that night, I made a red lentil curry for dinner, following a recipe that I'd used for years. I briefly turned on the news but then decided to listen to a record instead, something from my mother's collection. *Ella Fitzgerald Sings the Irving Berlin Songbook.* I hummed along to "Suppertime" as I chopped ginger and garlic and onions. People say vinyl has a warm sound, other people say that's pretentious nostalgia, and someone I once interviewed claimed listening to old records was physically better for you, that all that compressed music streaming through computers was addling our brains. Everybody has their theories; maybe they were all right. Maybe they were all wrong. All I knew was that Ella's voice was like honey sliding off a spoon.

While the rice cooked, I sent an email to Jenny. I was feeling magnanimous after hearing the plants sing; I wanted to tell her that her therapy was real. I wrote a short, vague note that was more an invitation than anything else. As soon as I sent it, the message volleyed back was a vacation responder whose formality made me laugh. All Best, Jennifer Hex.

I checked her Instagram feed to see if she really was out of town. For the first time in two months, there was a new post, showing the cliché shot of an airplane wing, midflight. The caption said, 16 hours to heaven. I wondered if she'd posted in real time, and if she was in the sky at that moment.

I scrolled back through Jenny's feed until I found the picture that had first captured my attention, the portrait of her sitting beneath the sycamore tree, with the dappled light. The photo still appealed to me, though now I wondered if the tree had cast the spell—the way the peeling bark of the sycamore, which left whitish, circular marks on the trunk, echoed the play of sunlight on Jenny's shirt. I scrolled further back, watching the years rewind; Jenny's aesthetic sense seemed to devolve as the filters became more limited, reflecting the early days of Instagram. Suddenly all the photos looked like vintage Polaroids. And then I saw it, an actual snapshot from the nineties, uploaded for Throwback Thursday. It showed Jenny in high school. She was wearing a jade silk shirt with frog fasteners. I knew the shirt well—it was from The Limited. I had the same one in fuchsia. All the girls had them. The caption: As you can see, I've always loved the color green.

The bizarre thing about this photo was not that Jenny looked so young, so unvarnished and charming with her toothy smile and her messy hair, so essentially glamorous despite her unstudied appearance and unspecial clothes; no, the unbelievable thing was that *I* was in the photo, right next to her on the same bench. We were sitting at what looked to be a cafeteria table, probably the spot where she used to hold court in the morning before school started, except it was more crowded than I remembered, there were several kids there, and I was clearly more interested in someone sitting across from me, out of the frame, because my smile was directed toward this other person; I wasn't looking at Jenny. I didn't notice or care that she was being photographed by whomever—a yearbook lackey? I had no memory of the day or the crowd of people I was among. I wanted to reach into the photo and reclaim the nascent Leigh, but she was laughing and elusive, living her private life.

I put my phone down and went outside.

The sky was the silky gray of early evening. Walter was beginning to produce his second growth of leaves, and it was a paltry showing, but I was proud of him for making the effort. Next door, weeds were abundant, pushing through the cosmetic grassy sod: clover and dandelions, burdock and wild onion. I wondered how much would grow if we encouraged them, how green we could get.

"I know you're singing," I called out to all the nearby trees and plants. "I can't hear you, not consciously, at least. But what is consciousness anyway?"

"It's the fabric of existence stretching across space and time that connects all living things!" Walter called back.

He didn't really say that, at least not in my language. But I felt his reply. I really believed it this time. I walked down to the front yard and touched one of the new leaves he'd put forth to collect light, air, and water. Together, we watched the sun set. I felt his energy slowing, and the eyes of his heart close. I felt all the green things around me begin to relax into the night. It was magnificent, and it happened every day.

"Walter," I whispered, "I'm glad to know you."

ABOUT THE AUTHOR

Photo © 2023 Zoe Fisher

Hannah Gersen is the author of *Home Field*. Her fiction has been published most recently in *Electric Lit*, *Visions*, the *Southern Review*, and *New England Review*. Her essays and criticism have appeared in the *New York Times*, *Poets & Writers Magazine*, *Lit Hub*, *Granta*, and *The Common*, among others. She lives in Brunswick, Maine, with her family.